Spirit of the Wolf

Also by Vonna Harper

Surrender

Roped Heat

"Wild Ride" in *The Cowboy*

"Restraint" in *Bound to Ecstasy*

Night Fire

"Breeding Season" in *Only with a Cowboy*

"Night Scream" in *Sexy Beast V*

Going Down

Night of the Hawk

"Mustang Man" in *Tempted by a Cowboy*

Taming the Cougar

Falcon's Captive

Years ago, my husband, two sons, and I spent a week camping in eastern Oregon. My husband wanted to scout the area in anticipation of antelope season, and we wanted our young sons to experience something far from civilization. While driving along rutted, two-lane roads, I occasionally noticed isolated farmhouses surrounded by cattle grazing land. At one point I spotted a rawboned, middle-aged woman hanging clothes from a clothes line in front of a weathered house, a lean dog at her side. Except for the dog, she was utterly alone.

I dedicate *Spirit of the Wolf* to that strong, independent woman and the pioneering spirit she represents.

1

Lose yourself in the land. Breathe the cleanest air you'll ever know. Scan the cloudless summer sky for a glimpse of a hawk. Stay in the moment. Remember why you live here. Let the breeze quiet you.

Despite the high-desert heat, Cat Alward drove with the window down and her elbow out, undoubtedly adding to her sunburn and risking a collision with an insect. Air-conditioning would be nice, but there was none in her old Ford pickup. Fortunately it had the necessary pulling capacity. As long as it could haul what she needed hauling, she'd find ways to keep it running.

A glance in the rearview mirror assured her that, yes, the horse trailer was still tracking behind her.

Ginger, an okay name for a horse, had been chosen by the mare's former owner in deference to her light mane and tail. The last thing Cat wanted to do was confuse the three-year-old by changing her name.

Matt.

She was taking Ginger to Matt Yaye—a job fulfilled, a cattle rancher supplied with the well-trained mount he needed to do his job. Nothing more.

The hell it was.

Thoughts of Matt's land and work-hardened body slipped like hot silk through her and settled, as she knew would happen, between her legs. Matt, early thirties, a tad over six feet with hands like new leather, dark eyes permanently squinting against the sun, and a rumbling voice that stirred her as she'd never been stirred.

If she dared grip the steering wheel with a single hand, the left would go between her legs and press against her jeans. However, with no power steering and a single-lane dirt road conspiring against her, she knew better. Squeezing her pussy muscles only worked what didn't need to be worked.

Damn Matt. Damn his cowboy body and take-no-prisoners cock.

It's not all him, she reminded herself. A Greek god couldn't crawl under her skin and into her body if she didn't allow it to happen. And she allowed. In spades. When it came to Matt.

Who, if she was being honest, was little more than a stranger.

The so-called road leading to Matt's place was a good two miles long. Between rocks and potholes, what was left of the Ford's shocks was going down for the count. Her back ached, and she wouldn't be surprised if her butt sported bruises. However, because dirt roads were more common than paved ones in central Oregon cattle country, she gave it little mind.

Unlike her parents, who'd declared that the high-desert land was worthless.

They had been and still were wrong.

Resigning herself to a leaking pussy, she let her attention drift to the low summer-gray hills to her right. They rose treeless into an achingly blue sky sparsely painted with clouds incapable of bringing rain to the parched area. To the uninitiated, this area was lifeless, dead. Capable of sapping the soul from anyone trapped here.

"Get out," her mother had demanded when she and her father had come for a visit nearly two years ago. "Before you shrivel up and die in this godforsaken land."

What her parents hadn't understood was that she'd never felt more alive. Maybe too much lately, full of screaming energy and the deep-seated desire to take wing and fly.

Find peace in the hills. They've always offered you comfort and fulfillment and will again if you let them. Tamp down this restlessness. This tension. Call those things out for the nonsense they are.

Or was it nonsense? she questioned as the trailer shuddered, and Ginger whinnied a protest. Maybe something was trying to get through to her. Maybe she needed to get away from work, turn off her cell phone, listen to herself. Call up instinct. After all, hadn't she gone with instinct when she'd first come here? Hadn't instinct gotten her on her first horse when she was still a toddler?

And hadn't instinct told her she was going to fuck Matt the moment she met him?

Okay, maybe it was time for her to clean out all the junk in her mind and open it to what waited on the land she loved with every cell in her being, because whatever it was, it wanted a piece of her.

Matt Yaye cranked on the fence puller, tightening the barbed wire. In deference to the heat, he wore a once-white undershirt with the sleeves rolled up, revealing tanned strength. His ever-present Western hat rode low, as did the faded and dusty jeans clinging to narrow hips. Equally dusty boots dug into the earth.

Although he must have heard her approach, he didn't look at her because he was intent on replacing a fence section that ran along the dirt road. Traveling at little more than a crawl, Cat divided her attention between driving and the man— mostly the man.

There was nothing easy or soft about Matt. He faced life as if it were a Brahma bull, not with bravado but wrapped in self-confidence. He accepted without question or doubt that thousands of beef cattle lived or died because of the decisions he made, of his understanding of them and the possibility for danger.

Coming alongside him, she stepped on the brakes and waited as the man she'd been looking forward to seeing for a week secured the top strand to the metal fencing. Sweat tracked down his neck. The wind teased what showed of his too-long black hair under the gray hat, making her ache with a powerful need to run her hands through the strands. What did it matter that equal parts dust and sweat coated his hair? Those things were part of him, part of both of them.

Rolling his shoulders, Matt turned toward her. His features were quiet, his emotions hidden, and yet something simmered in him. "You're here."

"Later than I said. I'm sorry." Like every other time she'd seen him, her throat didn't want to work. Her body hummed.

"Something came up?"

"Doesn't it always?" He needed a shave, damn him. Did he have any idea how sexy the added shading made him look? "Chet over at the Lazy M called. He wanted my opinion of letting his horses go unshod. He said he'd read that horses did just as well without as with."

Matt shook his head and licked dry lips. His gaze drilled into her, looking for what? "Chet's cheap. He doesn't want to pay a farrier."

There were only two farriers in the county, and both brought a lifetime of experience and compassion to their jobs. They charged fair. Short of learning how to shoe himself, Chet wasn't going to get a better deal anywhere.

"That's what I told him." She smiled for the first time, wishing it was easier but knowing how she was around Matt—flying apart. "An unshod horse in an irrigated pasture or in a barn's one thing. Riding all over hell and gone keeping up with range cattle's another."

"He didn't like hearing that, right?"

She shrugged. At least they were talking, albeit about things that didn't matter. With Matt, she never knew what was going to come out of his mouth, if anything. "He asked for my opinion; I gave it. You want to see Ginger?"

"In a few." Stepping closer to the truck, he closed rough fingers over her elbow. His eyes dared her not to react. "Your arm's hot," he unnecessarily announced. "Prickling from the sun, not that you care. You're as bad as me when it comes to facing the elements. You take whatever Mother Nature throws at you."

"I guess." Most of the time, Matt was as quiet as the stereotypical open-country cowboy. This much from him was close to a record. Now, suddenly, thanks to his touch, it was she who couldn't put two words together.

Quite possibly, they were the only two human beings for miles around. No one would ever know what they said or whether they did anything about the rage between them. Granted, Addie might be at Matt's and her ranch, but the older woman couldn't see clear out here. Even if she did, she'd undoubtedly declare Matt was an adult and then some. What he did with his life was his business.

"Tell me something," she came up with, because the question had been stuck in her craw. "If you didn't need a new horse, would I have heard from you?"

"Sure."

Back to one-word sentences, was he? But then wasn't that part of his appeal? The mystery? "When you were horny enough?" she challenged.

"Unless you got that way first."

He hadn't released her elbow. The pressure should have been enough, no other contact needed—surely nothing deep. After all, conversation hardly defined their relationship, but something else was at work this afternoon, something new in the air maybe.

"I'm wondering if there's going to be a storm," she said, because it was a given that they were going to have sex. No further definition needed.

"Yeah?" Lifting his head, Matt scanned the sky. Done, he met her gaze again. His eyes made her think of obsidian as they always did, but today she caught a hue she'd never seen. Maybe the sun was responsible, and there was no need to ask where the hint of scarlet had come from. "What makes you think that?"

Pulled back by the question, she shifted into neutral and eased her foot off the clutch. Pins and needles traveled up her leg. "You don't feel the energy? Like static electricity."

"Sorry," he said on the tail of a shrug, yet there was something artificial about the word, a deliberate dismissal, perhaps.

"Look, Ginger's been in the trailer long enough." Much as she wanted to, she didn't place her hand over his. "You want a ride back to the house? If you aren't done, I'll put her in the corral and—"

"I'm done for now." That said, he released her, hoisted the wire puller over his shoulder, and walked around to the passenger's side. He got in, placing the tool of his trade on the seat between them. "I was going to quit working when you got here."

Because there was something he wanted to do more than ranch upkeep—specifically, fuck the county's only female horse trainer.

A couple of conversation possibilities skittered through her mind, only to evaporate under the masculine presence an arm's length away. She'd known about Coyote Ranch long before meeting Matt at a Lakeview bar last fall. Her friend Daria had been singing Matt's physical praises for years, but with Addie's husband, Santo, handling the Coyote Ranch's horses, there'd been no business reason for their paths to cross. Besides, Cat hadn't been hurting for male companionship—one of the perks of being single, lean, and strong in a land where strength counted for a lot.

Then somehow Santo had gotten himself thrown by the tall, gentle mare he'd been riding for years. He'd landed on rocks, breaking ribs and an ankle and, according to the coroner, prob-- ably sustaining a concussion. Also according to the coroner, he'd lived the first of the two days he'd been in the backcountry. It had taken Matt, Addie, and the men searching with them that long to find him.

The moment she'd first seen Matt Yaye in the Rangerider Bar, Cat had become like a mare in heat. With Daria handling the introductions, Matt had quickly gone from "Glad to meet you," to "Can I buy you a beer?" to "I've heard about your reputation with horses. You're damn good."

Everything had gone fast between them. Fast and furious, as the saying goes. Close to cold sober, they'd sweated and screamed through the quickest sex of her life in the bed of his pickup that first night. Maybe someone had heard them having sex, but hopefully everyone had been in the bar. Either way, it hadn't mattered then. It still didn't because every time she got within a few hundred feet of Matt, she was ready to jump his bones.

Like now.

Five minutes after picking Matt up, she pulled into a large area that was surrounded by wooden fencing and a couple of corrals to the right of the old Coyote Ranch house. The barn used mostly to house pregnant cows and sickly newborn calves was to the left. Guessing Matt would want to take Ginger through her paces—even sex took a backseat to business with him—she'd saddled and bridled the mare before coming out. Now, however, she couldn't find the words to explain her thinking. Five minutes of watching him rub his left thigh and wishing to hell she was the one doing that, but minus the denim, had her opening the truck door and facing into what breeze slipped over the nearly treeless acreage.

She had to get a grip. Somehow. Otherwise, despite what was bothering his thigh, she'd back him against her rig and start clawing at his zipper.

A metallic creaking let her know he was already opening the horse trailer gate. Joining him, she watched as Matt stepped into the trailer. Scant seconds later, Ginger's rump and tail came into view. She'd been a little concerned that Ginger would need time to adapt to having a strange man handle her, but as soon as the mare was out, she pressed her head against Matt's chest.

"Standoffish," he observed as he rubbed behind both ears. "Skittish and shy."

"She knows when she's being handled by a man who understands what a woman wants."

A black-eyed glance in her direction left her with no doubt Matt had picked up on the subtext.

Hands meant for physical work ran up and down Ginger's neck. Instead of dozing off as horses often did, the mare remained alert.

"I wish I wasn't doing this," Matt muttered.

"Having to retire your old horse?"

"Not that so much. Buck deserves to relax. I'm talking about Santo."

Until this moment, she'd believed Matt didn't want to talk about the man. Knowing he'd been part of the group that had found Santo's body, she hadn't pushed. "From everything I've heard," she ventured, "he was a good man."

"The best." Still stroking Ginger, Matt turned his body and attention toward her. He stood on widespread legs, drawing her attention to the bulge beneath his snug jeans. "Came to the U.S. illegally to get away from the poverty in his village so he could support his parents. He said he got his papers, but I never saw them." He shrugged. "Didn't matter to anyone around here, especially me."

Especially him? Strange he didn't mention Santo's American wife, Addie. "You miss him, don't you?"

"I'm not sure I'd be alive without him."

Rocked by the unexpected glimpse of what there was of Matt beneath the surface, she struggled to come up with something to say. Damn both of them for making sex first, second, and third in their relationship—if what existed between them could be called that.

"People, ah . . . Some wind up having more impact on us than we expect." She winced at the stupid words.

"Yeah, they do."

Leaving Ginger, he headed toward her, his boots landing soundlessly on the packed earth. Solid thigh muscles beneath old denim caught and relaxed. "How soon you have to be back?"

"Before dark. I need to feed the horses."

"Hmm." His breath slid hot over her forehead, entered her bloodstream. "An hour drive. You have time."

Although he hadn't yet touched her, the promise and challenge coated the air. Another woman, one whose body hadn't been imprinted with his, might think he was asking permission, but she knew better. Matt would haul her jeans down over her hips when he was good and ready. When he'd gotten her to the boiling point—which she was already approaching.

"Who's here?" She nodded at the house that, like most around here, hadn't seen a paintbrush in years because other things took priority.

"No one."

Just us. Just like I hoped. "What about Addie?"

"Staying here's hard for her. She's off seeing her sister in Vegas."

As a child, she'd briefly lived in Las Vegas with her parents. Hated everything about it.

"When's she coming back?"

"She's not sure."

Matt didn't want to talk anymore; he was ready for action. So was she, and yet there were things she wished she could ask him about his relationship with Addie—and with Santo before the older man's death. The three of them had lived together in the house, sharing work, meals, and companionship. According to her friend Daria, Addie's parents had been the ranch's original owners. When Addie was a teenager, her parents had hired Santo. Before long, the two young people had fallen in love. Daria didn't know how Addie's parents had felt about their only child hooking up with a man who spoke broken English, but no one disputed Santo's competence when it came to running a cattle ranch. After Santo and Addie married, Santo had moved into the house. For years, the two couples from different generations had worked together to keep Coyote Ranch going.

First Addie's mother and then her father had gotten cancer, dying within a year of each other. Santo and Addie hadn't had children—rumor was they'd had nothing but miscarriages to show for all their trying. The ranch became their life.

Then, as Santo had done, Matt had come along. One rumor was that Matt had escaped from a juvenile-detention facility and found refuge on the ranch. Another rumor was that Matt's folks had owed Addie's parents some kind of debt. They'd paid it off by indenturing their strong teenage son to them.

Matt had never said what the truth was.

"What are you thinking?"

Startled by the unexpected question—where had her thinking taken her?—Cat blinked Matt into focus. Damn but he was close.

"About you," she admitted.

"Me too." The hands she'd stared at when they were on Ginger landed on her shoulders. His fingers slipped under her tank top's shoulder straps. "I've never seen you in a sleeveless whatever-it's-called before, have I?"

"Probably not." *Today I wanted my clothes to speak to you, to say what I don't have the words for.*

"I like. Especially the low-cut part." Licking a forefinger, he ran it over the V-neck where cotton met cleavage.

"Thought you would."

The corners of his usually straight mouth lifted. "Have you wondered what it would be like if we didn't live so far apart?"

Out here, an hour between properties wasn't that much, but he had a point. "Think we'd get any work done?"

"Depends on your definition of *work.*"

Done with trying to keep the conversation going, she pulled his shirt out of his waistband so she could run her fingers over his middle. When he sucked in a breath, she crouched and lathed what she'd just exposed with her tongue. He continued to hold his breath.

His jeans rode so low his navel was exposed. Wondering what happened to her when she was around him, she slipped her tongue into the indentation.

Shuddering, he grabbed her long, single braid and pulled her head back. She had no choice but to stare up at him. "Damnation, woman!"

"You don't like?"

"I like too much and you know it."

If not for the growing heat between her legs, she might have admitted that his reaction to foreplay was one of the few things she knew about him. Clenching her teeth, she straightened. Her hands remained at his waist.

"What about Ginger? You going to ride her?"

"When I'm done riding you."

"Just like that, you're going to ride me?" she challenged. "Don't you believe in courting a woman?"

"I know what you want."

Anger sliced through her, but whether she was pissed at herself or him she couldn't say. She wanted more than sex from him, didn't she?

Maybe not. Uncomplicated itch scratching had a lot going for it.

"What do you, in your infinite masculine wisdom, believe I need?"

His features sobering, he pulled the straps over her shoulders, so she risked ripping the fabric if she tried to raise her arms. Leaving her with her arms pinned to her sides, he dove a thumb into the valley between her breasts. "Bra's in the way."

"That's your problem, not mine."

"Oh, I don't see it as a problem." His other hand went to a front pocket, and he held up a small folding knife.

"You wouldn't!" Maybe the scenario called for her to back away, but she didn't.

"Don't be so sure. You'd have to drive home with your breasts bouncing."

"You'd like that, wouldn't you?"

"You know the answer."

Of course she did. She might have told him if not for the distracting thumb still between her breasts. He returned the knife to his pocket—not that it mattered. Studying his chest beneath the shirt, she noted that his breathing deepened. Instead of the quick rise and fall that said he wanted to fuck her here and now, his breaths lengthened almost as if he was falling asleep.

"What?" she whispered.

When he gave no indication he'd heard, she lifted her gaze to his face. He'd turned his head and was staring at the hills. These weren't the same as the ones near her place, the ones still giving up their secrets to her. Maybe Matt's did the same for him.

Trying not to think too much about the heat of his hand against her chest, she blinked his eyes into focus. Yes, there were the intense, shining black eyes she'd fallen in lust with, eyes with midnight buried in them.

And again the scarlet.

"What are you seeing?" she asked.

2

Cat had said something, the words spoken in a lilting tone with a hint of the deep behind the lift. Her body, less than a foot from mating with his, cried out, and his listened.

Why, then, was it so hard to stop studying the horizon?

Something rolled through Matt, a kind of cool heat with sharpness behind it. A sound accompanied the sharpness, a solitary and hollow note coming from an animal throat. The wind caught the sound and threw it about, sucking out the heat and leaving only the cold.

"Did you hear that?" he asked, not taking his attention from where the sound had come from.

"What? Matt, I didn't hear anything."

Matt. Yes. That was his name.

Shaking himself free of what couldn't be but what had made him think of a wolf howl, he looked down at Cat. In winter, her long hair was a dark brown. Summer lightened things a bit so it turned reddish. He hadn't mentioned it because he didn't know how to bring up sun and women's hair and what those things did to him. At least once he'd told her he liked the way her breasts filled his hand. She'd shaken her head when he had and laughed a less-than-real laugh. Then she'd told him he had to work on his seduction skills.

Hell, he didn't have any.

Just today's hard-on.

Cat was giving him a head-tipped-to-the-side look that indicated it was his turn to say or do something. Speaking was more than he wanted to concentrate on. Action, however, he could do.

Plan formed, he gripped her shirt hem and yanked the pale blue garment over her head. Her hair snapped with static electricity. He tossed the top onto her truck's dusty hood. Good thing she was okay with everything the earth offered. At least he thought she was; he hadn't asked.

Placing her long, slender fingers under her breasts, she lifted them. "Still meet your approval?"

Hell, yes. Even more so once the damn bra wasn't in the way. Loving the enhanced swell above the white fabric, he slid his fingers over what she'd just offered him. Her breath caught, and she showed clenched teeth. Not thinking about what he was doing, he retraced his earlier move with a little more force and his nails making contact.

"Easy," she warned.

There was dirt under his nails, and under no stretch of the imagination could he call what he had a manicure, not that he'd ever had one. His cock felt tied in a knot. Unless she'd turned 180 degrees from what she'd always been, she was feeling the same. The sun's heat bore down on them. Maybe he should cover her breasts with his hat.

Where to take her? Out here with the mare watching—unless she slept through the whole thing. Or in the calving barn, only there weren't enough hours in the day to keep it clean. Decisions to make when he wanted to unzip and enter.

"Are you going to talk?" she asked.

"Not much to say."

Her fingers were now around his wrists. Tan lay over tan, two sets of hands branded by their shared world.

"No, there never is."

There was that *off* tone to her voice, not hard and hurting like Addie's when she talked about Santo, but something he should do something about. Maybe he would if he understood what the hell had prompted it.

He was good at sex. He wasn't being boastful or bragging, just a conclusion reached as the result of compliments from the women around here he'd slept with, not that there were that many. Cat had never rated his performance. Her cries, a little like a hunting cougar, as she climaxed said he'd done what she needed doing. A few times women had told him he needed to slow down and enjoy the ride, but Cat hadn't asked him to put on the brakes.

Hell, sometimes she'd beaten him to climax.

Cat's fingers tightened, cutting off the circulation in his wrists. "This get your attention?" she asked.

Much as he wanted to shake free, he put it off. "Yeah. What do you want?"

"Funny, Matt, funny." She lightly kicked him in the shin. "I don't have to spell it out."

Maybe she knew what she was putting him through, because her grip let up so blood flow resumed. They'd fuck outside, he decided, where the sometimes breeze reached them and he could see the hills—including the one where Santo had died. All that was left to decide was the specifics.

"I saw Beale in town the other day," she said, leaning forward so her breath warmed and dampened his shirt. "He said one of those mega beef corporations offered to buy you out."

"Did he?" She wanted to talk now?

"And that you sent them packing. Told them you'd go to your grave before you sent your grass-fed, open-range beef to a feed lot to be pumped full of growth hormones and protein supplements."

His goal was to die a participant in the natural beef industry, but life had taught him to take nothing, including parents, for granted. "Beale's a hard worker."

"Just not the sharpest knife in the drawer. Unlike you."

Not expecting a compliment, he took hold of her arms and pushed her back so he could get a better look into her eyes. Nearly as green as spring grass, they'd take hold of him if he wasn't careful. What he wanted from her was sex—same as she did. But sometimes, like now, when he was thinking about how deep her eyes went into him or the occasional dream about waking to find her beside him, he wondered if there could be more between them.

If he'd tell her what had brought him to Coyote Ranch.

"What are you looking for, cowboy?" Her question was light, but her expression made a lie of the light.

His mouth opened. He actually thought he had something to say. Then the distant hills again drew him. Holding her within inches of his cock, he stared. The sun made him squint. From this distance, each hill looked the same, gray and done in. They were different up close, of course. Not only were hundreds of his cattle in the valleys and on the slopes, but also antelope shared the area with them. Also the coyotes Addie's folks had named the ranch after. Also lizards, mule deer, butterflies, horned larks, prairie falcons, burrowing owls, gopher snakes, rattlers, and if he looked close enough, old arrowheads.

He knew those things, so why—

The wind changed, energized. Not only that, but also color returned to the hills so they appeared the way they did in spring, green and living with wildflowers laying down yellow, red, and blue streaks.

Yes, the wind. Not energy today so much as anger. Like in winter when storms howled and tore, forcing cattle to turn their backs to the sharp gusts. It wasn't winter; he knew that. He felt as if he were getting drunk. Gust after gust tore at his flesh and blinded him. Just the same, he knew this wasn't happening, which was the hell and fear of it.

"Matt? What is it?"

A different sound in the boiling wind. Not new so much as what he'd heard earlier and had denied.

Howling. A solitary predator voice, then another, weaving together like tall prairie grasses. Pushing past his skin, sliding over and then into his muscles. Creating fissures in his bones. Gnawing at his veins to make him bleed.

Taking him.

"Matt. You're hurting me."

Despite Cat's warning, Matt continued to grip her arms hard enough to leave bruises. Self-preservation told her to fight him, knee him where it'd get his attention, but their *encounters* had always been rough. Maybe he was simply kicking things up a notch.

"What about your ranch hands? Any chance they'll show up?"

"Huh?"

Noting that he was still staring off into the distance, she leaned into him until her breasts brushed his middle. Sliding a leg between his, she rubbed the inside of his right thigh.

A shudder washed through him in fits and starts.

"Look at me, damn it," she said. "Don't tell me you've forgotten what was on our agenda?"

His lips parted, prompting her to prepare for another "huh," but he closed them without saying anything. Slowly, as if he didn't want to, he turned his head toward her. No way could she make herself believe the glow in his eyes was caused by the sun.

Right now, Matt wasn't the man she'd thought he was. Hell, at the moment, she wasn't 100 percent sure he was a man.

"Let me go," she commanded. "This isn't funny."

Another shudder struck him. "What are you talking about?"

"You don't know? Lighten up on your grip or I'll make you."

Instead of pointing out that her strength didn't hold a proverbial candle to his, his fingers relaxed. Pain relaxed into pressure, which she could handle.

"That's good." Needing to better balance her weight, she removed her leg from between his. "Don't forget, I'm not some green-broke filly."

"Hmm."

Damn it, the Matt who'd shoved her sex life into overdrive that first night remained buried beneath the surface of whoever he'd become. If she didn't know better, she'd conclude he was zoned out on something.

When she tried to pull her arms free, his hold briefly let up, only to increase again. Alarmed, she twisted to the side. "This isn't funny, damn it."

"I didn't intend it to be."

One second she was staring up at him; the next he'd let her go, clamped his hands around the sides of her waist, and hoisted her up and onto his shoulders so she was upside down. Her breath whooshed out.

"What the hell—"

"Shut up."

He'd never said anything like that to her. Always before he'd been polite and well mannered—right up until civilization no longer mattered to either of them. Arms dangling and hands nearly touching his buttocks, she tried to lift her head, only to stop because she feared sliding off. Wrapping an arm behind her back, he started walking. She thought about asking where they were going, but chances were he wouldn't answer.

Maybe he couldn't.

Dismissing the crazy thought, she relaxed. Or rather that

had been her plan until he slid a hand between her legs, high where it counted. Desire oozed through her, prompting her to massage his ass cheeks.

Head down, blood pooling behind her skull. Getting light-headed but not caring.

He took one long stride after another, deep yet rapid breaths escaping a masculine chest.

When he stopped moving, so did his hands. More nervous than excited now, she waited. Instead of letting her down, how-ever, he continued to rub her pussy. Little by little she relaxed, or rather he took her to that place. Despite the growing heat, she remained attuned to him, trying to guess what he was thinking—if he was.

Finally, even with the grand melting sensation throughout her cunt, she could no longer ignore the pressure in her head.

"Let me up." *Please.* "I'm getting a headache."

"Hmm."

No, this wasn't the Matt he'd been. That man would have expressed concern and apologized. Using her hips as his an-chor, he pulled her off him. Dizzy, she had no choice but to hold on to him. Instead of waiting for her balance to recover, he reached behind her and yanked on her bra.

"Easy," she warned. "There's a knack to that."

Another hard yank, and the support was gone, causing her breasts to sag. He dropped the maybe-ruined bra to the ground.

"What the hell . . . Damn it, Matt, if you've—"

"Doesn't matter."

Although she didn't want to, she had no choice but to study his expression. He was in there and yet he wasn't, the physical presence the same and sending undeniable messages to her body. However, she couldn't say the same about the look in his eyes.

"I'm willing to do this," she said, determined to exert some control over the situation. "I wouldn't have come out here if I hadn't hoped sex would be part of it, but to say I'm crazy about how things have been going up until now would be a lie. If you're playing macho man because you think it's a turn-on, you're entitled to another think."

Unless she'd missed something, he was listening to her, or at least trying to. His arms were by his side, for now.

"About the silent-type role you're playing today, it's not working. I need more than grunts from you."

"Like what?" His voice sounded rusty.

"Foreplay would be nice. No need to pile it on—just enough to turn me on."

By way of answer, he held his right hand up to her face. "No need to. Your jeans' crotch is wet."

Point taken. "What I felt was more friction than a massage. Promise you'll do better once the jeans are out of the way."

He didn't. Instead, he flattened his palms over her breasts, exerting so much pressure that she was forced to take a backward step. There they were, standing near a small wood corral. If she wasn't careful, she'd bang into a metal box on the ground next to the fencing that she guessed held tack.

Determined to stand her ground, she tried to pull his hands off her. "Still not funny."

Shifting his hold, he closed thumbs and forefingers over her nipples. "I don't do funny."

No argument there.

If he wanted to, he could inflict serious pain on her. She'd never call what he was doing right now comfortable, but at least . . . at least what? Hadn't she just announced that she intended to call the shots?

"Let me go. And pick up my bra before one of us steps on it."

Grunting, he kicked at the bra, causing it to skid along the dirt. No way would she put it back on today.

"Not funny," she snapped, careful not to move. The pressure on her nipples radiated out to envelope more and more flesh. The sensation headed for her belly. Despite herself, she sighed. Her fingers fisted, and she widened her stance.

Matt began lightly rolling his fingers back and forth, adding to the heat in her breasts and elsewhere. He was getting to her all right, stimulating her. Working her.

She sighed again. "Damn you."

Not long ago, maybe the last time they'd had sex, she'd said those very words when, instead of letting her climax, he'd drawn out the delicious agony. He'd responded to her curse by saying, "Yeah, damn me." Today's silence unnerved her.

Fighting something she couldn't put a name to, she wrapped her fingers around Matt's waistband and tugged. To her surprise, he stepped closer. His hold on her shifted so he was supporting and lifting her breasts. Although she looked down, thinking to study what he was doing, the edges blurred.

Say something, she wanted to yell at him, but did she really want to deal with words? It was easier, and more exciting, to rub the backs of her fingers over his belly and feel it tighten. When he increased his hold on her breasts, she pulled his jeans toward her and slid a hand under the denim and over his belly. Finally she ran her fingers into the coarse, dark hair there.

"Enough!"

His exhaled breath fairly singed her forehead. Grabbing her around the waist, he lifted her, propelling her back and to the side as he did. When he let her down, she realized she was standing on the metal box.

Her sex aligned with his.

"Good thinking," she managed. She'd dispensed with snap and zipper before she put her mind to what he was doing.

He'd been waiting for her to finish, his thumbs hooked through her waistband and his stance wide. Determined not to give up until his jeans were down around his ankles, she started to give them a tug.

"No."

Pain arched through her wrists. Gasping, she acknowledged his hands pressing against the slender bones there. "What—"

"Am I doing? What I damn well want to."

When she winced, he jammed her arms against her sides. Although she tried to tell herself that he had no business stopping her from placing her hands where she wanted them, she didn't move.

He reached for her jeans. Maybe she was mistaken—she wanted to be—but was a snarl lifting the corner of his mouth? Not breathing, she waited as he yanked at her waistband. Fortunately, unlike her bra hooks, the jeans' button easily gave up its hold. He didn't look at her as he pulled down on the zipper.

No pause, no checking to see if she was on board with what he was doing. Instead he hauled her jeans down over her hips. He took her bikini panties at the same time, said nothing about the deep red pair she'd ordered online and had just arrived. Denim chafed her thighs, briefly hugged her knees, wound up around her ankles. Because her boots were still on, she had no way of freeing herself from the bondage he'd created.

Caught.

By him.

Her head had sagged forward while he worked on her. Lifting it so she could keep an eye on him took more courage than she wanted to admit. Somehow, without her paying attention, he'd positioned his jeans around his hips. His erection remained hidden behind his briefs.

Why aren't you exposing yourself? tugged at her mind. Then he slipped a workman's hand between her legs with the side of his thumb against her sex, and only that mattered. Arching her back, she thrust her pelvis at him.

Leather against silk defined what she was feeling. Her lids drooped. Although she knew it was coming, she started when a masculine finger slid into her. This was the foreplay she'd spoken about, yet the word didn't go far enough. Didn't reach deep enough into the experience.

Matt had impaled her on his finger. Hung her out to dry. Only *dry* was hardly the word. Wet. Hot and sopping and beyond gone. Nipples hard and hurting, her legs trembling while her arms remained submissively by her side.

Submissive?

Not her.

And yet—

Ah, he was going deeper, finger simulating cock, not as thick or promising as the real thing but—

Wait!

"Matt?" Speaking burned her throat. When he didn't respond, she said, "Condom."

"Yeah."

Although he didn't add *damn it* to the little he said, she sensed the words anyway. From the beginning of their *affair* she'd made it clear that although she was on the pill, she expected him to provide the added protection. After all, they'd had other sex partners and in today's world . . .

How could she have lost contact with what he was doing? Whatever the reason, she again locked herself around the masculine invasion. Tightening her sex around him, she searched for something, anything, to distract her from a premature climax.

Ah, the hills. Dry and done until spring softened the harshness. Someday, maybe, Matt and she would explore them together. He'd show her what made the ones on his property unique. And, maybe, once he had, she'd take him into those around her place and show him *the cave* she believed only she knew about.

"Enough."

Startled by his outburst, she stared at him. "What's enough?"

"Messing around."

His finger sucked out of her, emptied her, left her dripping and shaken. Wishing she didn't have to, she grasped his shoulders for balance. After wiping her sex juices on her naked flank, he hauled his cock out of its hiding place and rammed it into her.

Just like that. No asking if she was ready. No condom.

"Wait!" She wanted to pull back but couldn't make the move. "You promised—"

"Shut up."

Again with the command. Even more unsettling, he dug his fingers into her hip bones. Using his hold to keep her in place, he powered into her. If not for his grip, she would have fallen off the box.

And her hands gripping his shoulders—don't forget that.

One powerful thrust, then another. Hammering at her and her caring about nothing except his cock's commands.

She could fight, claw at his shoulders, scream maybe.

But she didn't want to, damn it.

She needed this man's cock plowing deep and strong and full into her, over and over, both of them sweating, the sun beating down, his hat sliding forward and then falling off.

More. Even more. Her knees locking and now her ankles chafing from the denim. Back protesting from arching deep. Careful to keep her pussy in alignment.

"Shit!" he bellowed. "Shit!"

Matt was coming. Hard. Wet heat spewing into her. Coating her channel with his cum.

Determined to keep up with him, she went deep inside, looking for the release she craved, touched it, lost it.

"Shit!"

More of his ejaculate filled her. When he pulled back, some escaped to dribble down the inside of her thigh. Until now, she'd been denied this part of sex, had told herself that was how it needed to be. But this was the real thing. Primal sex.

"Ah, shit."

He again rammed into her, grunting as he did, his fingers vising her hips. She returned his strength with all she had, and her fingers ground into his collarbone. She belatedly remembered to clamp down on his cock, but it was too late. He was beginning to soften.

Was done.

3

Being dressed again—well, minus the bra—helped restore Cat. At least she no longer felt so vulnerable.

Unfortunately, having her body covered did little to shake off her unease and tension.

Like hers, Matt's jeans were back up around his waist. He'd retrieved his hat. As she shook what dust she could off her bra, it occurred to her that he hadn't removed his shirt. Had that been because he'd been in such a hurry to get to the main act, or had he deliberately stripped her while remaining virtually intact clotheswise himself? Granted, this was far from their first quickie, but if her memory was serving her right, they'd always done equal amounts of stripping.

Shaking her head, she tucked her bra into a back pocket. Only then did she allow herself to focus on Matt. He'd walked over to Ginger and hoisted himself into the saddle without first letting the mare smell him. As a result, Ginger's head was high and white showed in her eyes.

"Careful," she warned as she joined them. "Give her a chance to figure out who you are."

He didn't look down. "I know what I'm doing."

"Do you?" she snapped. "You couldn't prove it by me today. What are you going to do? Take her for a run?"

He frowned. Before he could respond, if that had been his intention, his cell phone rang. After pulling it out of a front pocket, he shielded the faceplate so he could read what was displayed there.

"Beale," he said.

Although she wasn't concerned that Ginger would take advantage of Matt's inattention, Cat took hold of the reins so Matt could concentrate on the conversation. He did more listening than talking, his responses punctuated by three *damns*. Finally he said, "I'm on my way," and hung up.

"What is it?" she asked.

"Dead calf." He pointed toward the hills. "Slaughtered."

"No! Does Beale know what—"

"Not human."

A cougar attack was a remote possibility, although usually cougars concentrated on smaller game. Coyotes could have done the deed but probably only if the calf was already down.

"Dogs?" she ventured. "I've heard there's a pack..." She didn't bother to finish because Matt was dismounting. The instant his boots hit the ground, he started for the house at a run.

"I'm getting my rifle," he said over his shoulder.

"What are you doing?" Matt asked when he emerged from the house. Cat was loading Ginger into her trailer.

"I'm going with you. I figure we can drive most of the way, then take horses." She jerked her head at the adjacent pasture where he kept his working stock. "Which one do you want me to saddle?"

She was right. It would take time to hook his truck up to his trailer. Not only that, the trailer tires were bald; he'd been going to replace them.

"Why do you want to do that?" he asked as he headed for the pasture gate.

"I want to see for myself."

"It won't be pretty." After propping his rifle against a post, he opened the gate and whistled. Although the three horses in the pasture were a fair distance away, they lifted their heads. He whistled again and they trotted toward him.

"I know it won't. Matt, in some respects I've insulated myself from the reality of what ranchers have to deal with. I need to face that."

Misty, the smallest and steadiest of the horses, reached him first. Taking hold of her halter, he led her through the gate. The others looked disappointed, but Misty was probably best for Cat to ride.

"Where's the saddle and bridle?" Cat asked. "What if I get her ready while you fill some canteens?"

As he pointed at the tack box he'd placed her on for sex such a short time ago, he acknowledged that this maybe-120-pound woman could hold her own. Under the surface she was soft and feminine, but if he ever needed a woman watching his back, she'd be his first choice. He walked Misty over to Cat, who'd started digging into the box he'd had built because sometimes he wanted tack right where the horses were. Holding a saddle against her chest, Cat straightened. The saddle dragged her top precariously low, nearly revealing her breasts. For a moment, he didn't understand why she wasn't wearing a bra. Then the memory surfaced.

His skin felt strange, his muscles unfamiliar. Releasing Misty, trusting her to stay put, he headed back for the house. Why hadn't he thought about water when he was getting his rifle? And what about extra bullets?

The year after he'd come to live here, he and Santo had added insulation to the attic. As a result, despite the heat, the old house was cool. It hadn't occurred to either man, but Addie had talked them into replacing the small front window with a large one, which provided them with a broad view of their surroundings.

Walking into the kitchen, he reached under the sink for the canteens he kept there. As he filled four with cold well water, he let his thoughts drift to the damn hard work of digging a new well two years before Santo's death. Despite the dirt and strain, he didn't regret the time he'd spent with Santo.

Done with his first chore, he entered his bedroom, decorated with paintings of cowboy scenes he'd brought in Pendleton while participating in the roping events at the rodeo there. His favorite, over his bed, depicted two rearing stallions with the sun setting behind the combatants.

Yeah, he'd think about the stallions, not why he was digging in his top dresser drawer for ammunition. Neither would he ask what the hell had happened to him before and when he and Cat were having sex.

Cat.

Intriguing name. Why hadn't he asked how she'd come by it?

By his reckoning, he'd been in the house less than three minutes. In that time, Cat had saddled and bridled Misty and loaded her into her trailer. It was a tight fit for the horses, but they'd reach the end of the road in less than a half hour.

Cat stood, resting her hip against the trailer. "Do you want to drive?" she asked. "You know the way better than I do."

Again with the practical, logical observations. If not for her nipples pressing against the soft white fabric, he might think he was discussing plans with one of his hands. Beale was the only one in the hills today, which meant only the young buck would get a look at Cat's breasts.

No doubt Beale would wonder why she was out and about braless.

"I'll drive. Just let me get my rifle."

"It's already in the cab. Sorry, I don't have a gun rack."

But she hadn't hesitated to handle the weapon. "Do you know how to shoot?" Yet something else he didn't know about her.

Pushing away from the trailer, she headed for the passenger's side. "It depends on how you look at it. The way I figure, I learned enough to be able to plug a rattler if I need to. And if it isn't moving too fast."

Giving her a shrug by way of response, he walked over to the driver's side. Her pickup, like his, looked like crap. He hoped the engine was another story. Maybe he should take a look under the hood before—

Distant movement in the direction of the hills caught his attention. Those usually gray mounds were part of his world, and yet he didn't take them for granted. To his way of thinking, the hills' greatest value came from the grass they provided. The movement belonged to a solitary vulture. Yeah, like it or not, this vulture and others of its kind saw the dead calf as nothing more than food.

Beale had sounded shook up and had been glad to hear that his foreman was going to be joining him, but truth was, Matt wished he was going anywhere else. For the first time since this land had taken hold of his heart, he wanted nothing to do with it.

He didn't fear it; nothing like that.

Then what?

As Cat settled herself in the cab, he wondered if he was making a mistake by letting her accompany him. Instead of saying anything, however, he looked through the dusty windshield. A second vulture had joined the first.

Unfortunately, the scavengers weren't the only things out there. There was something else, instinct told him, a force, something that lifted the hairs at the back of his neck. Damn it, was he endangering Cat's life?

No, instinct told him. Who or whatever was out there wasn't interested in her.

Him, then?

Long before they reached the end of where the truck could go, Cat had come to the conclusion that she should have insisted on driving. Lucky Matt. He had the steering wheel to hold on to. As for her, her tailbone was going to be talking to her for hours.

They silently unloaded the horses. When she was in the saddle, Matt handed her two of the canteens, mounted, and urged Ginger forward. He wore his rifle slung across his back, looking too much like a man out hunting.

Up close, the landscape revealed the closely guarded secrets of what lived here. Sagebrush, of course, with its pungent aroma, tough bunchgrass, dry and dead-looking meadows that would turn moist in spring. What there was of trees mostly consisted of white-bark aspens. No matter how many times she'd seen the aspens' rich fall silver hues, she had yet to go through a November without riding around to take pictures.

They weren't here to pull out their cameras. For the first time since Matt had invaded her world, the focus was on something other than sex. Spotting several cows grazing in a small, narrow valley to her right, she wondered if the death of one of their number impacted them in any way. If the responsible predator or predators were still here, wouldn't they be nervous?

Experience had taught her that horses sometimes keyed into human emotion. If she was calm, they were too. If she brought tension into the barn, they became harder to work with. In addition, they seemed to have a connection with other animals, specifically dogs. That's why she insisted that potential horse buyers introduce their dogs to the horse. Twice a dog's aggression had nixed a sale.

Leaning over the saddle horn, she stroked Misty's neck. "You'd tell me if there's a pack of wild mutts around, wouldn't you?"

Yes, she concluded. Misty would be trying to buck her off so she could gallop away from danger.

Newly alert, Cat straightened. Compared to the hills around her place, Matt's looked as if they'd been sanded. Instead of sharp angles and rocky spires, these had a muted quality. She'd be surprised if there were any caves.

Heat attacked the back of her neck, making her regret not having worn a hat.

Riding was getting to her unrestrained breasts, or rather the unaccustomed freedom stirred her awareness of herself as a woman—that and Matt moving ahead of her. His cell phone chirped, cutting through the music of birds and wind. "We're almost there," he said into it. "Me and Cat." He was silent. Then, "Guess we'll find out."

"What was that about?" she asked when he'd returned the phone to his pocket.

"Beale asked how you'd react."

The carcass was a mess. The calf had been dead long enough that its legs were rigid. Despite that, its eyes remained big and black and, to her mind, scared-looking. Beale, a pistol strapped to his side, sat nearby while his mount, minus its bridle, grazed a short distance away. Cat was proud of Ginger's reaction. Although the mare's head stayed high and her ears kept moving, she continued walking until Matt reined her in. Misty needed knee pressure against her sides to venture close. Warned by Misty's shudders, Cat remained alert for sudden panic, something horses—that at the core were prey animals—were known for.

Matt dismounted and wrapped Ginger's reins around the closest bush. Instead of reminding him that the mare ground tied and had no need of a restraint, she decided not to distract him. Besides, Ginger had, to her knowledge, never come face-to-face with a violent and bloody death. After dismounting, she did the same with Misty, taking time to tie a secure knot.

By then Matt was standing over the dead calf with a somber-looking Beale beside him. Beale glanced her way. His attention slid to her breasts. Eyes wider than they'd been a moment ago, he frowned.

"Even before I found the calf, I had this feeling," Beale began. "I can't explain it, just this sense that I didn't want to come here."

"Why did you?" she asked. A look from Matt reminded her, too late, that she was suppose to be a bystander.

" 'Cause I had to," Beale said. "It's my job."

If Beale was twenty-one, he hadn't been for long. He had the not-quite-settled look of someone who wasn't done growing, but his family had been in the ranching business for generations. Obviously Matt had hired him for his upbringing, not for the breadth of his chest.

Matt squatted next to the calf, pushed back his hat, and ran his hand down the animal's neck as if looking for a pulse. Now that she'd had time to steel herself, she acknowledged that the calf had been disemboweled. In addition, the wounds in a hind leg left her with no doubt that it had been hamstrung.

"I'm not much good at reading prints," Beale told Matt. "You are. I was careful not to walk around much and tied my horse"—he pointed at the roan gelding—"where it wouldn't mess things up."

"Good." Matt stood, walked over to the calf's rear legs, and crouched again. The first time, his touch had been gentle. Now Cat saw only a clinical approach, a man searching for the facts. Mindless to the gore, he pulled at the ruined skin.

"What are you looking for?" She kept her voice at a whisper.

He looked over his shoulder at her. "Figuring out how many attackers there were."

By the time she'd assimilated his short explanation, he'd returned to his study of the carcass. Remembering the pain that had lurked in his eyes, she realized that beneath the hard exterior, Matt was a man who loved his animals. Although she wished he would share what he was learning with her, she kept her questions to herself. After examining what was left of the calf's belly, he slowly and gracefully stood and circled the carcass. He kept his head down and several times leaned over for a closer look at something.

Finally he returned to where she and Beale waited. "This wasn't done by a dog."

How can you say that? she came too close to blurting. Instead she clenched her fingers to keep from touching him. He looked not just grim but also tense.

"I didn't think so," Beale said, "but I didn't want to say anything until you'd come to your own conclusions. Too clean for curs, right?"

"Yeah." Matt rammed his hands into his back pockets. "Damn, I wish I'd brought a camera."

"I have one." Beale nodded at the gelding. "My girlfriend keeps asking me to show her what I do."

"I'd like to borrow it."

Looking pleased to be able to do something for his boss, Beale hurried toward his mount.

"Who are you going to show the pictures to?" she asked.

"I haven't decided."

Although Matt had met her gaze during the short exchange, she sensed his attention was elsewhere. He had the look of a man backed into something he wanted no part of. Different from before.

And the sexiest man she'd ever seen.

What is this reaction about? she pondered as Beale demonstrated how the digital camera worked. Matt's rugged quality had been a huge part of his appeal to her. He was no less rugged and untamed today, but there was a new layer. Mysterious. Dangerous?

Not rushing, Matt took at least a dozen shots of the sad remains. He even aimed the camera at the sky and captured the buzzards circling overhead. That done, he stepped away from the kill site and started walking in a slow, contemplative circle. He stared at the ground, occasionally brushing grass aside with a boot. Although she hoped the activity—she guessed he was looking for tracks—would calm him, tension continued to ride his shoulders.

"You ever seen something a pack of dogs has gotten to?" Beale asked her.

"No."

"It's ugly. They don't know what they're doing; hunting's been bred out of their DNA or something. They rip and tear until not much is left. This"—he jerked his head at the carcass—"is the work of a real predator."

"Cougar?"

"No," Matt responded. "Cats go for the throat."

Matt knew or suspected more than he was saying. So, she gathered, did Beale. Much as she needed to know what that was, she'd wait for them to explain. Watching Matt lean down and snap a picture of something on the ground, she acknowledged that the prickling at the back of her neck hadn't gone away. It wasn't just the carnage or even the men's moods—not that she had a handle on Matt's.

Their surroundings contributed.

Were they being watched?

Going by Matt's actions, she surmised he'd found the trail made by whatever creature had killed he calf. She didn't understand why he found it necessary to take shot after shot. Before he'd finished, he'd covered nearly a hundred yards. Rubbing the side of his neck, he started back. Then he stopped, new tension evident in the lines of his body. Unfortunately, he wasn't close enough for her to read his expression.

To her surprise, he turned ninety degrees to the left and took a dozen slow, long-legged steps. Stopping, he drew his rifle from his back and stared at the ground. Didn't move a muscle. The better part of a minute later, he squatted, holding the rifle in one hand and the camera in the other. She couldn't see what he was doing beyond studying something on the ground. Everything about him called to her. He was no longer the determined cowboy who'd recently turned down a corporation's offer to buy him out. That man had been replaced by a creature ruled by instinct.

After standing, Matt took more pictures, using one hand this time. Done, he slung the rifle over his shoulder but made no move to rejoin her and Beale.

"Damn," Beale muttered.

"What?" she asked.

"Last time he acted like that, a storm was about to hit in the middle of calving season."

"But this was just one calf." She wasn't sure who she was trying to calm, maybe both of them. "He can't be thinking the rest of the herd's in danger."

Instead of agreeing with her, Beale started toward Matt. Although she wanted to see what had captured Matt's attention, she couldn't make her legs move. Reaching out, she patted Misty's side.

At length, Beale reached his foreman. She didn't think they said anything before Beale knelt as Matt had done. A few seconds later, Beale stood. His hand hovered over his sidearm. Even at this distance, she knew the man inside Beale had been replaced by the child he'd been not long ago.

They started back toward her, walking side by side, looking

all around instead of where their boots landed. Shadows caused by their hats hid their expressions, yet their body language said a lot of things she wished they didn't.

"You know what did this, don't you?" She glanced at the calf.

"Yeah." Matt fingered his rifle.

"Are you going to tell me?"

The two men exchanged a look. "Wolf," Matt said.

"Wolf." She took a calming breath. "Then the rumors... They're here, aren't they?"

"Yeah."

Years ago, wolves had been reintroduced to Yellowstone as an experiment in restoring the balance of nature that had existed before man declared wolves a menace and all but wiped them out in the United States. She loved the idea of having the predators back in the wild.

The original pack had grown, divided, moved. The first wolf had appeared in eastern Oregon a few years ago, but because wolves were territorial, they'd continued to head west. Once a pack became established in an area, the alpha pair chased off the juveniles, forcing them to claim new turf.

Central Oregon's ranchers had known that time was coming. Why, then, did Matt and Beale appear so shocked?

"All the scat's a day old. There's no reason for me to stay here," Matt announced.

Surprised, she opened her mouth, but he knew his world better than she possibly could.

"What do you want me to do with the carcass?" Beale asked.

As Matt explained that it needed to be buried to discourage wolves from returning, she noted how few words had been exchanged between the two men. Instead they seemed to be communicating via locked gazes.

"That's that, then?" she asked. "You don't have any concerns for the rest of the cattle?"

"Of course I do. That's why Beale's staying here, with my rifle. And why I'll get one of my men to get my dogs up here."

That made sense, especially since Matt had trained his two Australian shepherds to protect and herd livestock.

"I want to upload the pictures tonight," Matt said. "I'll get your camera back to you after that."

"That's fine."

Squaring himself, Matt looked from Beale to her and then back again. "I don't want either of you saying anything about this until I give the word."

Nodding soberly, Beale stared at what was left of the calf.

"You can't be thinking about keeping this to yourself," Cat blurted. "The other ranchers have a right to know—"

"I know what I'm doing, Cat. Believe me, I have damn good reasons for it." Grabbing her upper arm, he propelled her toward her truck. "Time for us to go."

4

Driving took up only a small part of Matt's attention. Mindful of Cat sitting beside him, he occasionally took in his surroundings. Although he'd known how the calf had died the moment he spotted the carcass, seeing that first wolf print had sent a chill through him.

Things had changed.

Maybe the life he'd fought so hard for had been upended.

Damn, he didn't want to feel like this. From early childhood, the predators had fascinated him. Unlike him, wolves were strong, resourceful, independent. On the few occasions when he had access to research material, he'd soaked up everything he could about them. Back then he hadn't seen his fascination for what it was—escape from the real world. He did now, not that self-analysis had lessened his interest. Wolves were unique, intelligent and deadly, complex and, in their own way, loving. As pack animals, each member had a well-defined role. They relied on each other, raising pups as a group, watching each other's backs, hunting and killing together.

If wolves and wolves alone had been out there, he could live with that. He'd contact the authorities and spread the warning through his fellow ranchers. He'd even speak to the media, because that was what a responsible man did.

However, that last paw print had turned everything on end. Maybe short-circuited his mind.

To his disbelief, he no longer felt comfortable in his own skin.

"A pack's moved into the area, hasn't it," Cat said. "I wonder how many there are."

"Hard to say."

"Matt, I have a right to know something. Are you considering not telling Fish and Wildlife?"

"Hmm."

"Don't." She touched his arm only to jerk her hand back and hug her side of the cab. "I hate it when you give me a nonanswer. Telling us not to say anything—I don't understand your thinking."

Me either. "This is my call. Let it be."

"The hell I will. I can't."

Although he didn't look at her, her glare bore into him. Even with her waiting for his response, he couldn't give it. Damn it, she was right. A responsible man would have already dialed 911. Let people swarm over his land.

Maybe that's what it all came down to. His land. Not wanting anyone on it. Leaving the wolves—and the other thing—alone.

Maybe.

If only he could pull his thoughts together.

The truck and trailer filled him with movement and sound. The woman beside him . . . Hell, he didn't know what to think of her, so he buried himself in the act of driving through land that had become his parents and family, his life, his soul.

One mile became another and then a third until he spotted the ranch and outbuildings. The horses whinnied, obviously looking forward to getting out. Usually he felt the same way, because being confined in a vehicle made him more than a little claustrophobic. Today he didn't know what he wanted.

Fighting the urge he didn't have a name for, he pulled Cat's truck close to the wooden corral and turned off the engine. Faced her. She sat with her head resting on the seat back and looking at him.

"I'm still trying to wrap my mind around what happened and the way you're acting," she said, "but maybe it's a fool's mission." Sighing, she straightened. "You turn me on like I've never been turned on. I'm not telling you something you don't know." Another sigh. "I tell myself you feel the same way and we're riding this whatever-it-is for all it's worth, but this is crazy—you know it is."

Her words were a song, sounds brushing over grass. His attention was drawn to her neck and throat. And her breasts. She was female, he was male. Heat speaking to heat.

She continued. "I'm going to take a break from us. Get my feet back under me. Figure out who I am because I sure as hell can't figure you out."

Now the words came at him one at a time and disjointed, meaningless. In a wolf pack, only the alpha pair mated. They were the strongest, the leaders, and passed on superior genetics. Unlike humans, who hooked up for countless and often meaningless reasons, wolves did what they did for one reason: to maximize the creatures' chance of survival.

He was strong and healthy. So was Cat.

Something primal had brought them together.

Even with the windows down, the air inside the cab started heating. Sweat bloomed on Cat's temples.

"I give up," she said, and reached for her handle. "There's no talking to you today. If—"

His hand, which no longer felt as if it belonged to him, snaked out and clamped onto her knee. "Stay!"

"Stay? Matt, I'm no— Hey, that hurts."

Her sharp tone barely registered. Teeth clenched, she dug her nails into his wrist. "What the hell? Let me go!"

Pain triggered something in him. Growling, he slid from behind the steering wheel and shoved her against her door. Eyes wide, she glared at him. Was that fear behind the glare? Didn't matter.

"Let me go." Her every word had a drumlike quality. "This is so damn not funny."

Although she trembled, she made no move to try to free herself, only looked at him as if she'd never seen him. The day had heated her bare arms, and what he could see of her chest looked sunburned. Cotton covered her breasts. He'd expose them and handle what belonged to him. Take her hard and fast. Leave his imprint on her. Remind her of his superior strength and great need.

"Matt? Can you hear me?"

Her lips remained parted. Behind them, he glimpsed straight, white teeth. They'd kissed, of course, but not much and not for long, because they'd always been eager to get to sex itself. As a consequence, he knew little about her mouth.

Time for that to change.

Leaning across her while still gripping her upper arms, he aimed. To his relief, her features went out of focus. This way he no longer had to face her questions, her disquiet. Fighting the force trying to break free inside him, he managed a light touch of lips against lips. In contrast, his hold remained firm.

She turned her head to the side. "What the hell is—"

"You know you want this."

"Damn you." She swung her head back toward him. "Damn you for—"

He cut off her words with another kiss, this one stronger and less in control. His muscles contracted and expanded, and his heart pounded.

Another shudder struck her. Then, breathing quick and unsteady, she returned his crude attempt at a kiss. Dimly aware that it was getting even hotter in the cab, he increased the pressure. His suddenly erect cock pressed against his jeans to hammer home the fact that she was his mate, the female fate had chosen to accept his seed. The animal taking over inside him didn't care whether she wanted the same thing.

His mouth still locked with hers, he let go of her arms only to press his hands over her thighs. His brain expanded, pushed against the inside of his skull, risked exploding. Shaking off the possibility of that happening, he clung to the belief that she was his. When, where, and how he wanted.

Images formed and faded behind his nearly closed lids. He *saw* a wolf running along the top of a ridge with a dying sunset all around and small animals flattened against the ground so, hopefully, the predator wouldn't see them.

Something waited for the wolf, a shadow among shadows.

"No! Damn it, no."

Cat had again turned her head to the side and was trying to push him away. The image in his mind faded, yet enough remained to stir the question of its meaning and what it had to do with him. She drew back her hands, then struck his chest with both fists.

"Now!" she commanded.

Despite the distracting pain, he fought to keep the mindscene with him. The shadow belonged to another wolf. Huge. Fangs bared, it faced the first one. A single howl drifted through him.

"Matt? Matt, are you listening?"

Whether it was her question or another blow that got his attention didn't matter. Straightening, he stared at her. She was nothing like the wolves he's just *seen*. The predators had nothing to do with this moment.

"What?" he managed.

Instead of answering, she reached behind her and turned the handle, practically falling out as the door opened. She got her weight under her and stumbled back when he joined her. Still confused about what had happened, he rammed his hands into his back pockets to let her know he had no intention of touching her again.

He didn't, did he?

"I don't want to talk about this," she told him. "Right now I don't want to hear your excuse, if you have one. Excuse?" She pressed the heel of her hand to her forehead. "No, it isn't that, is it? Something..."

The horses were impatient to be let out. Cat and he should end this stare-down and tend to them. Instead, he continued to study her. Everything from her bruised lips to her lack of a bra, even the sweat on her throat was his doing. From the night they'd met, he'd felt things for her he hadn't known he was capable of. Things he'd always refused to examine.

"Matt?"

"What?" Instead of telling him to go to hell, which she must believe she had a right to do, she was still speaking to him.

"I want to see the pictures once they're uploaded." She extended a slow, maybe hesitant hand toward him and touched his middle.

The prints. "No, you don't."

"I saw the real thing. How can photographs be any worse?"

How little she knew. "Don't ask."

Confusion and perhaps compassion spread over her. "Everything feels as if it's breaking apart today. Somehow I'm going to put it back together and get some answers. The thing is, I don't see how I can do that without your help. Are you willing, Matt? Are you?"

Was he capable? "The horses." He started toward the rear of the trailer. "They need out."

He didn't hear her footsteps, but somehow she was there, ready to step into the trailer as he unhooked the latch.

"Talk to me." She planted her hand over his. "What's going on?"

"You don't want to know," he said, when the truth was, he couldn't see past the darkness still clinging to him.

She backed away, looking at the ground as if expecting something from it. "We're not getting anywhere. I'm going home. The next move's up to you, maybe."

Good thing she added *maybe* to her comment, Cat thought as she pulled into her driveway with the empty trailer rattling behind her. She'd done a fairly good job of shutting down her mind during the ride home, but now it was waking up, as was her body. After parking beside her six-stall barn, she got out. Hungry whinnying served as a reminder that she was late in feeding her horses. Her own stomach growled, but that would have to wait, because the critters that paid the bills came first.

But not so first that she was oblivious to her body, she admitted as she headed for the hay stacked under a lean-to. One hand went to her mouth, and she ran a rough nail over her lower lip where Matt's impact remained. She hadn't expected him to kiss her. Given everything that had happened since they'd had sex earlier today, she'd believed making out would be the last thing on his mind.

Making out? It had hardly been that; more like an attack.

And not just a bruising kiss, she acknowledged as she took wire cutters to the wire around the closest bale. There'd also been a matter of him backing her against the truck door and holding her in place.

Rough foreplay. If she wanted to evade the truth, she might be able to get away with calling it that. Unfortunately, foreplay was a lie.

Something had come over Matt. Whatever that something

was had made him believe he had the right to manhandle her. He'd plowed over manners and civilized behavior. She could buy that he'd been reacting to finding one of his calves torn apart, but did that really explain things? Wouldn't most men punch something, curse, maybe blast away in the direction the killers had gone?

Most wouldn't jump the bones of the only member of the opposite sex within jumping distance. Not that he'd accomplished the act.

Shaking her head, she concentrated on the horses. Things were set up so they could go in and out of the barn as they wanted. Come night, she'd lock most of them in individual stalls for security. When she'd showed up, they'd all been out in the two-acre pasture adjacent to the barn with their heads over the top railing and staring at the road, waiting for her.

Now all were bunched where she always dropped their hay. "I'm working as fast as I can," she informed them, and heaved hay over the top rail. Her breasts jumped.

Why'd you do that to my bra, Matt?

She quick-stepped back to the lean-to and got another pitchfork full of hay. There probably was a more efficient way to handle feeding time, but the manual labor kept her in pretty good physical condition.

She'd never match his strength, she admitted, and threw the horses another pile. If he wanted to rape her, she wouldn't be able to stop him.

Could it come to that? she pondered when she stepped into the shower a half hour later. Despite their sex's frenzied quality, until today she'd believed she had nothing to fear from the man. Now she didn't know.

Lukewarm water slid over her hair and back, freeing her thoughts. Today aside, her relationship with Matt had been everything she'd ever wanted from a man physically. His body was hot; he was hot. A look, a touch from him and she was off and running.

Shampooing her long hair was no one-minute task. Sometimes she wondered why she didn't simply chop it off. But her folks had insisted on keeping her hair short and stylish throughout her childhood, and hardheaded or not, she'd be damned if she'd follow the path they'd tried to lay down.

Enough with my parents, she ordered as she began rinsing. They were—where were they now anyway?—doing their self-absorbed thing. They certainly weren't worrying about her.

So if any worry was needed, it was up to her to do it.

Matt. Body carved from an unforgiving land and never-ending work. Eyes that hinted of things unsaid. A cock made for wrapping more than just her pussy around.

Straightening, she backed away a little so the spray struck her breasts. Lifting one and then the other, she watched the water attack them. Matt wasn't gentle with her, never had been. No kid gloves. Crazy determined to match his frenzy, she approached his body as if it were a prairie-wild bronc. She clung to his cock. Sometimes she planted it in her mouth and raked her teeth over sweet steel and satin.

Mostly she took it into her starving, impatient core.

Groaning, she braced her back against the small shower stall and slipped a hand between her legs. He hadn't worn a condom today. For the first time, it had been skin against skin between them. Wonderful. Memorable.

Breaking the rules.

Damn him.

Her eyes closed. The sound of running water became everything, that and the fingers gliding over flesh that jumped and wept with every touch and thought.

Decision time. She could either set out a list of rules of behavior for Matt to adhere to from this moment on or leap into the unknown and embrace whatever happened next. Maybe die happy.

What about the wolves? Where did they fit into all this?

Wolves. Sex doggy style. Mating simply to reproduce, unlike humans who came together for pleasure and sometimes a sense of belonging.

Bombarded by the reality of how little she and Matt shared, she didn't fight her tears. Lonely and a little scared, she splayed her legs, tilted her pelvis upward, and worked two fingers deep inside. Her thumb unerringly found her clit, stimulating it and turning her stupid. Surrounding her in pressure followed by the harsh, wonderful climb to the top.

Her nerves twanged, her sex muscles gripped, and as her hard climax rocked her, more tears fell.

"I'll be back early next week," Addie said. "Maybe as soon as Sunday."

Now that the calls to Fish and Wildlife and his fellow ranchers were behind him, Matt had been looking forward to a cold beer and the evening news, which was something he seldom had time for. Although the beer was in his hand, Addie's call had changed any hope he'd had of being able to put the day behind him. Sooner or later, Addie needed to know what had happened.

"You sound eager to get back," he told the woman who'd slowly and lovingly shown a confused and angry teenager the meaning of trust. "The last time we talked, you were excited about all the places your sister was taking you."

"Was I? Now I'm just exhausted and getting broke. Carole's a shopaholic. I don't get it. What's the excitement in collecting stuff?"

Addie sounded like what she was, a farmwife accustomed to putting the land and the livestock's needs before hers. To her way of thinking, buying for the sake of buying was flat-out insane. She'd told him that she and Carole had had several good conversations that helped bridge some of the gaps caused by lives that had gone in different directions since childhood. But Carole kept pushing her to hold back nothing about Santo's death. According to Carole, the only way Addie was going to get over her husband's death was by talking and then talking some more.

Addie didn't want to talk about burying the man she'd loved more than she'd known it was possible to love. Her grief was hers and hers alone, part of the memories of a solid marriage.

"Carole didn't know Santo more than superficially," Addie said, her voice thick with tears. "You did. When and if I feel like letting down my hair, I want it to be with someone who doesn't need a picture painted. So, anyway, if I show up on your doorstep in the middle of the night, you'll know why."

"It's your doorstep more than it is mine," he said. He stared out the kitchen window with its view of where he'd been today. He, Beale, Cat, a dead calf, and wolf prints.

"Let's not get into that, Matt. There's more of your blood and sweat in the land than mine."

"I'm not sure about that." Upending the can, he swallowed. "I figure it's pretty equal." He didn't need to mention how much blood Santo had shed. "I've been taking care of your garden. The refrigerator's full."

"I'm sure it is. Matt, is there anything I should know about?"

"What makes you say that?"

"Have you forgotten we live under the same roof? Something's going on, right?"

"We'll talk when you get back."

"I thought so. I can always tell when something's on your mind."

He couldn't argue with that, he allowed as he hung up, but there was no way Addie could guess what he was thinking about tonight. Although he didn't want to, he again stared out the window. From this distance, the hills he knew as well as the back of his hand and yet didn't looked hazy. He'd never told anyone—hell, he'd barely admitted it to himself—but they'd always made him feel uneasy, not nearly as uncomfortable as the last time he'd gone to where his father was living.

He was a grown man, he reminded himself whenever unease about his surroundings caught him unawares. There was no such thing as a bogeyman, no evil spirits, nothing waiting to jump out at him from the shadows.

Opening the refrigerator, he reached for another beer, his limit because he never knew when he might have to make a decision or jump into action. Logic said his present tension was a result of thinking about where they'd found Santo's body, a place not far from where the calf's life had ended.

Santo and a calf were dead. He couldn't do anything about that, so why the hell was he letting himself get tied into a knot? Better to think of something pleasant, something that spoke to the man in him.

Cat.

Who, after what he'd done to her, might want nothing to do with him.

5

He was naked with a jacket slung over his shoulder. Cold misted his breath and chilled his bare feet. It was night, moonless, and yet he could see. What he was doing here briefly concerned him. Then a wind kicked up, and he stopped thinking about anything except jamming his arms into the too-small jacket. When he shrugged, trying to make the jacket fit, the garment ripped down the back, but that was all right because he now wore boots.

Nothing but boots.

And a knife belted to his waist.

For a moment he thought the night had started breathing, then realized the sound was coming from just beyond what little he could see.

"Who is it?" He wasn't sure whether he'd spoken aloud or had thought the question. "What are you doing here?"

No one answered, and he acknowledged that he hadn't expected anything. Grateful for the weapon, he pulled it out of the sheath. It started out being heavy only to lose weight until it felt as if he were holding on to feathers.

Looking down, he saw blood dripping off the ends of his fingers. Fear bit at him, only to fade. Now he didn't know what he was feeling, maybe nothing. Maybe impatience because he suspected something was going to happen and he, by damn, deserved to know what it was.

Why? It wasn't as if he knew what to do.

Morning bloomed around him. The sunrise wasn't perfect; it left shadows here and there, but he was in the hills at the east end of his property. No, that was wrong, because the ones he was looking at weren't smooth and rolling with plenty of grass but liberally shot with sharp rocks and a steep peak only a mountain climber would attempt.

As he studied the peak, it melted a little so it no longer looked so formidable. At the same time, it gave birth to other mountains until they surrounded him. Interesting, he thought. A moment later, interest turned into tension and shivers down his naked back. Wiggling his toes reassured him that his boots hadn't deserted him. He wasn't sure about socks. Who needed a coat when it was so hot?

Hot? Hadn't it just been cold?

Shrugging off weather concerns, he did what he'd been putting off since night deserted the scene. These weren't morning shadows painting the sides of the mountains away from the sun after all. Instead, he was looking at cave after cave. Some were barely pinpricks. A few appeared perfect for a she-wolf looking for a place to give birth. The closest sported a narrow opening and beyond that a large, well-lit room complete with some of the furniture he'd seen at Cat's place.

Cat. Was she part of whatever the hell this was?

As if answering his question, feminine fingers stroked his cock. A hand gathered up his balls and held them as if they were precious.

Was this Cat? The woman he'd once thought he knew had

always grabbed his sex as if determined to wring every bit of cum out of him. Feeding off her, he did the same, lightly twisting her nipples and slapping her mons. Then he rammed a knee between her legs and lifted, forcing her to ride him.

"You can't answer your question about who has hold of your cock and balls, can you?" Cat's voice asked. "Wanna know why?"

"Yeah."

"Because you don't know me. Hell, you never asked where I came from or why I wound up here."

Loving the feel of her hands on his most important organ, he prayed she'd keep the touch light. Otherwise, he'd go off.

"You're not the only one with dark places in their background." He didn't know where the words were coming from, surely not his mind. "What the hell do you know about me?"

Releasing his cock and balls, she threw herself at him, nearly knocking him off his boots. Funny how he could feel arms, legs, breasts, and belly and yet not see her.

"Isn't that a pisser," she said. "Strangers fucking each other's brains out. Going at it like rabbits."

She wrapped her arms around his neck and hauled on it until he was forced to bend toward her. Somehow her legs were around his waist with her damp, hot sex plastered to his middle. We can't fuck like this, he wanted to tell her, but her mouth clamped onto his and he couldn't speak. Couldn't breathe.

Seriously, couldn't breathe.

His head began pounding, and his lungs burned. Something had plugged his nostrils. No matter how desperately he fought to wrench his head to the side so he could open his mouth, nothing happened.

Light-headed, he struggled to keep his legs under him, but her body was becoming heavier. They'd melted together, would go down together.

He swayed forward and back, forward again. Then just as his knees started to buckle, the weight was gone. Feminine arms no longer gripped his neck. Most telling, the sex moisture she'd smeared over his belly started to dry.

Gone. Lost. Nothing left behind except the few words she'd spoken.

She was right. They were strangers.

Thinking—if it could be called that—that the dream had come to an end, he ran his hands over his waist to discover that the knife no longer existed.

Cold returned. Alert and more alarmed than he wanted to admit, he looked around. His attention settled on the cave that had had Cat's furniture in it. Now only her bed remained.

Thinking she might reappear and be on it if he touched it, he started toward the bed. Something sharp jabbed his right instep. What had happened to the boots?

Knowing there weren't any answers, he looked up. A dark, four-legged form blocked the cave entrance.

"Damn it, not that."

A long muzzle opened to reveal countless teeth. He wasn't sure but thought the wolf—yeah, that's what it was—had been normal size at first. Now it was massive. Not as large as a horse but nearly twice as big as a mortal wolf. Growling, it started toward him.

Terrified and fascinated, he held his ground.

"Welcome," the wolf said.

Cat woke with a headache that two cups of coffee did nothing to alleviate. She had two students coming this afternoon, teenage girls looking to improve their roping skills so hopefully they could earn more ribbons at the periodically held local rodeos. She was looking forward to their enthusiasm and willingness to learn. As they'd told her, their parents didn't have the patience or knowledge. Cat suspected some of the problem was the girls didn't give their parents enough credit, but as long as they listened to her, which they did, she didn't care.

She hadn't heard from Matt. The local morning news had led with the wolf attack, proof that he'd spread the necessary news. She'd heard from several neighbors eager to rehash what little the reporter had said. Maybe she should have mentioned that she'd seen the dead calf, but that would lead to questions she wasn't up to answering.

When she'd first gone outside, it had been cool enough that she'd regretted not wearing a jacket, but giving the horses their morning hay had warmed her. Instead of saddling her newest acquisition, a two-year-old quarter horse gelding with a tendency to shy every time he saw a lasso, she sat on a hay bale and stared at the rocky outcroppings to the north, which were on what had once been Paiute land.

Other than the occasional hiker, the rimrocks held little appeal, and her one attempt to take a horse there had taught her it wasn't worth the risk. After the failed horseback ride when she'd discovered that the terrain was even steeper than it had looked from a distance, she'd argued with herself for months. She had no reason to go there. Her boots were hardly made for climbing, and she had more than enough to keep herself busy. Only lizards, spiders, and maybe snakes made their homes there.

But the former Paiute turf continued to call to her. Why had ancient Native Americans lived there? She could understand scouts staying there so they could keep an eye on strangers, but not building homes. However, the little she'd learned from the local historical society led her to believe the tribe had spent extended periods of time there.

One spring day last year, she'd gotten up, driven to the end of the road, and, armed with water, granola bars, binoculars, and her cell phone, she'd started up a narrow deer path. She'd climbed and explored for hours. Despite scratches, bug bites, and aching limbs, she'd followed curiosity or instinct or something from one intriguing spot to another. The whole time she was up there, she imagined she was a Paiute woman on a spirit quest. Modern life no longer had a hold on her. She'd become someone ancient and tied to the land, a primitive and trusting human being who believed everything the shaman said about mystical forces such as the sun and moon gods. They ruled Native American life by rewarding righteous behavior and punishing those who didn't follow *The Way*.

She'd never told anyone what she'd found that day.

Shaken by memories of the eerie time she'd spent in the cave, she scrambled to her feet. Enough with getting hung up with what she didn't understand and hadn't shared with anyone. Action time had arrived.

Still fighting the hold the cave exerted over her whenever she thought about it, she headed toward the horse pasture. She'd lifted her hand to shield her eyes and was looking for the quarter horse gelding when she heard an approaching vehicle.

Ramming her hands into her back jeans' pockets, she waited. Told herself it wasn't Matt and even if it was, she didn't want to see him.

Today Matt had on a Western shirt with pearl snaps that hugged his torso before disappearing into old, faded jeans. In deference to the heat—or maybe because he wanted to test her resolve—the shirt was open at the throat down to the fourth button. Dark, curling chest hair challenged her not to touch it. He'd rolled up the sleeves to just above his elbows. Damn those hard-as-hell forearms.

He held up a flash drive. "You wanted to see the pictures I took."

Something about his tone said she'd regret this, but what was she going to do, chicken out when she already knew what she was going to see?

"You could have e-mailed them to me," she said.

"No, I couldn't. Do you have time?"

She'd make time. She just hoped she could keep her emotional equilibrium about her. Matt had parked his pickup next to hers in such as way that she'd have to do a lot of maneuvering in order to move her rig. Deliberate?

"I see you called Fish and Wildlife," she said over her shoulder as she led the way to her house.

"And the police. Also some of my neighbors."

"I know." She laughed. "The rumor mill's on overload today. Did any of the authorities say you shouldn't have touched anything, give them a chance to look at the carcass?"

"Sheriff Wilton started to but stopped when I e-mailed him the pictures."

Which he hadn't done when it came to her. Feeling a tension she didn't want to acknowledge, she opened the front door and stepped inside. In some ways, her place and Matt's were clones. Both had been built in the 1950s with sitting porches, small living rooms, and kitchens at the rear. Her house's former owners had done a pretty good job of keeping up the house; the outbuildings and pastures hadn't much concerned them. In contrast, Santo and Addie had spread their attention equally throughout the property and had built a wing consisting of a bedroom, bath, and office for Matt. She envied him his modern sleeping/work quarters.

Careful not to look in the direction of the bedroom where she and Matt had sometimes torn at each other on her double bed, she went to the desk and filing cabinets she'd set up in a second bedroom. Her laptop was open on the desk.

"Good-sized screen," Matt said, and sat in the office chair.

As he plugged the flash drive into the USB port, she contemplated planting her butt on the table next to the laptop; however, not only would it be hard to see the monitor from that angle, but also she wasn't ready to commit to getting that close to him.

For the first time since their relationship began, he hadn't touched or tried to touch her. In fact, he barely seemed aware of her, as if watching things load was the only thing on his mind. His fingers looked too big for their task, but she knew what they were capable of. The things he could make her feel.

Opting for standing behind him and slightly to the side, she looked over his shoulder as the first picture appeared. Even without the sounds and smells that had been part of yesterday, the close-up of the calf's sightless eyes saddened her. It might help if she placed her hands on Matt's shoulders, but chances were then she wouldn't be able to concentrate on what was obviously important to him.

And to her, too, she amended as the slideshow continued. The seventeen-inch screen allowed for too much detail. Yesterday she'd looked down at what a wolf pack had done to a living creature. Today reality was being played out in close-up.

"The sheriff said he was satisfied with what I sent him. I haven't heard back from Fish and Wildlife. They might want more."

"They're not going to get the carcass, are they?" The calf shots were over and had been replaced by telling paw prints visible despite the surrounding weeds. "I mean, Beale buried the calf, right?"

"Yeah."

Matt still wasn't looking at her, and his hands were beneath the table where she couldn't see them.

"Then there's not much point in them going there." She pointed at the screen. "Besides, I'd think that what's important is learning where the pack is now, not where it was."

Matt gave no indication he agreed or disagreed. When he leaned forward a little, she noted the tight tendons at the sides of his neck. Not giving herself time to question what she was doing, she started massaging them. A sigh rolled out of him only to end abruptly as if he regretted letting her know how he reacted.

Touching him to comfort instead of excite was a new experience. Instead of pressing the heels of her hands against the base of his neck as she would have done in the past, she lightly ran her fingertips into his hair. She tried to keep her touch firm enough that she didn't risk tickling him.

"Not a good idea, Cat," he muttered.

Instead of heeding him, she leaned into him so the back of his head touched her middle. "I can't help myself."

"The hell you can't. You know exactly what you do to me."

She slid her hands around his neck and touched her thumbs to his windpipe. She'd never try to cut off his ability to breathe. Quite the opposite—feeling him swallow let her tell herself they were sharing something.

Can we take another run at it? she wanted to say. *Put part of yesterday behind us and go back to what's been good between us. Maybe see if we can reach deeper, touch deeper.*

His long, strong shudder reminded her of a horse about to buck. Confused and a little hurt, she settled her arms by her sides. "Sorry," she muttered.

"So am I." He rubbed his forehead, didn't look back at her. "Here's where I started placing my hand beside the prints for size comparison."

Hating the effort needed to do anything, she blinked and concentrated. After a half-dozen shots, she concluded that wolves of different sizes had been responsible. Matt's hand was longer than any of the prints. She wasn't sure about the width, but what struck her was how easily she could distinguish the rear pad from the toes. The claw marks seemed small until she reminded herself that a wolf's deadliest weapon was its fangs.

"That's remarkable," she said. "Maybe I shouldn't think that, but seeing proof of the animal that's the object of so much controversy in this country thrills me."

"Hmm."

Touching the mouse, Matt stopped the slideshow.

"That's it?" she asked as she again locked onto his unmistakable tension. "I thought you took some out near that sagebrush just before you turned around. Maybe they didn't turn out."

"They did."

With his tone warning her to wait, she wrapped her hands around her elbows.

"Those wolves were walking," he said. "When they run, their tracks become larger because the foot spreads, elongating the toes and widening the pads."

"How do you know that?"

The chair protesting, he swung around so he now looked up at her. Despite the difference in their height because she was standing, she felt his greater size. His hands gripped the armrest, turning his knuckles white.

"I did a lot of online research last night. When I wasn't dreaming."

Don't ask me about the dream, his eyes said, so she didn't. As long as he kept that to himself, she wouldn't mention waking drenched in sweat with her hands between her legs and her taut nipples aching.

"I don't blame you," she said lamely. "No matter what they did to your livestock, wolves are fascinating creatures."

"Are they?"

She wasn't going to get in an argument with him. Neither was she going to give in to the impulse to try to smooth away the new deep lines between his eyes. Maybe he knew what she was thinking and had decided to push her limits, because he closed his hands around her hips and drew her toward him with hands that trembled.

"What?" Letting go of her elbows, she impulsively gripped his shoulders. Bone and muscle capable of riding a Brahma bull spoke to her and nearly allowed her to dismiss his mood. Then his gaze met hers and she knew that wasn't going to happen.

"What?" she repeated.

"The pictures—there's two more."

Going by his tone, she sensed she wouldn't want to study them, but if Matt could take them, she could study.

"That's why you came here, isn't it? You wanted to watch my reaction to the last ones."

"It's more than that."

6

Instead of prodding Matt to continue, Cat worked her fingers under his shirt. Life and energy and something she couldn't define met her. Then his hands went to her buttocks, and he pulled her close and nothing else mattered.

Dragging her attention off his features, she studied the growing bulge between his legs. As if triggered by it, her breasts pressed against her bra—the one that replaced the one he'd destroyed.

Although he remained sitting, she didn't trust him. Didn't know this man with his leathered body and darkening—yes, darkening—eyes.

She wasn't going to tell him he was scaring her. A woman who'd weathered high-country winters could stand on her own. However, storms and vulnerable horses weren't the same as strange wild vibrations from a masculine body.

Somewhere deep inside was the truth of him, the reason for the recent changes in his personality, an explanation for the dusky shadows seeming to surround him.

Maybe there was only one way to get to the core.

The teenage girls she'd agreed to work with wouldn't be here for several hours, which meant it was just her and Matt until his world interrupted them.

Hot friction along her thighs drew her attention there. He was rubbing her legs—hadn't he done the same yesterday? She must have slid even closer because her legs now rested between his with her knees pressing against the chair seat.

Saying nothing, certainly not asking permission, he unsnapped her jeans. Answering his silence with her own, she dug her nails into his shoulders. Next came her zipper, followed by tugging her jeans over her hips. When she lifted her head from her study of what he was doing, she found herself looking into eyes devoid of emotion.

Of humanness.

Take the risk. Wrap yourself around what he offers. And maybe in the doing, understand.

Exhaustion closed in on her until she lacked the strength to continue holding on to him. Leaving her hands to drape uselessly over his shoulders, she again watched what he was doing. Stray dogs were a fact of ranch life. Some were frightened, others aggressive. She'd been able to approach several, while others ignored her crooning voice and offered food. Matt might get mad if she told him she was comparing him to one of those creatures, but right now he seemed more like them than a man.

All except for his cock.

And muscles.

And the hands gliding over her newly naked flesh.

"This is what brought you here?" She couldn't get her voice above a whisper.

"No." Despite his closed mouth, she could tell he was clenching his teeth. "I told myself I wouldn't let this happen."

"Not working so well, is it?"

"You could stop me."

"Don't throw responsibility in my lap," she snapped. The

instant the words were out, she forgave him. Maybe she shouldn't, but with his hands touching what needed to be touched, did she have a choice?

Looking down, she noted the contrast between his tanned hands and her pale belly. After that first night with him, she'd debated shaving her pubic hair—something she'd never done before—but it seemed like too much work. Besides, how much more exposed did she dare allow herself to become?

"Is this to distract me?" she managed. "A way to put off letting me see those last two pictures?"

"Let? *Make* is more like it." When he gave his head a weary shake, she wished she could tell him this wasn't necessary. She didn't need to see the shots; there was no need for him to put himself through some emotional wringer she didn't understand.

Curiosity and more kept her silent.

He sighed. "You're right. I can't put off the inevitable. Your safety . . . Hell, I don't know what I'm saying."

Safety? "Show me," she ordered.

Looking trapped, he swiveled away from her and rested his hand on the mouse. She hooked her thumb over her waistband but didn't pull it up. As she'd done earlier, she looked over his shoulder.

If it wasn't for the layer of dust over the rocks, Matt might have missed the second-to-last paw print. At first there didn't seem to be anything unusual about it, but as he'd done with earlier shots, Matt had placed his hand next to what a wolf had left behind.

She couldn't keep her mouth closed, couldn't think how to do anything except breathe. Even that took effort.

"Ready for the last one?"

His voice had a disembodied quality to it, as if he'd distanced himself from this moment.

"No. Yes."

Color and definition blinked out and were replaced by another paw scene. This time the wolf—wolf?—had stepped on dried grass and flattened it. Matt's hand, slightly blurred as if he'd been shaking when the picture was taken, was to the track's left.

"I don't know what to say," she managed. No longer simply holding on to her jeans, she gripped them so tight her fingers protested.

"I didn't think you would."

Comprehend or not, she couldn't deny that the last two shots highlighted a *wolf* print at least twice as large as the earlier ones. Claw marks bit deeper into the ground, and pads left distinct impressions as proof of greater weight. Disbelief and denial warred inside her, but this was no joke, no illusion.

"Now do you understand why I needed to share this in person?"

"What . . . what did the sheriff say?"

"I didn't send them to him."

"What? Why not?"

"Neither have they gone to Fish and Wildlife."

She'd been too shocked to pay attention to his tone. Now she was calming down a bit, either that or resigning herself to the unbelievable. There was no emotion in his voice, nothing to indicate his underpinnings had been rocked the way hers had.

Bottom line, while trying to determine where the wolf pack had gone, Matt had come across the prints of a monster-sized predator. This couldn't be. There was no way in hell the prints should exist or make any kind of sense.

And yet . . .

She was having trouble breathing. In contrast, Matt, who had turned toward her, was locked away emotionally. At the same time, something in his eyes made her take a backward step.

"Where are you going?" he asked in that dead voice.

"Nowhere. Just..." She started to pull up her jeans. "I was startled, that's all."

"Hmm."

She hated trying to put a label on what was in his eyes, but lying to herself might be more dangerous than facing the truth. Okay, so maybe she was delusional; she wanted to be. But if that wasn't a predatory glare, she didn't know what one was.

Having her waistband back up where it was designed to be restored her self-confidence. A little. But what about the glare, the sense that he wanted to attack her?

"Matt?" Hoping to pull him back to reality, if he'd indeed distanced himself from it, she'd deliberately spoken his name. Hopefully patting his cheek would speed the journey. "Why haven't the sheriff and government officials seen those? Did you think they won't believe you?"

He gave no indication he heard, prompting her to slide back a few more inches. "They won't conclude you're trying to pull a joke on them. This is much too serious for... You didn't, did you?" *Please let the too-big prints be a hoax.*

"No."

"Good."

He was getting to his feet. Behind him, a paw print filled her monitor. Her office was small with barely enough room for two people to be in it at the same time. Yes, that's what she'd do, walk out of the cramped space and into the larger living room where they'd discuss... Hell, what could they possibly talk about?

"Don't."

She hadn't started for the other room, but maybe he'd sensed what she had in mind because his hands shot out, clamped on to her still-unzipped jeans, and hauled her to him. Her fingers fisted, she aimed them at his chest, only to stop. She wouldn't hit him, not yet, not until—

"What the hell is this about?" She glared at his hold on her.

"Damn it, Matt. You came to show me those pictures, not . . . What's going on?"

He glanced over his shoulder at the paw print. When he faced her, the lack of expression had been replaced by an intensity that made her think of a hunter stalking prey.

Was the hunter human or animal?

"Putting your hand next to the prints shook you, didn't it?"

Instead of answering, he yanked on her jeans and forced her against his hard and ready cock. She barely had time to start to lift her arms, which meant her forearms were now trapped against his chest. His right arm clamped around her waist. They were too close for her to aim a knee at his groin, something she'd never imagined ever doing.

"I want you to let me go." She aimed for the tone she used to get a horse's attention. "I have students coming in a few minutes. They—"

"The hell you do."

Despite his grip, she managed to free her right arm, only to wonder what good it was now over her head. She tried to grab his hair but failed.

"I'm not lying. I do have students coming."

"But not for a while."

Had she told him about today's schedule? How could she expect clarity as long as his powerful arms all but chained her to him? This close together, his features had blurred. She wondered if his view of her was the same, or if he cared.

"I'm not going to fight you or try to get away," she said, not sure she was telling the truth. "We need to talk, Matt. About the oversized prints and your reaction to . . . What's happening isn't normal." She struggled. "You know it isn't."

"Doesn't matter."

She couldn't remember when touching his cock hadn't caused her heart to hammer and her temperature to raise. Right now was different from anything she'd ever experienced, a lifetime away from the man / woman relationship that had kept her in a nearly perpetual state of arousal, and yet . . .

Damn it, and yet the woman in her was responding to the male in him.

Hoping that reacting as she had in the past might make an impression on him, she rubbed her belly against him. Her arm was still above her head. Any other time she would have laughed and called for a strategic realignment of body parts.

This wasn't any other time.

"I'm all for spontaneity," she said. "You know I am. A quickie behind or in the barn, maybe in your truck bed—you've caught me off guard; that's the problem."

"Be quiet."

This wasn't happening, absolutely couldn't be. "What's going on inside you, Matt?"

"I . . . don't know."

He'd spoken so softly she wasn't sure she'd heard correctly. She was far from the world's most intuitive when it came to understanding people, but she'd always been able to key in to horses. Now she used that skill to decide what to do next. Contrary to what a lot of people thought, horses were complex creatures. Some responded to a firm hand while others needed a gentle touch. Matt's hold bordered on the painful. She could either treat like with like or let him believe he held the upper hand.

He does. Don't ever for a minute forget that.

"I'm glad I was there yesterday." She smiled to reinforce her soft words. "Even with the gore and death, the experience was unique, life in the raw. I'd hate to have missed it. What about you? I imagine you—"

"You don't know anything about me!" Even before the words were finished, he shoved her away. She slammed into a wall.

Stunned, she straightened, whirled, and bolted for the doorway. Where the hell was her cell phone?

He caught her from behind, circling her waist with both arms and effortlessly pinning hers to her sides. Grunting, he lifted her off her feet. She kicked back at him. Her boot glanced off his leg. Despite her struggles, he easily carried her to the couch and threw her facedown onto it. She tried to plant her hands on the couch in preparation for pushing off it only to have him snag her wrists and pull her arms behind her.

"You don't want to be doing this, damn it! Goddamn, you don't!"

For all she knew, he didn't hear a word. Bending her elbows, he pulled her arms higher on her back, crossing her wrists over each other as he did. He released her, but before freedom registered, he closed one large hand over her wrists and anchored them.

She'd landed with her face on the couch. Desperate for breath, she turned her head to the side. She couldn't make out his features, not that she wanted to. What if the look in his eyes was inhuman? Driven by the possibility, she fought to free her wrists. Damn his strength!

"Don't force yourself on me, Matt," she hissed. "I'll never forgive you if you do. It'll be the end of everything between us."

Always before all it had taken was a cautioning word from her and his handling of her gentled. This time, however, there was no apology, no asking what she wanted from him. Nothing of the Matt she thought she knew.

Head pounding, she stared at his torso. He'd become a chest, waist, belly, hips, cock. Because of the couch, it was as if his legs no longer existed. Neither did his intellect, his mind, his compassion for living things.

He pulled up on her arms, forcing her breasts deeper into the couch. The strain in her shoulders brought tears to her eyes, and yet would it do any good to tell him? Maybe it would make him even angrier—if indeed that's what ruled him.

Sudden male strength and warmth pressed against the insides of her thighs. No doubt what he had in mind, none at all. Whimpering, she clamped her legs together. "Matt, don't."

"No!" He slapped her right buttock. "Don't fight me."

"What do you expect me to do, damn it? Matt, you're crazy."

When he didn't reply, she again wondered if he'd heard. No matter how many ways she spun what was happening, it made no sense. Matt was a sexual creature. Hell, that was his greatest appeal where she was concerned. But he'd never been cruel. Never wanted anything but for her pleasure to equal his.

What had happened?

Maybe he knew how much strain he was subjecting her shoulders to because before she could say anything, he stopped drawing them up. Burning relief ran through her, and she nearly thanked him. Then he grabbed the ankle closest to him and yanked it toward him, and the impulse died. Once again she resisted, but he had no trouble pulling the leg off the couch and down, so it now dangled with her boot on the carpet.

Of course. This way her legs were separated and her crotch within easy reach. Bottom line, he'd splayed her out for his use.

Her consideration unimportant.

"I mean it, Matt," she said, determined not to let panic have the upper hand. "You don't want to do this."

"Yeah, I do. Have to."

"*Have?* What do you mean?"

He didn't reply, but instead of pressuring him, she lost herself in what was happening to her body. In ways she did and didn't want to think about, it no longer belonged to her. He'd taken control. She could either fight or surrender.

Surrender? Jump flat-footed into the exciting fantasy of becoming some man's sexual possession?

Turn today into something incredible?

A simple touch to the denim over her sex and she went limp. Pressure built against her core and with it came a kind of dummying down of her will and mind. Simply because Matt was rubbing her crotch, she lost touch with the woman she'd been moments ago. Having her waistband loose and the zipper unzipped made it easier for him to touch her deep. Deep and long. Long and full of delicious friction.

Not wanting to give away her responses, she held her breath as long as she could, but at length it escaped in a gasp. When he gave no indication he'd heard or cared, she gave herself a mental shake. She *had* to take control. Despite the warning, however, she remained lost. This was no longer her couch, her living room. Somehow Matt had turned it into a foreign place, maybe because he himself had become a stranger.

A stranger who knew all her triggers.

One lingering, hot cunt stroke after another stripped her muscles. She stopped trying to lift her head, half believing she was looking at his naked body beneath the practical clothes. He was slightly bent over, giving rise to images of tight thigh muscles. Everything from his ragged breathing to the insistent and knowing hand between her legs screamed that he was aroused.

How long would he be willing or able to keep his need under wraps? Surely at any moment he'd haul off her jeans and panties and bury his fingers in her sex. The moment he did, she'd be gone. She wouldn't try to escape or demand an explanation. Propelled and controlled by his commanding fingers, she'd press her body against his and tighten her cunt muscles around those invading fingers. If he tried to pull loose—which she couldn't imagine him doing—she'd hold on with all her strength.

Do me, she'd demand. *Finish what you started. Forget what I said about not forgiving you.*

Halfway through her silent message, relief spread over her shoulders and at the base of her spine. At first she couldn't put one and one together. Then she realized he'd released her wrists. One arm now hung over the side of the couch while the other was trapped between the couch back and her side. She should sit up. Gain control of the situation. That's what the woman she'd always prided herself on being would do.

Before she could move, however, Matt grabbed her jeans and yanked them down over her hips, pulling her about as he did.

"It doesn't have to be this way." Where were her words coming from? "I can help."

"That's not how I want it."

After getting nothing but silence from him for so long, his voice startled her. What was it he'd said, a command maybe?

The couch felt wonderful. As long as she lay on it like this, she didn't have to worry about how to sit or stand with her jeans hobbling her. Okay, so her ass was naked. It wasn't as if he hadn't seen it before.

"How do you want it?" she asked.

7

The buzzing in Matt's head had quieted a little. Either that or he'd become accustomed to the strange sound. He tried to shake it off, only to close his eyes in frustration and surrender. When, finally, he opened them, they focused on the pale feminine form before him. Enthralled, he touched.

A woman's buttocks.

Cat's.

How did this happen, and where are your clothes? he wanted to ask, but he sensed he'd done something that demanded an explanation, and he didn't know what that was.

Ah, soft and warm flesh.

Swallowing, he splayed a hand over each ass cheek. His intention, maybe, had been to study the contrast between his tanned and work-scarred hands and her offering to him.

Was that true? She'd turned her body over to him?

Maybe. Maybe not.

The inner buzzing built again, only he was wrong to call it that. A growl was more like it. Or a howl.

Yes, a howl.

Something vised his cock; it took all he had not to cry out. Determined not to let the *pain* overtake him, he clenched her buttocks. She gasped and tried to turn over, prompting him to press down. Yes, the female trapped under him.

He growled.

"Shit, Matt, this—"

Caught in what had claimed his mind, his fingers bit into her pliable flesh and left indentations that touched a half memory. Where had he recently seen similar marks? Not ones left by a human hand but . . . something.

Shaking his strangely heavy head, he pressed the heels of his hands into Cat's buttocks until she made a sharp, nonsensical sound. Confused because she wasn't reacting the way he needed her to, he raked his nails over her flesh.

Another cry slammed against the battle raging inside him. What he was doing was wrong, and yet right. Necessary. Essential to his survival. His cock fought its prison. Determined to put an end to what caused him more pain than pleasure, he yanked at the jeans' snap. The zipper sound sliced the silence.

"Damn you, Matt."

Grunting, he lowered his jeans and briefs to free himself and ran his hand between her legs. One and then two fingers touched her sweet, soft, weeping core. That was the truth to her, not her words. Moments ago his muscles had been so taut he thought they might shatter. They loosened now, gentling him a little, not taking him back to the man he used to be but connecting him with something new and good.

Cat was his mate, his woman.

Teeth bared, he ran his thumb over her opening. She responded with a long, low whimper. He liked the look of her with her legs held together by her jeans. As long as he did what she wanted, she'd stay like this.

But what if he pressed her too far? Gave in to the dark impulses? She'd fight, hate him.

Didn't matter.

He ruled her.

Owned.

Shaking his head against the darkness nibbling at his mind, he grasped her legs and hauled her on her belly toward the end of the couch. With no plan in mind, he lifted her legs over the armrest. Her arousal swamped his nostrils and slammed into his veins. Panting, he positioned her so the armrest pressed against her crotch and lifted her buttocks. Leaning down, he lapped at her rear opening. Tasted her.

"Holy shit, Matt. If this is a dream, don't wake me."

No dream. Just something he didn't understand. Action he had no control over.

About to drink from her again, he caught sight of his cock. Mesmerized by its length and breadth, he clutched it in his right hand so he could feel its weight. Warm strength flowed through his fingers, encircled his wrists, moved into his forearms.

"My jeans." Her voice sounded both uncertain and excited. "Get rid of the damn things. Spread me. Please."

Too much to think about. An end to mastery when primal impulse drove him. Wishing he could remember how to laugh, he slapped her buttocks with his cock. The resultant jarring spiked through him and tore his mind apart.

He slapped her again, then positioned himself between her legs as best he could and guided his cock forward. She braced herself on her elbows so she could look back at him. Her arms started to tremble.

He loved her helplessness.

Using one hand to guide his cock, he pulled her ass cheeks apart with the other. Holding his breath, he touched his tip to her puckered rear opening.

"Oh, shit! Matt?"

Tension? A sign that she didn't want this? Incapable of asking her, he went in search of her pussy lips. They welcomed him with a heat and wet only his cock fully understood. Arching his back, he pressed.

"Yes," she whimpered.

One word. The only one he wanted to hear.

Barely aware of what he was doing, he glided his cock over her sex. Making mewling sounds, she scooted closer and struggled to lift her buttocks. Her soft, pale ass cheeks contrasted with her riding-honed thigh muscles. She could ride him until he came close to dying. Hell, she'd done so enough times that thinking about her strength threatened to overwhelm him. However, today she was at his mercy. He in control and she ready, willing, and helpless.

Her juices coated him, covered him, challenged him to determine where she left off and he began and he entered her.

She sounded like a bitch in heat, whimpering and growling and the sounds blending into nonsense. When his mouth opened, he thought he might be about to echo her sounds only to nod in acceptance and satisfaction at the deep, low growl rolling out of him.

"Matt?"

Matt? Who was that? Some man who had something to do with him, a casual acquaintance maybe, a civilized and responsible human whose mind and body belonged to him alone.

Who hadn't heard the wolves howl.

Greed overtook him. Threw him about. Filled him. Clasping her ass cheeks, he pulled her apart and stared at his nearly buried cock. Her drenched tissues surrounded him. Embraced him. For a moment, he wondered if her sex wanted to eat him, but that couldn't be and if it was true, he'd show her! Take her down deep into that fiery place with him.

Yeah, fire! Raging at him. Clutching his body and shaking it, building strength onto strength so she shook every time he pummeled her. Her sounds kept changing until the whimpers died out. Feeding off her faint growls, he covered them with deeper, louder ones of his own.

"Do me! Goddamn you, Matt. Do me!"

He attacked repeatedly, rocking her body and his, his head whipping up and down like some puppet, his legs on fire, his buttocks clenched, and his fingers digging into her.

"Oh my God, yes!"

Her speaking? Maybe. Didn't matter. Only the screaming need did.

A sound that spoke of civilization scraped at his nerves, only to fade. He closed his eyes, then opened them when he started to lose his balance. Urgency climbed through him, and he recognized the hard rushing sensation that came during those final seconds before he lost himself.

The torrent slammed against him, shaking him and forcing him to tighten his hold on her. Seeing nothing and everything, he howled. His body turned against itself and rocked him with its power. Then everything became good and hot and wet.

The force slowly released its hold on him. In the past, weakness had broken him down. This time, however, he remained strong. Even as his cock slowly shrank, he reveled in his power.

Reaching under her body, he closed two fingers around Cat's clit. Shrieking, she climaxed.

Good. Remind her of how much he knew about her.

Of his power over her.

His cell phone was ringing; that's where the thought of civilization had come from. As Cat's pussy tightened repeatedly around his dying cock, he told himself to ignore the damnable sound. But only a handful of people knew this number. Most of them worked for him.

Stepping back from the still-climaxing Cat, he hauled up his clothes and jammed his hand into his pocket so he could retrieve the cell.

"What?" he snapped. Was that his voice?

"Matt? It's—" Coughing cut off whatever the man—that was all he knew about the speaker—had been about to say. "It's Beale."

"Beale? This connection sucks."

"That isn't it. I'm on my"—a deep and far-from-steady breath—"way back to the ranch."

Concerned the wolf pack might return to where they'd buried the calf's carcass, Matt had assigned Beale to remain near the herd. "What's going on?"

"Attack."

"Damn. You mean the wolves went after another calf?"

"No. Me."

Matt stared at Cat, who had gotten to her feet without him knowing when or how. Truth was, although she was part of his world, an important part of it, at the moment he barely recognized her. As for why her jeans roped her legs—

"What is it?" she asked.

"You're serious?" he said into the phone. "The wolves attacked you?"

"Yeah. Matt, I'm sorry about leaving the cows but..."

Still staring at Cat, who looked as if she'd been struck by lightning, he told Beale he was heading for the ranch and would meet him there.

"What happened?" Cat glanced down at her naked body, then back up at him.

"Beale." His head pulsed. "The wolves went after him."

Following the dust trail created by Matt's truck, Cat worked to keep pace as they bumped down the drive to his place. He'd barely responded when she insisted on coming along. Because she wasn't sure when he'd be able or willing to take her back to her place, she'd taken her own vehicle. She'd called to let the teenagers know that she couldn't work with them today after all and rescheduled. There'd been no time to clean up.

Gripping the wheel with both hands, she acknowledged the moisture drying between her legs. For the second time, she and Matt had had sex without protection.

Sex? No way could she slap that simple label onto what had taken place on her couch. Most of the time she'd been all for it. Hell, why wouldn't she want to kick the kinky up another notch? But there'd been moments when she hadn't been sure Matt was fully aware of what he was doing. When she hadn't known him.

His growls were part of it, and those lengthy silences of his didn't help, but mostly it was having to ask herself if he knew he cared about her. Right when he was positioning her over the couch arm, she'd questioned whether he'd known what he was doing.

The hot, heavy, and unnerving fuck had begun while he was showing her the wolf-print photos. True, something had felt a little off about him from the moment he'd shown up, but she'd chalked his mood up to concern for his herd's safety—or something. Then the oversized prints had filled her monitor, and he'd said he hadn't shown them to law enforcement. Instead of explaining why not, he'd became someone new. Sexual. Primitive.

As the ranch house came into view, she faced the question she'd put off the whole time she'd been driving here: Should she show him what she'd discovered on the cave walls?

If looking at a huge wolf print had turned him wild, what might ancient Paiute drawings do?

Beale's horse was in the corral. Whatever had happened to the young ranch hand, he'd removed the saddle and bridle, but both lay on the ground inside the corral, something no responsible hand would do.

Matt was already out of his truck by the time she pulled alongside. Through the settling dust, she noted that he was looking at the discarded items while striding toward the house.

Wondering if her presence meant anything to him, she hurried after him.

They found Beale in the bathroom. The lanky cowboy was sitting on the edge of the tub as if he was contemplating taking a bath, but his clothes—or rather what remained of them—were still on. His pants legs were ripped as were his shirt-sleeves. All were blood-soaked.

Looking numb, Beale stared at them. "Where do you keep the first aid? I . . . don't remember."

"Don't worry about that," she soothed to counter Matt's silence. "That's what we're here for, right, Matt?"

"Yeah."

Concerned, she turned her attention from Beale to Matt, who stood looking down at his employee as if barely comprehending what he was seeing. *He's shocked,* she told herself. *Of course he is.*

"Matt? Beale needs help."

"What?" Matt shook his head as if trying to wake up. "Yeah, right."

Leaving Matt to get bandages from the medicine cabinet, she knelt before the injured man and pulled off his boots. Although she did her best not to jar him, he winced. "Stand up," she said. "The jeans have to go."

She thought Beale might object to stripping in front of her. Instead, he took Matt's offered hand and stood on unsteady legs. She looked up to see Matt staring down at her. Like Beale, he was all but expressionless. What the hell was going on?

With Matt helping to support Beale, she gently pulled off Beale's jeans. Several deep puncture marks in his thighs leaked blood.

"Sit back down," she encouraged. "If you can."

Going by how Beale was acting, she believed his buttocks had been spared. Hopefully his boots had protected his ankles and feet. Taking the soapy washcloth Matt offered her, she began gently cleaning Beale's leg wounds. Although the young man sucked in several ragged breaths, she hoped shock stood between him and feeling true pain. If that was the case, she intended to finish the initial cleaning up as soon as possible.

Matt had taken off Beale's ruined shirt and was lightly scrubbing the long scratches on his arms.

"They didn't bite your arms," Matt said. "Just scratched them. I wonder why."

"Matt, I won't have to go to the emergency room, will I?"

Instead of pointing out that infection was a strong possibility and that Matt and she were just providing first aid, she gave thanks to the emergency medicine training she'd taken through the county's search and rescue when she was getting her business going. She'd expected to maybe have to deal with broken bones and bruises, compliments of a client being bucked off, not this. Some of the punctures and scratches would need stitches, but Beale had survived, somehow.

Matt handed her a bottle of iodine, his gaze saying what she already knew. This was going to hurt Beale.

"Take your time," Matt said to the nearly naked and shivering Beale. "I need to know everything that happened."

As soon as Beale started his explanation, she guessed Matt was deliberately trying to distract his employee from the stinging antiseptic.

Between gasps, the young man painted a simple and chilling picture. He'd spent the night in his sleeping bag, something he'd done any number of times since coming to work here. Being the only person out in the middle of nowhere at night didn't bother him. He liked studying the stars and trying to identify the various night sounds.

"The cows were acting strange. I figured it was because of the calf killing, but now I'm not so sure. Same with my horse. I hobbled him so he couldn't run off. I know you don't like—"

"It's all right. So the livestock were restless?"

"Not that so much. More like nervous. Scared." Beale lowered his head. "Got me a little riled myself listening to them."

"I don't blame you," Cat said. She'd been blowing on the wounds as she applied the iodine, and this was the first she was able to talk. "I would have been uneasy myself. Okay, I would have been spooked."

"The wolves attacked at night?" Matt asked. He sounded so matter-of-fact that she again studied him. There was a distant look about him, as if his thoughts were somewhere else. "It took you all this time to get back?"

"Not at night," Beale all but mumbled. "I, ah . . . After a while, the wolves started howling. That kept me awake all night. That's something I don't understand. Why did they wait until daylight? Dark would have made it even easier."

Beale's tone had become uncertain as he explained the last. Guessing that shock was giving way to vivid memories, she took his hands and sat on the hard tub rim beside him. Feeling him tremble, she leaned against him, hoping that would help.

"You're right," Matt said as he placed gauze over the longest scratch. "Wolves tend to be nocturnal. How many were there?"

Looking at his hands linked with hers, Beale picked up the thread of his story. He'd eaten several granola bars for breakfast and was saddling his horse when he sensed something behind him. When he turned around, he saw four adult wolves.

"They were stalking me." Beale started rocking. "That's how it felt like anyway. Like they were daring me to try to get away."

How terrifying that must have been. When the time was right, she'd encourage Beale to get professional counseling for help in dealing with the trauma. The thought that Matt had been acting like a wild animal himself while Beale was fighting for his life made her sick to her stomach.

Couldn't be. Matt couldn't have possibly sensed what was going on and fed off it.

Shaken, she forced herself to concentrate on what Beale was saying. The wolves had closed in on him as if they had all the time in the world to do what they intended to. His horse had risked broken legs trying to get away, but much as Beale wanted to unhobble him and set him free, he didn't dare take his attention off the pack.

"Their eyes—I hope I never see anything like that again. All yellow and glowing. They hated me."

"Hated?" Cat and Matt said at the same time.

Beale stared at his ruined jeans on the floor. "That's what it felt like. Like they didn't see me as meat so much as something they had it in for. I didn't try to run. Maybe it would have made a difference if I had, but I was scared that would prompt them to attack." He swallowed. "They did anyway."

"Matt," Cat said when she found her voice. "We need to call law enforcement."

He grunted. "I did on the way here. I'm surprised they didn't beat us."

Relieved that had occurred to Matt when she'd been wondering if part of his mind had turned off, she took the gauze from Matt and, kneeling again, went back to tending to Beale's wounds. Someday she wanted to have children. Right now she felt like Beale's mother. She couldn't make the bogeyman nightmare go away, but she was determined to comfort him to the best of her ability.

Beale was explaining that, although the wolves remained around after the attack, he'd managed to crawl over to his horse when the sound of approaching vehicles caught their collective attention.

Matt's features tightened. "I'll get them," he muttered.

Watching Matt's retreating back as he left, Cat again tried to make sense of the way he was acting. She couldn't blame him for wishing none of this was happening—she certainly did— but was it that simple? Maybe, like her, he was trying to make sense of the wolves' behavior. As Beale had explained, the pack hadn't seemed to be interested in killing him, as one after the other bit his legs and clawed his upper body. It was more like they'd decided to play with him, had seen him as a hapless victim.

Or something else.

As Sheriff Wilton and a middle-aged man wearing a Fish and Wildlife uniform entered the bathroom later, she tucked the crazy thought into a corner of her mind. Still she couldn't completely silence the possibility that the wolves had wanted to make an example of Beale. Not kill him because then he couldn't tell anyone about what they'd done to him, about the hatred in their eyes.

Either having the others in the room helped remind Beale that he was indeed safe, or shock no longer gripped him as tightly as it had at first. Sensing tension ease out of him helped Cat relax a bit herself.

Once she and Matt had finished tending to Beale's wounds, they all went into the living room. Fortunately, Beale didn't appear concerned over his lack of clothing; the idea of him trying to pull jeans over his injuries made her wince. After sitting in the recliner and letting Matt put up the footrest, Beale told the newcomers what he'd already told her and Matt, adding details she wished she didn't have to hear.

As he described how the wolves focused on one limb at a time while positioning themselves between him and his horse, she forced her attention off Beale and back onto Matt. His concern and consideration for his young employee was genuine. Listening to him reassure Beale that he'd done what he'd had to to protect his life when he left the cattle, she wondered if he'd learned his compassion from his parents—parents she knew nothing about.

Why not? She'd stripped off her clothes and spread her legs for this man. Didn't his background mean anything to her?

Unable to admit that about herself, she reluctantly faced the other possibility. Matt had offered nothing about his family because he didn't want her to know.

Fine. Blame him. Except that she'd been no more forthcoming.

Male voices swirled around her to remind her what today was about. Damn it, her relationship with Matt wasn't what was important right now. No way would she let his supremely masculine body speak to hers.

As for the growing energy between her legs—forget it!

"No way," Matt said forcefully, jarring her. "I don't want armed men swarming over my land."

"You can't mean that," Sheriff Wilton replied. "Look, Matt, I'm not a rancher, but I know how important livestock is to one. Your herd's in danger. I'd think you'd want all the help you can get."

"That's what I have hands for. My land, my responsibility."

"Sorry," said the Fish and Wildlife man, who'd introduced himself as Chuck Ehlers. "Going by the size of your spread, I'd be surprised if you have more than three or four employees, right?"

"Four, counting Beale," Matt admitted.

"Besides, it's not that cut and dried," Chuck continued. "Word's going to get out about what happened. As soon as it does, you'll be inundated by hotheads waving their rifles around and after blood. You'll have a hell of a time trying to get them to leave."

Matt, who had briefly sat down but now stood near Beale, shook his head. "What are your plans?" He sounded trapped.

Chuck ran a long-fingered hand into his thick, graying hair. "I'm not sure yet. Nothing like this has ever happened. The government's set up to reimburse ranchers for wolf-killed livestock—"

"*If* the rancher can prove his case," Matt broke in. "There's a lot of red tape involved."

"I can't argue that, but back to my comment. I have to confer with my supervisors before anything's implemented." Chuck turned his attention to the sheriff. "Sorry, Bob. I know you're thinking this is your territory, but in this situation, the federal government trumps local law enforcement."

"Maybe."

"No maybe to it, unfortunately."

As Chuck spelled out the need to make sure his agency's plans met with federal approval, Cat again let her attention drift. Beale had adamantly nixed having an ambulance dispatched for him. He'd drive himself, he said, only to have his employer disagree. Matt was willing to go along with Beale's wish to stay out of an ambulance, which meant either he or one of his other hands would drive him into town. Because Matt's tense gaze repeatedly went to the window as he spoke, she had no doubt that he longed to go to where the attack had taken place and assure himself of his herd's safety. Equally important, he wanted to find the wolves. *Don't, please. If anything happened to you . . . We have things—resolutions—*

"This jurisdictional discussion is all well and good," she said to stop her thoughts. "But right now we have a man who needs to be seen by a doctor. Chuck, you're heading back to town, aren't you?"

Chuck shot her an irritated look. Obviously he didn't take kindly to a civilian telling him what to do.

"You'll take me?" Beale asked. "I don't mean to complain, boss." He looked at Matt. "But I'm hurting something fierce. If they'll give me a shot or something . . ."

It took more discussion than she thought necessary, but in the end, Chuck agreed to drive Beale to town but only because he had to wait for several officials to return his calls. The sheriff's mouth twitched a couple of times as he told Matt that he was counting on him to take him to where the attack occurred, now preferably. When Matt agreed, she sensed the two men respected each other.

There was nothing for her to do except go home.

And take a long, hopefully calming, shower.

Wash Matt's imprint from her skin.

8

The sheriff rode the mare Matt had saddled for him as if he'd been born on horseback, which didn't surprise Matt. After all, Bob had been born and raised in central Oregon, which meant horses were as much a mode of travel for him as a vehicle. Trotting alongside the man he'd known since not long after he'd come to live with Santo and Addie, Matt dug through his memory for the answer to how he'd learned to ride. One thing he knew, he hadn't hesitated the first time Santo had encouraged him to get into the saddle.

A few times he'd asked the couple he considered his substitute parents to help him understand why they'd taken a chance on a wild and half-crazy kid. As was his way when confronted with deeply personal situations, Santo had changed the subject. Addie had responded to his question with one of her own. Did he really want certain details?

With memories of his father's death pressing in around him, he'd said no. Better to keep those doors locked.

"So you know Cat, do you?" Bob asked when they slowed their mounts to a walk. "I'd heard rumors the two of you were seeing each other, but I didn't pay much attention to that kind of stuff. Believe me, I hear enough talk, most of it nonsense."

"I don't know if you can call it *seeing.*" He went on to explain why he'd been at Cat's place when Beale called him, at least the surface explanation. "We'd just finished looking at the photos I'd taken when Beale called." *Liar.* "Because she'd seen what happened to my calf, she wanted to make sure Beale was all right."

"Can't blame her. This whole thing with the wolves is a hell of a mess. Even before they migrated here, I knew there was going to be trouble. Not just this serious. I'm more than sorry it's happening on your property."

"You're not saying you'd rather someone else be in this mess?"

Bob grinned. "There are a couple of... Seriously, of course not. Matt, for all intents and purposes, this is your spread and has been even before Santo's accident. There's Addie. She's already had enough to deal with."

Staring ahead, Matt said, "I wish I didn't have to tell her, but she's going to be back soon."

"She's like a lot of ranch women. Either the land's always been more important than people or it just sucked up all her time. What I'm saying is, I don't know how much of a support system she's going to have." The sheriff stared at Matt. "Same as you."

"Yeah?" he said, because he had no choice but to find out where the sheriff was coming from.

"You're a loner."

Knowing the sheriff had hit it right, Matt continued to study the land he loved more than he'd thought it was possible to love. Right now it was trying to tell him something, nibbling at his mind and messing with his thoughts. Crazy as it was to have such a notion, he imagined himself running predator-like over the acreage. He wouldn't tire, would never grow bored. Hell, for as long as the land—had to be the land and not the other thing—touched his soul, he wouldn't need anything else.

Not even Cat.

Except sexually.

"What?" the sheriff said. "You think I'm wrong calling you what I did? Let me tell you something. This county might be spread out, but there aren't enough people in it that I don't keep track of everyone. Santo told me some about why you ended up living with them."

That belonged to the past. Had nothing to do with today, which, in part, was why he'd never said anything to Cat.

"Given what happened to your old man, I wondered if you might have a bit of his whatever-you-want-to-call-it in you. I never saw any sign of it, except for the keeping-to-yourself part."

Dragging his attention off their surroundings, he faced the sheriff. "I appreciate your concern. I'm sure my old man's story made for some crazy gossip."

"I wasn't interested in that. Believe me, neither Santo nor Addie blabbed. Just gave me the basics once I explained I might need that information." He nodded. "Good to see you turned out normal."

Normal? Thinking about how he'd plowed into Cat like some stud determined to breed, he wasn't sure.

Should he apologize to her? Maybe, but how could he explain his behavior when he didn't understand himself?

"No, there haven't been any more attacks."

Cat had been on the way from her kitchen to her office with a bowl of cereal when the voice on the morning news program stopped her. Gripping the bowl, she stared at Matt's image with his barn in the background.

She hadn't seen him for more than twenty-four hours and hadn't heard from him either. No matter how many times she told herself he was beyond busy and concerned for his cattle and Beale, the silence still hurt. Of course, she could have gotten in touch with him.

"Does that surprise you?" asked the reporter, a blonde who didn't look old enough to be out of high school. "According to Fish and Wildlife officials, wolves will stay around a reliable food source."

"You'll have to talk to those guys about that." Matt's words were clipped. "Like I said, my herd's been safe."

Smiling up at her subject, the reporter did her best to get some decent sound bites out of Matt, but he continued to respond as briefly as possible. He wore a cowboy hat and had on his riding boots, which led her to wonder if he'd been about to leave the ranch when the reporter intercepted him. Looking somber, he said he'd gone to the hospital to see his hand when the doctor decided to keep Beale overnight for observation. Matt obviously wasn't about to pass on anything he and Beale had talked about.

Finally, the obviously frustrated reporter thanked Matt for his time. Matt nodded, then turned his back to the camera and walked away. As the woman explained that Beale had been released from the hospital but his whereabouts were unknown, she stared at the strong retreating ass encased in durable denim.

The too-young reporter's voice faltered. No wonder, Cat acknowledged, even as she imagined reaching through the screen so she could give the blond tresses a hard jerk. That masculine ass belonged to her. She knew what it looked like naked. About a week ago she'd nipped at and left scratch marks on his flesh.

My man, she silently told the reporter, although the truth was, Matt didn't and never would belong to her. He was his own man, an enigma in many respects, hard and hot and mysterious.

As she ate cereal standing up, the scene switched to the Portland studio, where an older male anchor explained that Fish and Wildlife might hire a marksman to go after the wolves suspected of the attack. Both Fish and Wildlife officials and Sheriff Wilton warned people not to take things into their own hands. Matt's land was private property, and anyone spotted on it would be arrested for trespassing.

Knowing that what was happening hundreds of miles from Portland had reached the largest news organization in the state gave her pause, but maybe she shouldn't be surprised. After all, people were drawn to stories of man against nature.

Man. A single and solitary man who, from what she'd just heard, hadn't seen or heard anything when he and the sheriff visited where Beale had been attacked.

Or was that true? What if Matt had deliberately kept something from Sheriff Wilton?

Many more trips like this, Cat thought, and she could get to Matt's spread with her eyes closed. It was only a little after 10:00 a.m., but already what little dew formed this time of the year had dried.

The take-no-prisoners weather, among a multitude of other things, was why her parents would never understand why she lived where she did. As soon as she'd declared she intended to use her inheritance from her grandfather to buy ten acres out of Lakeview, they'd insisted she couldn't. She'd just turned twenty-one and was in her junior year of college. Surely she wasn't thinking of turning her back on all that hard work and bright future in the family business.

As a matter of a fact, she was. Her naïve plan to make her own way in the world instead of burying herself in the business once she'd gotten the degree she'd never been sure she wanted had been tempered by reality, which in retrospect had been a good thing. While waiting for the land sale to become final, she'd rented a small house in Klamath Falls, which was nearly a hundred miles from remote Lakeview.

That's where she'd met and come to respect Helaku, the elderly Native American who'd once been responsible for hundreds of wild horses grazing on public land. After a scant five minutes of watching the lean, dark man handle the bucking stock at a local rodeo, she'd known she was seeing something special. If there could be dog whisperers, why not the same when it came to horses?

Cat had thought she knew horses. Helaku, who she learned was a Paiute, taught her how to get them to open their hearts to her.

Blinking back tears, she mentally went back to the last time she'd seen Helaku, which, to her dismay, had been nearly a year ago. Time and a long-battered body had taken its toll on Helaku's regal bearing, and his eyesight wasn't what it used to be. He still lived in the cabin he'd built by himself, but these days a nephew who lived nearby took him to town and helped with the chores, and a local woman cleaned and cooked every Monday.

Helaku had bought himself a computer and, using two fingers, was writing down everything he'd learned from his Paiute grandparents. She had to see Helaku. Tell him about the cave she'd discovered. But first she'd take better pictures and blow them up as Matt had done with the prints. She'd ask Helaku if he knew what the drawings represented and get his opinion on the pros and cons of letting others know.

Something just ahead and to the left caught her attention. Putting on her brakes, she turned onto the road to Coyote Ranch. So much for knowing exactly where she was going.

Unless he was off doing whatever he needed to, she'd soon see Matt. Look at him. Remember how his leathered hands felt on her breasts and pussy. Trying not to hyperventilate, she slowed to lessen the risk of doing in her suspension system. Each bump jarred her sex. Moisture pooled, making concentrating on her reason for coming here even harder.

Why, really, had she arranged to have a neighbor keep an eye on her horses today? What would she tell Matt when he asked what she was doing here?

That she was scared for him when fear had never been part of their relationship?

That she'd gone without his touch for too long?

Matt stood with a hip leaning against a wooden fence and his cell phone at his ear, emotionlessly watching her approach. Seeing him surrounded by his world dried her mouth and sent fresh moisture elsewhere. He still had on the gray hat he'd worn during the TV interview. Then, except for the top one, his shirt had been buttoned. Now, as was his way when it was warm, the sun was free to bless much of his chest.

Her legs threatened to fail as she climbed out of the cab and walked toward him. Much as she needed him to say something, she wasn't sure she was capable of replying. Seeing Matt shouldn't be this *everything*. This hard.

"Figures, doesn't it," he said into the phone. "At least he didn't get cut up too bad. Rope a heifer and he'll follow her into the other pasture. Then you can get going on the repairs. Okay. Yeah, once you're done."

"A bull?" she guessed when he put the phone back into his pocket. "What'd he do, try to take out a fence?"

"Yeah, but that post needed replacing." Lifting his hat, Matt ran his hand into his rich hair. "Always something."

Their time together had always been about itch scratching. In reality, she had only a general idea what his life was like.

"I saw you on TV. It didn't look as if you were enjoying yourself."

"I understand people like the sheriff and the government guy needing to know things. The other..."

The fact that Matt was looking at the hills as much as at her concerned her. Was it possible he hadn't been able to dismiss the wolf attacks long enough to concentrate on his job? Maybe that's why he hadn't gotten in touch with her.

"Have you had to chase anyone off?" she asked. "Maybe some redneck hunters out for blood?"

"No. Not so far."

"Maybe that's because so many people are fans of wolves," she offered when she wished there was no need for words. Action only. "They don't want to believe what happened to your calf or Beale. Speaking of, how is he?"

"He quit."

"Oh, no. I'm sorry." Wondering if she had any right to do this, she touched Matt's shoulder. "Did he say why?"

Matt glanced at what she was doing, then went back to studying the horizon. "Scared."

"Of being attacked again? Of course he is," she amended. Dropping her arm to her side, she tried to see what had captured Matt's attention. "Maybe after he's had some time to get over it—"

"Maybe. Cat, I need to get going."

Don't take off like this. "Of course. I didn't mean to . . . I could have called. Should have."

"Why didn't you?"

Why didn't you? "I guess I needed to see you in the flesh. Reassure myself that the pressure isn't getting to you." He didn't so much as indicate he'd heard her, prompting her to continue. "Where are you going? You told the reporter that your cows were all right, but maybe you were just trying to get her off your back. You looked tense the whole time you were on camera." She paused, gathering what she needed to continue. "That's what brought me here, wondering if you needed someone to talk to."

"Talk?" A smile lifted the corners of his mouth but didn't reach his eyes. "That hasn't been our priority."

"No, it hasn't, but I'd like that to change." Another pause. "And I hope you feel the same way."

She had to be mistaken, of course, but was that a shudder on his part? "Cat, right now I'm not sure what I'm feeling."

"About me?" The question scraped her throat.

"About a lot of things." Frowning, he pulled his cell phone out of a front pocket and read the display. "Addie's been calling but not leaving messages. She's not crazy about cell phones."

"Maybe she wants you to know when she'll be back."

"That's what I'm thinking." The way he stared at her, she felt exposed all the way down to the juncture between her legs. "Have you ever been to Antelope Grove?"

Relieved because he hadn't told her something she didn't want to hear, she said, "I don't think I've ever heard of it."

"It's on my land, the south end. Mostly aspens, moist in spring but dry now."

Excited by the prospect of getting more than a handful of words from him, she pointed toward where he'd been looking. "It's out there?"

"About four miles. No road."

"You have cattle out there? The hand you were talking to about a bull—is that where he is?"

When Matt again fixed his attention on her, his intensity had her holding her breath. "None of my cows are—yet. I'm thinking of moving them there but not until I've checked out the area."

"Because of the wolves?"

"Yeah. I don't want to put them at more risk than they are now."

"Then you're, what, going to be looking for tracks? Maybe antelope and deer carcasses?"

"The possibility's there."

A moment ago she'd been hoping to see passion and need in his eyes. Instead, he seemed to be trapped, a man facing something he wished he didn't have to. It struck her that he might be questioning whether any part of his land was safe anymore.

"Why today?" she asked. "With Beale gone and a stubborn bull on your hands, I'd think you wouldn't want to add moving the herd—"

"Cat, I get one paycheck a year. It comes when I sell the calves. Their lives mean everything to my livelihood."

"But you aren't crazy about going to Antelope Grove. Don't tell me you are."

Straightening, he looked down at her. "You know me better than I thought you did."

Thank goodness for the wind. Otherwise, there might not have been enough air to fill her lungs. "Not well enough, but I'd like to." *That's why I'm taking you up on your offer, if that's what it was, not just because I hope something will happen between us.*

9

He shouldn't have asked Cat if she wanted to come with him. Damn it, he was a fool for risking exposing himself when he'd worked so hard to present himself as a man who had it all together.

However, the truth was, nothing about him had been together for, what, maybe a month before wolves got to that calf. He'd sensed something. It wasn't as bad as it had been watching his father splinter into tiny fragments, and yet the helplessness had felt the same.

That and wondering what, if anything, would be left of him once it was over.

Matt occasionally glanced at Cat, who rode alongside him, but mostly he kept his attention on the distance. As usual, Cat had pulled her hair into a single, thick braid, but maybe she'd been in a hurry because a bunch of strands had worked free. He wished he could run his hands over them, not that he needed the reminder of what that felt like.

She'd gotten to him with her comment about sensing his tension during the TV interview, but had he really expected it to be different? After all, the woman had yet to meet a horse she couldn't work with. Instead of relying on strength and sometimes stubbornness like he did, she got through to horses, even rank stallions, with instinct and intuition.

Her knees were bent with her boots toed into the stirrups. Granted, he couldn't see her thighs under her jeans, but it didn't matter because he knew what they felt like wrapped around him. Even more to the point, his cock would never forget what being inside her felt like. Mind-blowing. Mind-killing. Hell and heaven wound together.

"When do you have to be back?" he belatedly asked.

"I've arranged for someone to take over for the day." She didn't look at him. "If necessary, I can be gone all night."

Only they hadn't brought anything except for water and a few granola bars. Just thinking about having to spend the night at Antelope Grove tightened his belly.

"What about you?" she asked. "You're shorthanded without Beale, right?"

"Yeah."

She nodded but didn't press. After the better part of a minute, he relaxed. And went back to thinking about her body, because focusing on the physical—which had been the best he'd ever experienced—was easier than contemplating what she might be thinking about.

Even now he wasn't sure why he'd asked her to accompany him. Given how he might react once they were there, he should be alone. Alone and isolated and safe in ways he had no words for. Losing out on parents the way he had had done something to him. Either that or he'd been born what the sheriff had called him the other day—a loner.

But even a hermit needed someone in his life. A soft and willing woman body. Heat and urgency. Sex that stripped him stupid.

How deep had she been able to dig? he pondered as they

began the climb to Antelope Grove. She'd never said anything to indicate she'd discovered the holes in him, but Cat could touch a horse's soul. Surely she'd tried to do the same with him.

His head aching from the kind of questions he usually steered clear of, he risked another glance in her direction. She sat straight and tall in the saddle with her fingers light on the reins looking part and parcel of her mount. If she kept coming to his place like this, he'd suggest she leave one of her horses in his corral so she didn't have to keep on borrowing.

Some lovers left their toothbrushes at each other's place. In Cat's and his world, maybe horses served the same purpose.

"Where'd your name come from?" he asked, surprising himself. "I never asked."

"No, you didn't." She wasn't looking at him. "My folks named me after my wealthy aunt Catriona. She decided they'd done that hoping to get put in her will, which they did. My folks get off on chasing money. It's their ultimate high."

Blown away by what had just spilled out of her, he waited because he sensed she might close up if he pressed. Like he did.

"Anyway," she finally said, "even before she called their bluff, I hated the name and refused to answer to it. Cat felt right."

"I like it on you."

"You do?" Although her eyes were down to slits against the sun, he had no trouble reading her mood. She hadn't expected that from him. Hell, he hadn't known he was going to say it. Damn it, today was full of surprises.

"Kind of exotic and wild."

"And one of the first words I learned to spell. Kind of killing two birds with one stone."

They laughed together, something he hadn't done for too long. Although neither of them said anything after that, there was a welcome easiness to the silence. If he could do so without it being awkward, he'd hold her hand.

That's it. Just hold her hand.

Antelope Grove was at the base of what passed for a mountain on his land. The depression spread out long and narrow for a good quarter of a mile with boulders on the north and a gully to the south. Maybe the second time he'd come here, he'd spotted several antelope eating the sagebrush that shared space with the wild grasses. Santo had told him the area didn't have a name but he could give it one if he wanted. The hurting boy he'd been had nearly cried at the foreign notion of having something for himself.

This was where he'd come to mourn after Santo's violent death.

"What is it?" Cat asked. "All of a sudden you tensed. Again."

Careful. Don't let her look too deep. "Something just occurred to me."

"What?"

Pulling on the reins, he stopped his gelding and turned him so he could face Cat. She did the same.

"I'm just throwing this out," he said. "Maybe I don't know what I'm talking about, but Santo was one of the best horsemen I've ever seen, good as you."

Smiling slightly, she nodded. "I appreciate the comparison and the compliment. In other words, you don't understand how he could have gotten thrown the way he did."

Answering her nod with one of his own, he tried to shake off the uneasy sensation crawling over his back. Damn it, he'd known coming here wouldn't be a walk in the park. He should be prepared.

"Exactly. Besides, his mount is one of the steadiest horses on the ranch." Gathering his thoughts, he continued to meet Cat's gaze. "We found her more than a mile from Santo's body, still spooked. The way I see it, the only explanation I have is that she either bucked or reared, maybe some of both, when Santo wasn't expecting it."

"Do you want to say it or should I?"

"I started this. I have to finish it. What if his mare spotted a wolf or wolves? No matter that they'd never been part of her existence—self-preservation would have kicked in."

"And because it had, the only thing that mattered to Santo's horse was getting away from the danger, starting with getting rid of the load on her back. At the same time, Santo was trying to make sense of what was happening. He was distracted."

Feeling half sick, Matt kneed his gelding forward because he didn't want to look into Cat's eyes anymore. Damn him for not having put one and one together before this.

Only, how could he have?

"Don't blame yourself," Cat said as she drew alongside. "Back then no one knew there was a pack around."

"A pack?" He rolled the word around in his mind. "Cat, what if it was the other thing?"

"Other?" Eyes widening, she clamped a hand over her mouth. "Oh, hell, you're talking about the big tracks, aren't you?"

If he said nothing, could he keep the monster-sized wolf behind a locked door in his mind? Tell himself his imagination, or insanity, was getting the better of him?

Even ask himself if what had destroyed his father had latched on to him?

Oh, hell, what if that nameless monstrous thing had the power to reach Cat?

Someday, somehow she'd tell Matt how much his silences upset her, and yet would hashing over what they'd touched on make things better?

Closing her mind to the unanswerable question, Cat concentrated on the grove just ahead. Matt hadn't said anything about there being bunchgrass in addition to the sage, but seeing that didn't surprise her. What did was the feeling of dread she experienced when a grove where antelope congregated should have filled her with peace. From this distance, the grove was a pastel mix of everything from muted yellow to deepest green punctuated by stark-white aspen trunks. Among the many things she'd learned about this part of Oregon was that the land was perfect for sheltering the creatures born to it.

Hoping Matt was having the same thoughts, she slipped a glance in his direction. Far from looking at peace, every line of his body gave away his agitation. No, he shouldn't be alone.

Even if he jumped her as he had at her place.

Suddenly appreciative of the rifle attached to his saddle and the pistol at his waist, she again concentrated on their surroundings. Surroundings that were doing a number on both of them.

"Do you come here often?" she asked. "If your cattle aren't around, I don't imagine you have much reason."

"Or the time."

"Point taken. Not much downtime in this business, is there?"

"None. Calving time's the most intense, what with so many being dropped in a short period. Winter can be the hardest, especially if the hay runs out."

"What's your favorite part, if you have one?"

"Good question. Has to be calving. Having a hand in new life. Seeing those bright eyes open for the first time."

Listening to him, she acknowledged how rare a conversation like this was between them. There was something rare and different and maybe precious today—if they could keep it going. If nothing happened.

Despite the possibility, she had to admit that she was turned on and had been since she'd gotten out of her truck.

Had he brought protection? Not that a lack had stopped him the last two times they'd had sex. They didn't have so much as a blanket to lie on.

Did he want the same thing she did? Maybe whatever was crawling around in his mind had come between him and desire.

"I can already feel fall here," he said, and stopped again.

"Because of the higher elevation?"

"That's part of it."

Although she sucked in a deep breath, the air here didn't feel any different to her. "Only part?"

"There's something tired about the place this time of year. As if all that sun has drained it."

His observation shocking her, she slid her fingers over the reins. The horse under her was already relaxing. Unless the mare took it into her head to try to graze, she'd soon fall asleep where she stood. Good. If the instinctive animal could relax, so could she.

Wondering what might alert the mare, Cat openly studied Matt. In contrast to his gelding, with his already sagging lower lip, Matt had risen in the saddle and was looking all around. The hand not holding the reins rested on his pistol.

"What?" she muttered. "Do you hear or see something?"

"No. And that's the hell of it."

About to ask for an explanation, she admitted that something was biting at her spine. Tension. The feeling she got on those rare occasions when something woke her in the middle of the night. Maybe she was simply feeding off whatever was bothering Matt. One way to find out was by turning her back on him and imagining two naked bodies rolling around on the grass. The perfect distraction.

Unlike the last two times they'd had sex, today they'd be in sync. They'd move as one, turning onto their sides at the same time, her upper leg hooking over his hip. Sweat would bleed into sweat, her hair sticking to her temples while his danced with each thrust. She'd gnaw on his collarbone, lap at his chest while bracing for his assault. There'd be no howling on his part this time, no mindless masculine attack while she ricocheted between excitement and alarm. Only sex. Fucking. Back to what they'd had before the wolves arrived.

An image of long, tearing teeth and savage yellow eyes pulled her back to Antelope Grove. Her mare had lifted her head and pointed her ears at Matt. Although he was no longer standing in the stirrups, he hadn't relaxed. There was a resigned air about him.

"What is it?" she whispered. "When we were at your place, I got the impression you wish you didn't have to come here."

"Did I?"

Don't give me that silent-cowboy nonsense. "Why not? It sounds as if this used to be a favorite place of yours."

"It was."

"What changed things?"

Sighing, he dismounted and left the reins on the ground as a signal to his well-trained gelding that he was to stay put. She followed suit. Keeping to her own space would be easier, but if she touched Matt, she might get him to open up. At least he didn't back away when she brushed her knuckles over his cheek.

"I don't want you thinking I'd ever say you're acting crazy but—"

"Crazy? What makes you say that?"

"Nothing. Wrong choice of words. I'm sorry."

Despite her apology, he didn't look convinced.

"Matt, we all do things we have trouble explaining. That's all I was trying to say."

To her relief, he placed his hand over hers. "This isn't easy, Cat."

Her name coming from Matt tied her in a sensual knot. If only they could go back to what they'd had before. "Things have been rough the past few days. We're still reeling."

"That's not it, not the only thing. Hell, maybe if I don't say anything, I won't have to face it."

"It?"

"Yeah."

You're not helping. "Okay, I'll tell you what I'm thinking. If I'm wrong, you can straighten me out and I promise I'll stop trying to play shrink. Coming here should be a practical matter, right? Something you do all the time. But it isn't that simple. There's something going on inside you. I don't know what it is, don't know how to get you to open up. All I'm asking is for you to explain some things. You stood over a torn-apart calf and took some nerve-racking pictures. You aren't a man who scares easily."

"No, I'm not. Not anymore."

Before she could think how, or if, to ask him to explain, he closed his fingers around hers and brought their hands to his side. Her knuckles brushed his hip, adding fuel to her flames.

"Okay." He sucked in air. "I've been having this dream, if I can call it that."

"Dream?" she repeated, feeling stupid and near the edge of self-control at the same time. Having to acknowledge how a simple touch could get to her like this unnerved her.

Matt was returning her stare and yet he wasn't, his eyes holding with hers while she had no doubt his thoughts resided elsewhere. "The *thing* hits when I least expect it. That's why *dream* isn't the right word."

"I need more, please."

"I know. It happened twice last night, first when I was trying to figure out how much hay I was going to need now that I've increased the herd, then later while I was brushing my teeth. This morning I'd just stepped out of the shower when I forgot what I was doing. Where I was."

He'd been naked this morning, water dripping off his hard body, his hair glistening, thin rivulets rolling over his belly and parted by his cock. His erection. "What comes over you?" she asked around her thudding heart.

Releasing her, he took a half-dozen long-legged strides before facing her. *Trapped,* his body said. *No way out of this ex-*

cept the truth. "The wolf. The big one. Alone and staring at me. He's always at a higher elevation. Making me feel small."

Small? Matt? Never. She clenched her hands to keep them from shaking but couldn't do anything to quiet her short-circuiting nerves. The instant before penetration was like this for her, losing control of so much.

"How, ah, how big is he?"

Matt rocked back as if waiting for her to make fun of him, which was the last thing she'd ever do. "Hard to tell. My perception's off during those *times*. Part of me says this isn't happening, that I've been drinking when I haven't. The rest is so deep in the moment that I've lost objectivity."

A short-lived breeze made the aspens rattle. She wondered if they were truly alone. "How long has this been going on?"

"Since we found the tracks." His mouth became a harsh slash, and he shook his head as if trying to escape something. "No, that's not the truth."

This man with his god-sexy body and eyes that reminded her of thunder had nearly lied to her? No, not lied. Avoided exposing himself and frightening her.

"What is?" she asked when his mouth remained closed.

"Cat, I've been having images, or whatever the hell they are, since Santo's accident, if that's what it was. I chalked them up to losing him. Now I'm not so sure."

His slow and hesitant delivery filled her with longing. She wanted—hell, she needed—to touch him. To wrap her arms around him and protect him. But he needed to stand alone until he was finished. Otherwise . . . hell, they both knew what might happen once they touched.

"Is that it?" she asked, hoping to get him started again. "The wolf shows up. It watches you. Just that? There's nothing menacing in its behavior, no attack?"

"I wish."

Matt was positioned so the grove was behind him. It was

only her emotions getting the best of her; still, it wouldn't take much for the wild and remote area to surround and swallow him. Take him from her.

"You wish?"

"Crazy, isn't it." He dragged his hand down his face. "There's that damned word again. What doesn't make sense is I'm not afraid of him. Fascinated. In awe. I know that what's going to happen won't be good, but at first I just feel blessed."

Don't speak. Just listen.

"I'm pretty sure I'm the only one who knows about the wolf's existence. I don't understand why I've been chosen, but I can wait for an explanation. I know it's coming, just not when. I stand there waiting and watching as he slowly approaches." He shook his head. "When only a few feet separate us, I realize I don't feel his breath."

Maybe Matt wasn't aware that his voice had dropped, forcing her to lean toward him in order to hear. Something about the man now frightened her.

"That's significant?" she belatedly asked.

"Yeah. I think." When he again looked at her, she turned cold because his beautiful dark eyes now carried a light she'd never seen. "I hold my hand up to his nose and wait, but there's no breath, nothing to make me think he's alive."

Moments ago she'd been sweating under the afternoon sunlight. No longer. "How far are you from him?"

"Not far enough." He closed his eyes. "Suddenly his fangs sink into my shoulder."

"Fortunately, the bite doesn't hurt," Matt continued. "I tell myself that it can't be because I've started bleeding. Then he lets go, and I pull off my shirt."

"What do you see?" she asked when the silence again went on too long.

"Puncture marks."

"Do you feel pain now?"

"No. Instead of hating the wolf or spirit or whatever it is for what he's done, I'm grateful."

Spirit? Was that possible? Rocked by the notion that Matt might be losing his mind—he'd reacted to the word *crazy*, hadn't he?—she forced herself into his space and clutched his shirt at the neck. Forcing herself, she pulled it off his shoulder.

Nothing. Only the magnificent flesh, muscle, and bone she'd repeatedly lost herself in. Then Matt settled his hands over her hips, and two deep, dark red punctures appeared. Past trying to comprehend, she twisted out of his grip. Growling, he reached for her.

"No! Stop it!"

"I can't, damn it. Don't you understand that?"

She didn't understand anything, only glowing eyes in a face she no longer recognized. To her shock, heat slammed into her to steal strength from her legs. The too-familiar inner flames scorched her cunt and forced her to clamp a numb hand over herself there.

"What are you doing to me?"

"I don't know. Maybe the same thing that's been happening to me."

Impossible! Everything about these moments were part of a damnable nightmare. Even with sexual need searing her, she flattened her hands against his chest and shoved. As he backpedaled, his shirt slid back into place, and she told herself she hadn't seen anything.

Another howl raked her nervous system. "Stop it!" she started, only to jam a fist against her mouth. The sound hadn't come from him.

Cursing herself for not carrying a weapon—she spun away from the lover who'd become a stranger. Her desperate gaze first went to the aspens. Then, choice stripped from her, she stared at the sagebrush to the left of the aspens.

A wolf stood there, flanked by gray-green bushes.

"Matt?" Was that scared-little-girl voice hers? "Look."

"I know."

He knew? From the beginning?

Frightened to the point of being sick, she sprinted toward her horse. As the trembling animal started to whirl away, she grasped the reins, shoved a boot into the stirrup, and hauled herself into the saddle.

Matt could take care of himself. This was his land, his nightmare, his goddamned wolves!

Crying, she dug her heels into the mare's sides.

10

For maybe the better part of a minute—Matt had only a rudimentary comprehension of time—he watched Cat gallop away. *Go with her,* his nerves screamed. At the same time, a force he knew he'd never understand kept him next to his prancing gelding. Even with trying to prevent his mount from panicking, he managed an occasional glance at the wolf.

The predator was incredible, its thick coat a rich blending of brown, cream, and black. Its lips were parted to reveal fangs that appeared twins of the ones that had closed around his shoulder during whatever the hell had overtaken him. Maybe because it had yet to move toward him, he felt more awe than fear, but then a well-aimed bullet would more than level the playing field, wouldn't it?

Magnificent. Like stepping into the past to when man didn't belong on this land but the ultimate predator did. He longed to apologize for the bounty his ancestors had placed on wolves' heads. Instead of trying to coexist with the creatures and accepting them as part of nature's balance, man had blasted them out of existence.

Only, *civilized* man hadn't finished the job. Close but no cigar. And now many decades after the nearly successful bloodbath, the survivors' offspring and offspring's offspring had returned.

Once again, Antelope Grove and other places like it were the wolves' domain. Today he stood looking at one of them.

He was asking himself whether he should stay or follow Cat when the wolf flattened its ears and lowered its head in what he recognized as a submissive gesture. Another wolf? The alpha, perhaps.

Maybe something else.

His teeth and mind clenched against thought, Matt swung into the saddle and galloped after Cat.

Cat neither knew nor cared how long it took Matt to catch up with her. By the time he came alongside, she'd slowed the heavy-breathing and still-agitated mare to a jerky trot. She acknowledged Matt with a look but then kept her attention trained on where the mare was heading. Two things drove her. She needed to keep an eye out for holes before her mount lost her footing. Also, she couldn't think of a thing to say to her lover.

Lover? If only it was that simple.

The ride back to his place seemed to take forever, yet when she spotted her truck, she realized she hadn't decided whether to stay or leave. Right now she didn't care what he wanted.

Yes, she did, she admitted when he dismounted and took control of her mare. "Get down," he commanded.

A frisson of discomfort chased down her spine. Thankfully his eyes had returned to their true color, but she'd feel a lot better if they weren't so intense.

Intense? Hungry was more like it.

"What are you planning to do?" She remained seated. "I

need to get this out in the open, Matt. Right now I don't trust you."

"Then get the hell out of here."

The sharp challenge triggered something inside her, and no longer concerned with self-preservation, she swung a leg over the mare's rump. Hitting the ground jarred her. "Is that what you want?" she shot back. "For me to run off with my tail be-tween my legs?"

His mouth a slash, he grabbed her upper arm and swung her around so she had no choice but to face him. "What's between your legs is no tail."

They'd indulged in sex talk back when life had been simple and things between them primitive. This was different. As much of a challenge as his *warning* for her to leave had been.

"You should know," she came up with. "You've been there often enough."

"Do you regret it?"

They were so close his breath heated her scalp. Signing up for her first wilderness ride at thirteen had called for courage she hadn't known she was capable of, but that had been noth-ing compared to standing toe-to-toe with Matt. Her breasts ached, and she couldn't get her stomach muscles to relax.

"I hate the word *regret,*" she told him. "An adult should be capable of thinking things through beforehand."

"Damn it, Cat, you know what I'm talking about. Don't give me rational and reasoned."

The Antelope Grove wolf had exuded not just deadly strength but also a raw sensuality. The creature lived to hunt and breed; it was that basic. Right now it didn't matter whether she was being influenced by the brief and incredible moments when there was nothing except her and the predator.

That experience was being repeated, with Matt. With hunger taking bites out of her and turning her into as much of an ani-mal as the wolf.

"What do you want from me?" Her arm ached where his fingers pressed, yet the pain added to her need to fuck, to mate.

Where had those words and thoughts come from? Was the wolf responsible? Maybe Matt was.

"Look down," he commanded. She did but had to blink several times before she could focus. Not surprisingly, his jeans bulged.

"I see." Only inches separated them. If she arched toward him—

"That's what *this* is about." He tightened his hold. "What's it going to be, Cat? Flight or—"

"You're hurting me."

Rough sex had been an exciting part of their relationship, but he'd always been aware of boundaries, as had she. Staring at his fingers pressing into her flesh, she again acknowledged that he'd changed. Consideration no longer mattered to him.

Maybe it didn't to her either.

"Did you hear me?" she repeated. "That hurts."

"Make me stop, then."

Had the Antelope Grove wolf been male or female? Didn't matter; only the creature's world did. Not sure who she was anymore, she ran her free hand between Matt's legs and clutched his cock.

"Damn you!"

"You told me to make you stop. How's this working?"

Maybe she should have known what he was going to do; maybe she had, except the feel and heft of him had distracted her. Whatever the truth, when he planted a hand on her shoulder and shoved, she nearly lost her footing. Determined to have her arms behind her to cushion her fall, she let go of him. His heat and promise went with her, again splintering her thoughts.

Too late! The ground coming!

A half instant before she landed, he grasped her shoulders and pulled her upright, which caused her to slam against him.

Breathless and with her breasts flattened, she struggled to look up at him.

"We should have never met," he said in a tone she'd never heard. "That way you'd be safe."

"Safe? What—"

He twisted her away from him, his fingers raking her flesh as he did. Dizzy, she found herself staring at the corral where a half-dozen horses watched. She was still working on her equilibrium when he hauled her arms behind her so her elbows nearly touched. Even with the strain, she gave herself over to her body's insistent message.

It needed Matt's hands on her, controlling and confining.

"You're lucky you left the grove before I did," he muttered against her ear. "Maybe that saved you."

"From what?" Fighting, even if she wanted to, would be futile. Better, maybe, to stay in the moment.

"That's the hell of it. I don't know." Using his hold, he swung her from side to side. "It doesn't matter. Only this does."

Mumbling something she couldn't catch, he marched her toward the barn. With every step, the distance between her and her truck increased. They walked as one, his longer legs and stride forcing her to concentrate on matching him. Her breasts strained against her shirt to distract her.

All too soon, muted light surrounded her. The smell of fresh hay warred with that of wood, leather, and animal. Although the double barn doors now behind her were open, the walls, wooden stalls, and high roof trapped her. Her arms were becoming numb, the sensation at odds with her sensitized pussy. She wanted to know why being manhandled had turned her on so much and yet she didn't.

Matt stopped before a stall with a chest-high wooden door. After running an arm under her elbows to keep her against him, he unlatched the door and shoved her inside. Despite the fresh hay covering her boots, she managed to keep her feet. The far wall stopped her.

Feeling primal, she faced him. He stood in the opening as if challenging her to try to rush past him. She met his stare, echoed his motionless body, waited. Wanted.

His cell phone vibrated loud enough for her to hear. Drawing it out, he stared at the display, nodded, and then shoved it back into his pocket. Guessing she'd be wasting her breath, she didn't ask who it was.

Thanks to the deep shadows in the confining space, she could only guess at his expression. Vowing to match him, she kept her features neutral. She'd be damned if she'd let him know she hadn't come close to recovering from his manhandling. After taking a single step, he latched the half door behind him.

Wait. Let him make the next move.

When his hands settled over the fastening on his jeans, her mouth dried. He seldom wore a belt, and today denim clung to his nonexistent belly.

He unsnapped and unzipped without taking his attention off her. Much as she needed to hear his voice, to be given an explanation, silence was easier.

Reaching into the opening he'd created, he cupped his cock, briefs and all. Earlier today he'd directed one of his cowhands in how to deal with a bull. Now he'd become one himself.

Either that or a male wolf.

Shock squeezed her heart . Could it be? Was it possible that ... that what?

No! The wolf they'd seen earlier hadn't touched Matt. He was the same man he'd been this morning—maybe.

Knowing he was waiting for her to do or say something, she vowed to learn everything she could about him. His mysterious past had been part of his allure, shadows untouched perhaps. What a fool she'd been for not trying to fill in the gaps, but who would she ask? Not Matt because he'd gone to a place she couldn't comprehend and become someone she barely knew.

One thing she had no doubt of. He wanted to have sex with her. Hell, he'd insist on it.

She could fight him and in the battle lose him forever, or she could acknowledge her deep-seated need and meet him animal to animal.

Animal. Wolf.

Taking a deep breath didn't come close to settling her nerves, although the hay scent that was a core part of her existence helped a little. Then she took another breath and found something else, a feral quality perhaps.

Shaking, she freed her blouse's top button. The second bent a nail. Wincing, she tackled the third. *Take this, Matt. You want to play wild animal, you've found the right woman to play with.*

She wasn't sure how she felt when he yanked his T-shirt over his head. Intimidated—there was no way she could deny that, but seeing his naked chest lit something deep inside her. Either her eyes had adjusted to the quiet lighting or she was indeed becoming animal-like. Clothes were for a modern woman, not a creature, a beast.

Lifting her lip in a snarl, she pulled her blouse out of her waistband. Something tore as she hauled on the last two buttons. Done with the damned thing. Nothing between their bodies except for her bra.

Potent male legs killed the gap between them. Fear struggled to be acknowledged only to whimper and die as Matt's heat seeped into her. Not just heat. It was as if his strength and determination had found an inroad to her core. He closed a hand over her throat, pressing just enough that her attention went to breathing. Backing her against a wall, he stared down at her.

This time he was going to speak, and in the words she'd find ... what?

Instead, he reached into her right bra cup and hauled out her breast. He did the same to her left, then stepped back. Determined not to turn everything over to him, she drew down the straps. Much as she needed to touch herself, she fisted her fingers because if she gave in, she risked losing what little self-control remained.

His hand again. Capturing her shoulder this time and spinning her away once more. Before she could untangle her legs, he'd again shoved her against the wall and flattened her breasts. Holding her in place via the hand at the back of her head, he unfastened her bra. It remained trapped between her and the wood.

Hot moisture dampening a shoulder blade told her he'd leaned close. She made no move to lift her arms from her sides.

Matt's tongue gliding over her shoulder blade gave birth to a series of shudders. Not sure why, she clenched her teeth to keep from moaning. Leaving her shoulder damp, he bathed her spine from just below where his hand resided nearly to her waist. Floating in molten heat, she felt her knees start to give way.

"You're killing me."

"No." His mouth remained against her. "I'm not. Today."

Alarmed by his final word, she tried to look back at him only to forget when he worked his hand between her legs. He pressed against her cunt, forcing her onto her toes. The pressure continued, working its way deep inside and threatening to shut her down. She fought to concentrate on the hand at the back of her neck and waited endlessly for him to lick her spine again. Matt's fingers burning through her jeans' crotch claimed her.

Even with his hand in the way, the strain in her calves forced her onto the balls of her feet. She could escape if she felt compelled to—maybe. Surely he'd let her go at a command—maybe.

What the hell did it matter? She'd think about those things later, once his body no longer owned hers.

How well Matt knew her, damn him! Where and how had he learned to keep her suspended over this dark and maybe bottomless sensual pit? Her pussy was too sensitive, too tuned to him. Like a horse trained to respond to the slightest pressure, Matt's hand turned her stupid.

Stupid and wanting.

Lost without him.

When he abruptly withdrew, she wondered if he'd tapped into her thoughts and had decided to propel her, alone, into the pit he'd created. For too long she couldn't make herself face him, and when she did, it was with her arms still at her sides and her bra sliding down her body and onto the hay. She couldn't close her legs, not with ghost pressure still against her sex.

The other day Matt had discovered prints belonging to a wolf far larger than any wolf could be. Now she thought the same of him. Maybe his size hadn't changed; she wasn't sure of that. One thing she did know—there was more to him. More determination. More maleness. More power.

"You aren't going to let me go, are you?"

He shook his head. "Not yet."

Thanks for speaking. I wasn't sure you still knew how.

"What about after we're done with— Hell, you know what."

His puzzled expression surprised her. Was it possible he hadn't thought beyond their time together? Maybe, like an animal, he lived in the moment.

"Let's get it over, then." She punctuated her comment by freeing her jeans and hauling them and her panties down around her thighs. The air stroked her naked flesh.

She'd hoped her words and actions would get to him, but he gave no indication. Fine, then. They'd have mechanical sex, tab A entering slot A. Once it was over, what next?

As if in answer, Matt lifted his cock out of his briefs. As she gaped at it cradled in his palm, her mind closed down. Only impressions remained: him, potent and ready, giving no quarter, aimed at her.

"Down." His command whipped her. "On your hands and knees. Back to me."

"Just like that?"

"Either you do it or I will."

He'd played the Me Tarzan role before, but today there was no pretense to him. What if she screamed—not that anyone was around—or insisted that whatever happened would be against her will? Right. Like she could lie about what dribbled down her inner legs and knotted her nipples.

"On your knees," he repeated. "Back to me."

"Why? Because you don't want us looking at each other?"

"Now, Cat. Enough with the words."

Driven by his tight body and insistent cock, she dropped to her knees. Barely believing what she was doing, she stared up at him or rather she tried; his cock was in the way. Fighting an unwanted wave of vulnerability, she turned her back to him and presented him with her ass.

Her naked ass.

The hay shifted a little as he knelt behind her. Gripping her buttocks, he roughly drew them apart. Shocked and excited, she widened her stance, giving silent thanks for the layer of denim between her knees and the hay. Masculine fingers swiped over her sex lips and deposited what they'd collected on the base of her spine. Staring through a red-hued haze, she studied her hanging breasts with the dark and swollen nipples.

Another touch to her sex, this one by his cock, emptied her lungs and bowed her back. She was a bitch, a bitch in heat. Coating her man's cock in proof of her readiness for penetration.

Reaching under her, he claimed a breast. "You know what I want. Same thing you do, right?"

"Yes." *Damn you.*

His hold tightened. "Now, right? Nothing held back?"

You know me too well. That's the hell of it. Tears burned as she lowered herself onto her forearms and presented herself to him. This morning she'd been Cat, horse trainer. Now she was an animal.

Matt's bitch.

He'd let go of her breast while she was preparing herself for him. Familiar pressure against her opening filled her mind's eye with an image of Matt aiming his cock via a practiced hand. Instead of the harsh invasion she expected, however, he played with her by repeatedly rubbing his cock head from side to side and up and down. Not once did the union of cock and pussy break. Juices gushed from her. Her temple pounded; her breasts ached.

"Damn you. Do it!"

A growl layered over her outburst. Her heart hammering, she tried to look back at him only to nearly lose her balance as he rammed home.

Her inner tissues stretched, distancing her from everything else. Then her sex settled around what was both familiar and new. Fresh tears dampened her lashes.

Matt belonged here. In her. No matter what had taken place over the past few days, this was right. Perfect. What their relationship had been about. Lifting her head so she could fill her lungs, she tightened her muscles around him. Maybe he didn't know, maybe it didn't matter to him, but shortly after that first night with him, she'd started practicing with her inner muscles until she could clench them one section at a time in a wavelike action. Doing so fueled her, and she had to work slowly and methodically to keep her climax under wraps.

She didn't always succeed.

"Damn you." Matt slapped her right buttock and then her left. "Not so—Damn you."

Good! He wasn't as in control as she'd thought. Ignoring the sting and thrill of his repeated slaps, she tightened and released, tightened again. Energy filled her. Could she hold back until he climaxed? Throw him over the edge and then take her own sweet time while he struggled to become sane again.

Not love between them. Far from that. Something wild instead, a road she'd never taken. Her thoughts bouncing, she captured a mental image of them. He loomed over her, against her, staring at her ass. Because he still held her cheeks apart, even in the poor light, he'd have no trouble seeing her butthole.

How romantic. How glamorous.

How damn unimportant.

Joy rolled through her, touching off a long, low whimper. She tried to continue her assault, but every time she started to send a message to her muscles, he shoved into her. Screaming heat tore at her nerves. She was falling apart. About to rip in two.

Matt repeatedly buried himself so she was hard-pressed to keep her face off the hay. There was so much to do, so many things to try to concentrate on. What mattered most, commanding him or drowning in her impending explosion?

"You're mine! Mine." He hammered into her. "Belong to me."

Yes, that and more. Now.

"I ran you down. Brought you in here." A long, strained hiss spilled out of him. "Claimed you."

"Don't talk! Just do."

Something frightening and alive snaked through her. One instant she knew who she was and where. The next neither mattered. The explosion hit hard, fast, unrelenting, and incredible.

She rocked forward, lost her balance, and buried her nose in the hay. Her pussy on fire, she somehow got her forearms under her. She screamed repeatedly. Everything about her jerked. Again and again.

After a time without meaning, her exhausted muscles forced her to acknowledge the world. To face what was real. No matter how much she fought to hold on to her climax, she couldn't win. Resting her upper body on her elbows, she planted her chin in her hands and pulled air into her spent lungs.

Matt was still going at her, carving a home for himself. She should praise his ability to hold back so long, but maybe they'd only fucked for a few seconds before she exploded.

"Do it," she whispered into her fingers.

A hot flood seared her channel. She tried to tighten herself around him only to shake her head in defeat. Joyful and exhausted defeat. Repeated groans accompanied Matt's efforts, and his fists lightly tattooed her spine. She had him for these moments. He was lost, primitive and primal, unthinking. She could rope and tie him, keep what was left of him under her control. Tap into the wild animal he'd become.

"Enough." Still going at her, Matt again gripped her buttocks. "Damn enough."

Confused, she held her breath, but he didn't say anything else. Wise to his body's ways during sex, she believed he was nearly done. Instead, he paused as if gathering something around him. Reaching under her, he raked his nails over her belly.

"Shit! Matt!"

He scratched her again, forced something between pleasure and pain onto her. Thrilled and confused, she tried to scramble out from under him only to collapse when his weight dropped onto her. Spitting out hay, she went limp.

"Don't forget this. Remember who claimed you."

Get off me. Damn you, Matt. Matt? I don't know who you are.

His cock had slipped out. Empty, she struggled to clear her thoughts, but his body blanketed hers and his cum and her juices leaked onto the hay.

What might have been a long, long time later, he got to his feet. When she tried to do the same, he planted a foot on the base of her spine. Held in place, she looked over her shoulder at his shadowy and magnificently naked body.

"Mine." His teeth flashed.

11

A braless Cat walked out of the barn ahead of Matt. Hay stuck to both of them, and her hair looked as if she'd been sleeping. He wasn't sure how he felt about facing her or whether he could keep his expression neutral enough to fool her.

To convince both of them he wasn't losing his mind.

What had happened? He didn't remember making any decisions about their frantic and frenzied sex. One moment they'd been standing face-to-face either talking or silent, he couldn't recall. The next, she'd presented herself to him like a bitch in heat—hadn't she? Like the cur he was, he'd ridden her. Clamped his fingers over her ass cheeks and breasts and scratched her belly.

Damn him! Damn whatever creature he'd just been and might still be.

She circled her truck and reached for the door handle. "I don't want to see you for a while," she said without looking at him. "I don't think I have to explain why."

"Do you want me to apologize?" Could he and have it be the truth?

Shaking her head, she opened the door. "Right now the less said the better. Matt, be careful."

Always before, his body needed time to restore itself after sex. Now, however, he had the energy to race from one end of his property to the next, to see if he could outgallop a horse.

Most of all, he wanted Cat under him and him in her.

"Be careful?" he finally asked.

Running a hand into her hair, she faced him. Her eyes were haunted, alarmed, something. "You're changing. I'm not sure I understand the new you, or want to. Back in there"—she nodded at the barn—"it was damn good. Incredible. But, Matt, I felt as if a part of you, the man, was missing."

You aren't making sense, he wanted to insist, but she was right. Much as he needed to tell her what had happened after she'd left Antelope Grove, he lacked the words.

Maybe the truth was he was afraid.

"What part's missing?" he asked.

She stared at his jeans-encased cock. "I hope you aren't trying to make a joke because I've never been more serious. What is it? This business with the wolves has turned you on end? It's that simple? Maybe you're afraid your herd's in trouble and . . . We've had this discussion before, haven't we?"

It sounded vaguely familiar but at the moment even her voice sounded strange. In fact, he wasn't certain he'd ever had a conversation with this woman. Fucked her, yes. Gotten to know her, no.

"What do you want me to say?"

"If you have to ask— Hell, maybe nothing." Her shrug drew his attention to her full breasts. "Look, we've each got a lot on our plates right now—you more than me. You need to protect your herd and replace Beale."

"I'm not sure I'm going to." The truth was, he wasn't clear on what Beale's responsibilities had been.

"Oh? Well, what about that call you got when we were in the barn? It's an example of how things keep piling up, right?"

His mind a blank, he took out his cell phone and noted he had a new message. Still watching Cat, he accessed it.

"It's me," Addie said. "I'll be back tonight. I just turned south so that's, what, another six or so hours. Don't worry about having dinner ready. I'll get something along the way. God, it'll be good to be home."

"I heard that," Cat said. "Does she know?"

"About what?"

Disbelief claimed her features. "The wolves, of course."

"She caught the news and called." He didn't say when because he couldn't remember.

"And your explanation?" She tugged on a strand of hair. "Never mind. Matt, if something important happens, I hope you'll let me know. Otherwise, we need space and time between us. You agree, don't you?"

"Whatever you want."

"What I want is an idea of who you really are, starting with the basics like your background."

"Huh?"

"Oh, for— What is it, you want me to think you don't have a past?"

Not knowing what to say and not sure it would make any difference anyway, he watched her get behind the wheel. He'd never mentioned his parents because they had nothing to do with his life today and because, hell, he'd wanted things simple between them.

Just sex.

He held his hand over his nose and mouth when dust kicked up as she drove away. Yes, sex had defined their relationship, but that had been blown all to hell, and he didn't know what remained.

Time and space apart, like she'd said.

She wasn't yet out of sight when Matt knew he wasn't alone. Much as he hated the comparison between what he was feeling now and what he'd felt at Antelope Grove, he didn't dare ignore it. Something had intimidated the wolf Cat and he had seen. If whatever that was had followed him here . . . no, damn it! That kind of thinking had destroyed his father. He was better than that, stronger and rooted in reality.

Striding over to his gelding, he reached for the rifle still fastened to the saddle. Before he could draw it out, however, the well-trained horse reared and bolted, heading for God knew where. Cat's mare charged after it, and he had to force himself not to race for the ranch.

Months ago something had terrified Santo's mount. A man who couldn't be thrown had struck boulders headfirst.

Trying not to hyperventilate took effort. Although he ordered himself to study every detail of his surroundings, his attention skittered from shadow to shadow and possibility to possibility, none of them good. The now-distant hoofbeats reminded him of gunshots.

There. Under a trio of scrub oaks not a hundred yards away.

As a small boy, he'd crawled under his bed trying to hide from his guardians' demands. Long ago he'd told himself that child no longer existed. Still, if there'd been a bed here, he'd have to force himself not to scramble under it.

Shaking off the past, he shielded his eyes. The wolf standing under the oaks surprised him, and yet it was as if he'd been waiting a long time for this moment.

Even at this distance, he knew this wolf was different from the others. Bigger. Stronger.

Dominating.

"What do you want?" he asked the creature. "Me?"

"No, no, I don't want to rush you," Cat told Addie when she reached the older woman at the Coyote Ranch the next morning. "I'm sure you're still tired from all that traveling. I just . . . I feel bad because I haven't been a good neighbor."

"Neighbor is relative around here," Addie pointed out unnecessarily. "You had me with the offer of a drink at the Cattlemen's Bar. Who told you how much I like a cold beer?"

Truth was Cat hadn't known that about Addie. Her intention had been to set up a meeting away from Matt's ears. After the hellos were over, she'd suggested that Addie and she schedule their next trip to Lakeview for the same day. She'd mentioned the Cattlemen's because in the middle of the day, it was a cool and quiet place for a conversation.

"I hope you won't be offended if I order wine instead of beer," she said. "And if I ask questions or bring up things you'd rather not talk about, tell me to mind my own business."

Addie hesitated. "Santo's death still isn't easy to talk about, all right, but I'm learning that getting things off my chest is easier than bottling them up inside. As long as you don't hit me with psychobabble the way my sister did—"

"I'll try not to. Ah, Matt doesn't happen to be around, does he?"

"No. We'd hoped we'd have time to catch up, but he got a call last night. Some of the other ranchers and a few members of that rural Oregon hiking club want him to join them for a meeting."

"Oh?"

"I think they're going to put pressure on Fish and Wildlife to declare open season on the wolf that attacked Beale."

"The wolves have federal protection status."

"I know, but a deliberate attack on a human changes things."

"I guess," she hedged, because she hated agreeing with Addie. "How do you feel about the group's plans?"

"Confused. I can tell it's getting to Matt, and that bothers me."

She wasn't going to think about Matt, Cat told herself as she hung up. Hadn't she made it clear she had no intention of seeing him for a while?

How long was a while anyway? A day maybe if she couldn't stay away. A month if she knew what was good for her.

She'd been in the kitchen doing dishes when she called Addie, but now she had no choice but to go into her bedroom with the still-tangled sheets from one of the most restless nights of her life. Darn it, in the wake of barn sex, she should have had no trouble sleeping. It wasn't as if she'd had sexual tension to deal with.

Right.

Torn between giving herself a good chewing out and cutting herself some major slack, she made the bed and grabbed her riding boots. Today's agenda called for taking a mare and a pack mule into the foothills around her place for a daylong ride. The animals belonged to a governmental surveying pair set to do some mapping project. However, one of the men wasn't familiar with horses and wanted her to make sure the agency had provided him with dependable animals. Her salary for three days of work was nothing to be sneezed at. Maybe best of all, she'd been given a valid excuse for being alone.

And getting close to *her* cave. Hopefully taking more pictures, this time with her new digital.

Studying the images and maybe, somehow, answering the question she'd been trying to avoid.

Cat was placing a pack on the mule before she allowed herself to acknowledge her concerns. Thanks to the wolves, the hills might not be as safe as she'd always believed they were. At least, she reassured herself, her friend Daria knew her agenda as did the surveyors and the retired neighbor who was taking care of her small herd today. Her cell phone was charged.

Bottom line, she refused to run scared when there'd been no sign of wolves in the area she was going to. Swinging into the saddle, she repositioned her baseball cap so her eyes were shaded. Matt looked sexy in his Western hats, but she preferred something more compact.

Matt. It was always going to be about him, wasn't it? And because she couldn't get him out of her mind, she might as well let her thoughts go where they insisted. She hadn't thought to ask Addie where and when the meeting was scheduled. As a result, she didn't know whether it was over or not yet begun.

In many regards, Matt was the stereotypical loner cowboy. She wasn't sure how he'd react to the pressure the others might put on him. The truly sad thing was, she didn't know how deeply Santo's death and the attack on his ranch hand had hit him.

She should, damn it. She owed that to him.

Just as he owed it to her to open up, right?

The foothills closest to her place didn't have a formal name, but she'd heard them referred to as the Badlands, often accompanied by a string of profanity. Since the rugged land was pockmarked with lava outcroppings, the label seemed fitting. Scruffy junipers and sagebrush had somehow found room for their roots in what looked like worthless soil. Only *her* cave had value.

If she'd any say in it, she wouldn't have brought the two animals to where the footing was so precarious, but since this was the general area where the surveyors would be working, she didn't have a choice. Hopefully their responsibilities wouldn't bring them close to the cave.

Keeping the reins loose so the mare could pick her way over the lava chunks, she occasionally looked behind her to make sure the easygoing mule was keeping pace. Like the cautious mare, the mule walked with his head low. If either animal thought the human with them had lost her mind, they gave no indication.

Riding was hard. Okay, not in ways someone else might think, but her crotch definitely didn't need the vibrations. Despite the long climb, walking would have been easier. At least that way she'd be able to keep her legs closed. Her pussy wouldn't be open and vulnerable and turned on.

After readjusting her hat, she straightened and looked around for something to take her mind off her sex. During the explorations that had taken her to the cave and its rich treasurers, she'd twice seen mule deer. There'd been plenty of birds, jays, quail, hawks, and once buzzards in the distance but few ground animals. Either they were incredibly good at hiding, which was a distinct possibility, or not many rodents and lizards lived here. No wonder. As far as she was concerned, the vegetation sucked nutritionwise.

That was good. If critters and creatures had no use for the Badlands, wolves wouldn't either, right?

Right.

"So far so good." She patted the mare's neck. "I'll get you as close as possible to the cave, then leave you tied. I promise I won't be long. It's just something I need to do." Concerned the mare might not agree, she again patted her neck. "Either you're cool, calm, and collected, or you're oblivious to our inhospitable surroundings."

By way of answer, the mare gave her head a hard shake. Spotting a particularly steep section ahead, Cat leaned forward to keep her weight off her mount's hindquarters. Matt-thoughts went into hibernation as she assured herself that the mare was proving to be as strong as she looked. Hopefully she wouldn't figure out that the mule had the easier job.

When the mare reached a relatively level spot, Cat let her stop. Coming alongside, the mule nuzzled the mare's neck.

"You make a good pair. Respect's—" Alarm stopped her.

Yesterday—had it been such a short time ago?—she'd felt like this just before the Antelope Grove wolf appeared. Praying she wasn't telegraphing her tension to the animals, she forced herself to study her surroundings. An unseen jay protested her right to be here, but the wind barely made its presence known.

She was chiding herself for not having brought binoculars when her cell phone vibrated, startling her. It rang another two times before she could get it out of her front pocket. The display showed Daria's number.

"What's up?" Cat said, keeping her voice low.

"Just curious about whether you've heard the latest."

"What?" Did it have anything to do with Matt?

"I probably wouldn't know myself yet if I hadn't been over at Hart Mountain with the cattle truck picking up a bunch of stupid wandering heifers. You know the Albert Rim area."

Of course she did. The Rim was the largest exposed fault scarp in America. Thirty miles long, and 2,300 feet high, it was the home of Lake Albert, which she understood was the third largest inland body of salt water in the country.

"What about it?" she asked.

"A lot according to what a couple of women have been telling everyone. They were climbing up to the Rim when—"

"Climbing that? What for?"

" 'Cause it was there? How the hell do I know? They're part of that Oregon hiking bunch. Do I need to say more?"

"No." Hearing her friend's animated voice was calming her, thank goodness. No way was she going to let her imagination get the best of her. "So they were climbing. What happened?"

Daria didn't immediately answer, and when she did, she sounded serious. "The wolf pack was waiting for them when they got to the top."

Albert Rim was more than fifty miles from here as the crow flew. Just the same, she half imagined she was there. "How many?"

As her friend continued, Cat's mind filled with the image of two middle-aged women surrounded by no less than seven wolves. Apparently the wolves hadn't come closer than maybe 150 feet, but they'd stayed around for the better part of an hour. Every time the two women tried to start for the edge so they could climb down to where they'd left their vehicle near the lake, the wolves stepped between them and their escape route.

"The women were back at the road before I saw them, but they were still scared shitless. I've never seen someone who's supposedly healthy that pale. All they wanted to do was get the hell out of there."

"They said the wolves just watched them?"

"And not let them leave until they were thoroughly intimidated. Some other members of their hiking group were with them by the time I arrived. They were all excited and insisting the women stay put until law enforcement arrived. They wanted me to do the same, kept saying I had to put my two cents' worth in because I live here, yada, yada. Like law enforcement's going to listen to me." Daria laughed. "One good thing came out of that. There's two women who won't be coming back anytime soon."

"No, I don't suppose they will."

"Cat, did you hear about the emergency meeting that was set up so people could discuss finding a way to convince Fish and Wildlife that the wolves need to be blown away?"

"Addie told me. I understand Matt was going to be there."

"Considering what happened to his calf and a man who was working for him, I'm sure they want him raising holy hell. You're bonking him. Do you think he'd lead the charge?"

Bonking. "I doubt it. That's not his style."

"You're right. Unless he's getting it on with you, he prefers being by himself. Something I've been thinking about. What happened to the women will fuel the flames. Bottom line, they could have been killed. I don't know what stopped the wolves from attacking. It almost sounded if they were trying to decide whether to."

"It wouldn't have taken them that long to make up their minds."

"Then what—"

"I don't know, but learning the answer's important."

"How'd life get so complicated?"

Cat pinched the bridge of her nose. "It did, didn't it?" she muttered. "Are you still at the Rim?"

"Yep. Got the strays loaded and need to get them back to the ranch property. I just wanted you to know you don't have to worry about the wolves. They aren't anywhere near the Badlands."

12

Last winter a sharp but short-lived earthquake had stuck central Oregon. According to those who knew such things, the epicenter had been east of Lakeview, specifically in the Badlands. There'd been some minor property damage at a couple of houses outside the city limits. Back then the Badlands had been frozen and inhospitable, and no one had bothered to check things out. Cat might have been the first to come here in the spring. As far as she knew, no one had visited this steep-sided hill. Eventually someone would, and when they did, the cave would no longer be hers.

It needed a name, she decided as she tethered the animals to separate sagebrush. She could give credit to the Paiutes, but she wasn't sure they'd been responsible for the petroglyphs she'd found. Hopefully Helaku would know. For now, Ghost Cave seemed a good enough label.

After putting her new camera with its powerful flash over her shoulder, she started up the slope below the cave entrance. Her canteen bumped against her hip and stirred the part of her anatomy that riding had kept on edge for the past couple of hours. Within a minute, she realized that walking wasn't going to give her the respite she'd hoped it would. The constant rubbing factored in although she suspected Matt-thoughts were most responsible.

Despite everything, she wanted him to see Ghost Cave, now more than ever. In the past, she'd simply wanted to study his reaction to the ancient drawings, but now with the wolves turning his world on end, they'd have even more of an impact for her too. Surely he'd ask why she hadn't told anyone about what undoubtedly was an incredible find?

Good question. Logical question. Her answer, for what it was worth, was that she wasn't yet ready to share it with the world. This was *her* place, the ultimate example of what she loved about this land.

Do you think it's possible that the drawings are tied to what is happening now? she mentally asked Matt. *Will you agree with my assessment of that one wolf, that it's more than the work of an overenthusiastic artist? More than ignorance of perspective?*

The ground under her boots shifted. Determined not to risk a twisted ankle, she concentrated. Perhaps content to wait until she could focus on him, Matt remained at the edges of her mind.

As had happened just before her friend called, she felt a prickling between her shoulder blades. Well, no wonder. It was impossible not to imagine being in the two women hikers' position. They, too, had been in remote country. Granted, she knew more about the Badlands than they probably did about Albert Rim, but they'd had each other for comfort while she—

Damn it, she didn't need comforting. The wolves weren't anywhere around.

Because it was in shadow, the opening to Ghost Cave was hard to spot, and she had to stop a couple of times to get her bearings. The loose lava field the earthquake had shaken from its moorings all looked the same. Her guess was that before the quake, lava, placed there by ancient people, had obscured the opening.

Standing before the approximately three-foot-high opening, she wondered at the reckless curiosity that had compelled her to get onto her hands and knees and crawl in that first time. No way would she have if no daylight reached the cave. Or if she'd known about the flesh-and-blood wolves.

Okay, enough with the stalling. It was time to get in, take as many pictures as she thought necessary to accurately detail what was there, and get out. That done, she'd take the horse and mule to the meadow below her and to the south and let them graze for a while. Maybe tomorrow she'd go see Helaku.

More prickling joined what was already between her shoulders as she crawled inside, but that was to be expected. Ghost Cave was just that, ghostly.

As soon as she was past the entrance, Cat got to her feet. The cave ceiling wasn't quite six feet high, which meant Matt would have to stand bent over. Undoubtedly he'd share her awe of the nearly twenty-by-twenty-foot space with several nooks and crannies. He'd take notice of the bits and pieces of dried grasses still on the floor. Grass not thick enough for having sex on.

Darn it, Matt wasn't here. Drawing comparisons between now and the last time she'd been on her hands and knees was getting in the way of her mission.

Thanks to the sun's position, it was closer to twilight than night in here. Drawing the camera case off her shoulder, she took out the digital and turned it on. As soon as the flash signaled it was ready, she began taking pictures, starting to the right of the opening and working clockwise. It made sense to work like that and had nothing to do with needing to put off acknowledging the final drawing as long as possible. Unfortunately, her back was to *the one*.

The cool interior soon had her going from being too warm

to comfortable to slightly chilled. She tried to keep Matt-thoughts at bay, she really did. Nevertheless, he stood beside her in spirit, equally inspired by what had survived unknown centuries. Like her, the man in her mind was curious about who the artists had been and why they'd chosen these particular subjects.

There were five scenes consisting of stick figures. One showed people either standing or kneeling in a circle looking up at what she concluded was the sun, although it might have been the moon. Another depicted a battle complete with two prone figures with red staining the ground around them. The combatants were armed with spears and knives.

In the scene to the right of the battle one, a solitary figure knelt near the head of a body drenched in blood. Other people were grouped around the bowed kneeler, all with their heads down. Had the victim been a chief or religious leader?

Contrasting with the people scenes were animal and bird drawings, some very well done. Those of deer and antelope in particular impressed her because of the muscle detail. By the time she came to the one of a bear on its hind legs, her shutter finger ached. She took pictures of the bear—which she guessed was a grizzly and not a smaller black bear like the ones that lived here today—from several angles.

The region's petroglyphs that were viewable to the public were mostly made up of meaningless symbols, but everything in Ghost Cave made sense.

Finally, because she'd done everything else, and she needed to get back to the animals, she stepped in front of the final drawing. No matter that she'd seen it before, it again took her breath away. Six well-depicted wolves all looking in the same direction stood with their tails low and their ears flattened in what she understood was submission.

Leaning in, she snapped several shots of the clearly defined heads. Hopefully their gleaming yellow eyes would show up.

Then, holding her breath, she pointed her camera at what the wolves were looking at. Nearly twice as large as the pack members, this whatever-it-was had deep black, intelligent-looking eyes. It loomed over the others as if warning them.

Before Matt had shown her the oversized prints he'd found near the dead calf, she'd believed that whoever had drawn this had taken artistic license with his work. Now she wasn't sure.

Do you have the answer, Matt? If you saw this, would you understand?

The cave muted the outside sounds while the dim lighting made it too easy to imagine she'd stepped back in time. No longer a modern woman, she became a member of an ancient tribe that believed its survival depended on its reverence for a multitude of spirits as well as for the sun, moon, and the rest of nature's gifts.

Quite possibly, the ancients believed wolves were a key part of that spirituality. If they conducted themselves as their shaman and other leaders directed, wolves would guide them to successful hunts. Through prayer and spirit quests, they'd learn how to depend on senses sharpened by wolf spirits, and the women, children, and elders back home would sleep with full bellies.

Shaking her head, Cat turned off the digital and put it back in the case. Enough with losing touch with reality. Instead of heading for sunlight, however, she lightly ran her hand over the large wolf, starting with the top of the head and moving along the back to the bushy tail. It was her imagination, of course, nothing steeped in reality, yet she half believed she was caressing fur instead of hard lava.

She hadn't touched the fangs yet, didn't need to, no reason. Despite the inner voice warning her to get the hell out of here and back to the real world, she breathed warmth onto her fingers and stroked the killing teeth. In contrast to the wolf's soft fur, the teeth were sharp. Capable of tearing her apart.

Unnerved, she scrambled out of the cave and struggled to her feet. The sun should have warmed her. Instead, she shivered and goose bumps broke out everywhere. Her hand clamped over her mouth, she frantically looked for the way she'd taken to get up here.

Matt! I could really use you right now.

The sun caressed her hair and back, then moved to her buttocks and the backs of her thighs. Bit by bit, tension seeped out of her, replaced by memories. Matt had touched her much the way the sun now was. Although he'd been rough and urgent, she'd loved it.

She could cherish this moment with the cave behind her, the sun warming her, and Matt settled deep in her mind and body.

Squirming in response to the energy between her legs, she again tried to locate the route down. Talk about distraction! Heat where heat couldn't be ignored was getting to her. Forget keeping her distance from Matt! Right now she needed him way too much for logic and caution to factor.

A sharp whinny followed by a bray from the mule stopped her. From where she stood, she couldn't see the pair, but she knew animal sounds. They were alarmed.

Wolf!

Get over it! You know where they are. Just because you got carried away in the cave is no reason to . . . to what?

Despite the urgency, she took a long drink from her canteen that she'd left at the entrance in an effort to settle her nerves. Then, warning herself not to hurry and risk falling, she started down. Horses panicked when there was no need, and there'd only been that one outburst. Keeping her balance took her full attention. Her toes kept jamming against the end of her boots, and her thigh and calf muscles protested.

Sweat had made her top stick to her by the time she reached the bottom of the hill. Relieved, she took off her hat and fanned herself with it, then wiped sweat out of her eyes. So much for the glamorous life.

Neither animal acknowledged her presence. Damn it, that wasn't right. She opened her mouth to say something to turn their attention from whatever they were looking at, but just because she needed affirmation that all was right in her world wasn't enough reason to try to break their concentration. Holding on to the camera case, she looked in the direction they were.

Oh, shit.

Matt! Get here. Right now.

The solitary wolf stood far enough away that she couldn't be positive about its size—either that or she wasn't ready to acknowledge reality. *Magnificent* said it all. Proud and unafraid. Utterly at home in the wilderness.

Her body turned numb. At the same time, her mind sharpened. If the predator charged, she was in big trouble. Logic said it would prefer to turn the horse or mule into its next meal, but would a solo wolf take on a prey that size?

Maybe it wasn't in attack mode. Maybe it simply . . . what?

Her parents had never caught on to the concept that a child wasn't born knowing everything he or she needed to survive, but they'd given her a few ground rules such as not walking into traffic or crawling into a lion cage. They'd think she was fourteen kinds of a fool if they could see her now, because instead of jumping onto horseback and getting the hell out of there, she started walking toward the wolf.

"You're huge," she muttered. The sound of her voice startled her, yet she continued. "Like the Ghost Cave drawing."

A possibility stopped her, but the wolf was waiting for her, so she started walking again. After a moment, she gave her thought freedom. Was it possible she was looking at the model the long-dead artist had used?

"Why hasn't anyone seen you before this? I know they haven't. There's no way they could keep you a secret."

Sweat coated her palms. As she wiped them on her jeans, her right hand brushed her cell phone. Matt's number was on speed dial. She could—should—call him. Tell him what was happening.

But what if he wasn't alone? Did she want anyone else to know yet?

Was she ready to share this moment with Matt?

The still-waiting wolf lowered its head, revealing its fangs as it did. She thought she knew what a wolf warning looked like, not much different from a dog's, right? If she was correct, this wasn't it because its gaze remained curious, not threatening. But what then?

By now she'd covered about a third of the distance separating them. Between that and wrapping her mind around what she was seeing, doubt became certainty. Yes, this predator's eyes were black.

Like the one in the cave.

"Why aren't I terrified of you? Why don't I think I've lost my mind?"

As if contemplating her questions, the wolf cocked his head. Cat didn't know she was going to laugh until she heard the sound. "Thank you," she whispered. "I don't know why you've chosen me to show yourself to. Is it just because I found the cave or— Hell, I don't know what I'm saying."

She started to shake. Hoping to calm herself, she rubbed the heel of her hand over the cell phone. It would be so easy to connect with Matt but then what? Maybe even at "hello" he'd sense that something was different about her.

Different? Not even close to describing what was happening.

Giving up on trying to settle her nerves, she planted one foot in front of the other. She couldn't possibly know this, of course, and yet she had no doubt the wolf would remain where he was, for now.

"Are you part of the pack? Alpha male to the max?"

The beautiful head cocked again.

"What is it?" She laughed. "You don't speak English?"

Some fifty feet now separated them, and as she contemplated the scant space between them, her legs stopped moving. She rubbed her thighs. "This is close enough." *Even if I'm crazy, I'm not that crazy.* "Ah, look, if you're going to rip my throat out, just do it. Don't make me wait."

The wolf's ears swung toward her. His fangs slowly disappeared behind lowering lips, and he now looked more puzzled than anything. Maybe he, too, didn't believe what was happening.

"It's a dream." She wasn't sure which of them she was trying to convince. "We're having the same one. I'll buy that if you will."

A wind gust blew her hair against her mouth, prompting her to push it away. Maybe doing something ordinary had been the trigger she needed, because suddenly everything became starkly real. She, a woman trying to earn a living on unforgiving land, was standing on lava only a few feet from a wolf larger than any wolf had ever been. This creature had undoubtedly left its prints where Matt could find them, but why wasn't it at Albert Rim with the pack?

Maybe the pack had made it an outcast.

Maybe it didn't need the pack.

Maybe it wasn't real.

"I'm sorry . . . sorry but I can't . . . can't process this." Much as she needed to rub her eyes, she didn't dare. What if the beast attacked then? "I, ah, I'm going to leave. I want to turn my back on you but . . . do you want me dead? That way you're safe. No one will know you exist."

The white fangs returned.

Oh, shit! "If you understand what I'm saying—if that's possible—you need to know something. When they find my body, they'll come after you with guns. There'll be no stopping them."

Lifting its muzzle skyward, the wolf howled. The deep, drawn-out sound shook Cat to the core. She started to press a hand over her heart only to be distracted by the camera strap over her shoulder.

Do it!

Lacking the thought process to explain what she was doing, she fumbled with the case. Despite her uncooperative fingers, she finally turned on the digital and pointed it at the predator. She hadn't thought to activate the flash, but it wasn't needed out here.

"This isn't going to hurt." *Stupid thing to say! Just do it!*

Not bothering to look in the viewfinder, she pressed the button. The click was barely audible. Still the wolf again pointed its head upward and howled.

Another shot followed by another and then a third, all done as fast as camera and fingers allowed. Still holding the digital up, she started backtracking.

Thank you, thank you. Just let me live. That's all I ask, to make it back alive.

To show this to Matt.

13

Not quite twenty-four hours after reluctantly meeting with a small group of ranchers, hunters, and hikers, Matt watched as his next neighbor to the south bounced down the drive to his place. Cat had been the last person to come here. No way could he not think about that.

Closing his eyes, Matt welcomed an image of her into his mind's eye. Cat had been the best thing in his life, a soft and strong body eager to meet his, grope for grope and thrust for thrust.

Right now, as long as he mentally held on to her, he could keep other things at bay.

His eyes still closed, he went back to last fall on the day of the annual calf sale that represented his paycheck for the year. Beef prices had been higher than expected, and instead of each rancher going his or her way once the cattle trucks left, folks started talking about a celebration.

More than a hundred people had shown up at the Stensen Ranch. The women had cooked while tired, dirty ranchers—

him included—drank beer and reassured each other that hay supplies would hold out through the winter.

He'd called Cat and left her a message about the barbeque but didn't know whether she'd show. The sun had set before everyone congregated around the makeshift table in the large Stensen barn. After filling his plate, he'd looked around for a hay bale to sit on only to find Cat standing on one and nodding at him.

She'd nibbled from his plate while telling him she'd had the vet out today to check the stallion she'd brought in to service a couple of her mares. The damn stud had run himself into a fence post and was limping. Turned out he'd only sprained his right front leg and would be fine.

"So," Cat had wound up, "I've gone from cussing one stallion to wondering what another has in mind."

Five minutes later they'd had sex behind the Stensens' house. Fun and nearly civilized sex.

"You aren't going to believe this." His neighbor John Lawrence leaned out his truck window.

Reluctantly pushing Cat into the back of his mind, Matt watched John get out. Like most longtime ranchers, John's narrow face was rich with wrinkles. Going by the creases, Matt guessed John was in his midsixties, although his steady walk hinted at younger. Not saying more, John led the way to his truck bed.

John leaned a bony arm on the bed's side and faced Matt. "I heard fighting last night. Out a ways, not near my barn or the corral. It sounded like dogs mostly. Big ones."

Mostly?

A bloodstained canvas tarp covered something. Studying it, Matt's belly clenched, but then he'd been so on edge lately he'd had to fight himself to stay seated during yesterday's volatile and unproductive meeting.

"So it was the wild dogs we've been trying to trap?" Matt

asked. For a good three months now, a pack of four or five mutts, each weighting a hundred pounds, had been hunting closer than either he or John liked. The men had concluded that one or more persons had dropped off dogs they couldn't handle or feed. The mutts might have once been domesticated, but salvaging for a living had awakened the wild in them. John and he had given up trying to trap them to see if they could be redeemed.

A few weeks ago, the pack had ambushed and killed one of John's cattle dogs and Addie had lost several chickens to them. The men had reluctantly agreed they had no choice but to destroy them.

"The wolves got to those mutts before we could," John said, and pulled away the tarp.

Two dead scruffy dogs lay on the truck bed. Both had had their throats ripped apart. There were few other wounds.

"You're sure the rest of the pack didn't get to them?" Matt asked, putting off the inevitable.

"Look at what was done to them. Rogue dogs don't know how to attack. They rip and tear and make a mess of things."

Something dark curled through Matt. John, his truck, and the two carcasses ceased to exist, and he found himself in a pasture a good distance from John's weathered house. It was night, the air going toward cold. A dark brown dog slunk toward a doe and her twins. Just as the beast gathered itself to attack one of the fawns, something slammed into it and knocked it off its feet. Deadly fangs locked around the dog's throat.

"What do you think?" John pressed. "You agree with me that this was done by wolves?"

"Yeah," Matt made himself say. "What are you going to do?"

"That's the thing of it." After dropping the tarp back into place, John rubbed his whiskered chin. "I didn't go to yesterday's meeting because I don't agree with those who think we've got to get rid of the wolves. I don't want to lose any livestock to them, but damn it, Matt, wolves were here long before us. They have a right to be what God made them."

"You need to let people know how you feel."

John, who had been looking everywhere but at Matt, settled his gaze on him. "What about you? Where do you stand on this?"

Neck-deep in trouble, starting with not being sure who I am anymore. "It's going to tear the area apart with people on different sides arguing they're right and saying those who don't agree are fools. I don't want that."

"You haven't said—where are you?"

Decades ago, John had started out to be a college professor only to discover he hated the politics and bureaucracy that went with the job, and his parents had been right. He belonged on the land. Yet, much as he loved what he was doing, he missed having much opportunity to stretch his mind. Because he sometimes felt the same way, Matt was grateful for their occasional deep conversations.

"I agree that wolves have a right to return to land that humans denied them for too long," he said, "but the land's changed. It's no longer just antelope and deer living here."

"Our cattle are part of the change all right," John added. "The government... You heard about those women hikers yesterday, didn't you? A friend of mine called last night saying she was trying to correct the rumors going around. She saw the women. There wasn't a scratch on them."

Matt had been out checking on the youngest calves when the phones started ringing. By the time he got back home, Addie had sorted through everything and relayed what she believed was the straight story. Like John had done, Addie had talked to Daria—Cat's closest friend.

"What bothers me," he said, "is that those women are part of that hiking group. Their president and some other man were at yesterday's meeting." He shook his head. "All that talk about respecting the environment they dumped on us when they were asking permission to go on our land and now they're saying the opposite."

"In what way?"

"The president read a press release he'd already sent to the media. Everything was about freedom of movement, God-given rights, the importance of modern people being able to get in touch with nature. And being safe doing it."

"How?" John asked. "By putting bells around wolves' and coyotes' necks so they can hear them coming? Maybe they want all predators rounded up and put behind fences. Or dead."

Matt, who had been leaning against John's truck, pushed away from it. "That bunch won't come out and say so. They know better. But after the meeting, the two pulled me aside and tried to talk me into coming on board. Beale could have been killed, they said. A human life is more important than— Hell, you know their thinking."

"And now this thing with the pack intimidating those women is going to give them even more ammunition." John ran a deeply tanned hand under his hat. "Damn it, I just want to ranch. That's enough for any man to deal with."

Matt wished it were that easy for him. That, facing the two men, he hadn't wanted to rip their throats out.

Much more of this and she'd have to buy new carpet for her office, probably a new chair, too, Cat admitted. She'd been in and out of the room at least a dozen times since getting up this morning. Mostly she'd stared at her monitor instead of launching the software for her digital. Yesterday, just minutes after uploading the shots she'd taken earlier in the day, she'd walked out of the room and slammed the door behind her. It had taken her until morning to work up the courage or whatever it was to assimilate the magnitude of what she'd uncovered.

Tell Matt or not, call a press conference or not, go after her fifteen minutes of fame or not.

Mostly tell Matt or keep all this to herself?

That was the hardest part, trying to figure out how Matt would react. If she'd taken the pictures a year ago, she wouldn't be uptight right now. Matt would share her awe of what she'd found. Together they'd form a plan of action.

But Matt had changed.

Moaning, she planted her arms on her desk and rested her forehead on them. She supposed she'd gotten a little sleep last night because she couldn't remember every detail of the endless hours, but it hadn't been enough to restore her.

Well, what did she expect? She didn't come face-to-face with a massive wolf every day. She'd never had to decide what to do with that knowledge.

After another moan, she straightened and reached for her mouse. Her hand trembled, and her fingers felt as if they might cramp, but she did what she had to. When the slideshow launched, she leaned back, laced her fingers together, and stared. The pictures she'd taken inside Ghost Cave yesterday were a hundred times clearer than her first attempt. More to the point, the detail took her breath away. Every petroglyph was absolutely clear. She'd already called Helaku and told him she wanted to show him something.

"It sounds important," he'd said.

"It is," she'd responded, followed by explaining that she wasn't sure when she could get to his place.

If anyone could point her in the right direction with regard to what she'd found, it was Helaku, and yet she hadn't decided whether she'd show him the last series.

Her fingers started to ache. Looking at them, she saw that her knuckles were white, so shook her hands to restore circulation. The petroglyph of the oversized wolf filled the monitor. Knowing what was coming next, her right hand went to her throat, and she started to stroke her flesh, her vulnerable flesh. As the first outside shot came into view, her other hand slid between her legs.

The wolf. As real as real could be. With the surrounding vegetation and lava rocks offering perspective, there was no question about the predator's size. She couldn't remember whether she'd been using the zoom feature. Had she been that close to the beast?

The first picture faded to be replaced by another that showed a bit of fang. Coal-black eyes locked onto her. They seemed to be saying something, but what? One thing she had no doubt of, the massive wolf was trying to communicate with her.

Oh, shit! Enough with the indecision. She couldn't keep this to herself.

Hauling out her cell phone, she sent Matt a text message: *I need to see you.*

That done, she went back to staring at the slideshow. Her nerves jumped, and goose bumps assaulted her shoulders and the back of her neck. Desperate for the end to this terrible tension, she began rubbing her crotch. Some women were good at tapping into their imaginations to enhance their self-pleasure, her not so much. Sex toys did the job, if the toys themselves worked and she had batteries. Her fingers were more reliable, all except for wishing the fingers were masculine.

Sliding down in the chair, she separated her legs for easier access. Her jeans served as a damnable barrier, but after a few more seconds of rubbing, enough friction built up that heat spread throughout her pussy. Closing her eyes, she fumbled with her blouse buttons. That done, she ran her fingers under a bra cup. Gripping her nipple with thumb and forefinger, she pinched. Her other hand continued attacking her crotch.

Her phone rang.

Confused and disoriented, Cat shot upright and stared at the cell she'd left on her desk. The slideshow had started looping and now showed the stick-figure battle scene in Ghost Cave. With her hand still on her sex and her cheeks on fire, she flipped open the phone and held it to her ear. "Hello," she said. She hadn't checked to see who was calling.

"It's me."

"Matt." His name on her lips sent lightning through her. "I, ah, just left the text message."

"What do you want?"

You backing me against a wall and nibbling on my breasts. Maybe running your knuckles along the valley between them and from there to my midsection. Sliding your fingers into my pubic hair. "There's, ah, something I need to show you."

"I thought you wanted your space."

Talking took so much out of her that she had no choice but to stop rubbing her crotch so she could concentrate. "It wasn't that," she told him, angry at the spin he'd put on things. "Hell, never mind. Did you go to that meeting? Addie said—"

"Is that why you called?"

He wasn't going to cut her any slack, was he? "No. I could come to your place but if Addie's there . . ."

"You want us to be alone?"

Of course I do. I've wanted that starting with the night we met. "Don't read anything into this, Matt." The shot she'd taken of the wolf pack sharpened. "I didn't call because I'm horny if that's what you're thinking." *Well, there's that.* "Can you come here?"

His responses had been rapid-fire; now his silence caught her off-guard. "Not until tomorrow."

"Oh?"

"I'm short-handed, Cat, remember?"

How could she forget what had happened to Beale? Stumbling through the words, she let him know that tomorrow morning was fine, and no, of course shortly after dawn wouldn't be too early for her.

She didn't start shaking again until after they'd hung up. After several attempts, she stopped the slideshow. Then, although she'd just put a new color cartridge in her printer, she couldn't put her mind into printing out the pictures she intended to show to Helaku.

No, for now at least, she wouldn't include the ones she'd taken outside the cave. Those were for Matt. Only for him.

14

Cat had planted some roses and other bushes outside her place. The only time Matt had made the mistake of asking Addie why she bothered with flowers that took so much work and well water, she'd replied that her soul needed the color, and he should understand. Besides, they drew butterflies and bees. Studying the flowers, he debated telling Addie he must have a soul after all. She'd retort that of course he did.

Why did he do things like not letting Addie know how much he enjoyed and appreciated flowers? he pondered, only he knew the answer. He'd been protecting his emotions for so long it had become habit.

He shouldn't be here, shouldn't be turning off the engine and getting out of the high, dusty cab. He'd told Cat the truth when he'd explained about the extra work he'd taken on since Beale quit. Beale had called last night, not saying anything either of them could hang their hats on but letting Matt know that his wondering if he was a coward wasn't sitting too well with him. If Beale called again, he'd tell the young man his position hadn't been filled.

As recently as a couple of weeks ago, Cat would have been exploding out the front door and launching herself at him. Before she could so much as wrap her limbs around him, he'd be carrying her back inside. They wouldn't say so much as "hello" until after sex.

No, he admonished himself as he went up the stairs, he shouldn't be here. He didn't trust himself. The last thing he'd ever tell her was about last night's dream. In it he settled his lasso around her so her arms were pinned to her sides. Keeping the rope taut, he slowly, relentlessly pulled her toward him. That done, he held the rope over her head with one hand while attacking her jeans zipper with the other. Ignoring her protests, he hog-tied her, cut off the rest of her clothes, and jammed himself into her helpless body.

It had only been a dream, damn it. He'd never take her against her will. Would he?

He knocked, stepped back, and sucked in several quick breaths that made him a little light-headed. *Get in your damn truck. On your way out, call and tell her this is no good. You don't trust yourself.*

"Matt," Cat said through the screen door. "Hello."

"Yeah. Okay." Taking in her dim outline, he couldn't think of anything else to say.

Sighing, she pushed the screen at him. "Come in."

Cat's place always smelled good. When he'd commented on it, she'd said something about candles, incense, and essential oils—whatever those were. Today the scents swirled over and into him. Just like that, he had a damned erection when he needed to keep a lid on such things.

Except for not having put on shoes, she was ready for the day. His guess was she'd already had breakfast. After all, her life pace wasn't that different from his. If she hadn't headed for her coffee table, he might not have noted what was on it. Sitting on the couch, she looked up at him. He figured he outweighed

her by a good seventy pounds. Right now the difference between them seemed even greater. Energy all but exploded between them.

"This"—her hand hovered over a stack of photos—"is what
I need you to see."

Because she hadn't indicated she wanted him to sit next to
her, he settled his butt as far away on the couch as possible and
still see the pictures. Jamming his hands between his knees for
safekeeping, he leaned forward. One move from her and he'd
be all over her.

"I took the pictures several days ago," she continued, no
longer looking at him. "For a while I wasn't sure I was going to
share them with anyone, with you. But I can't keep what I've
discovered to myself."

Cat took life full-on, which was a big part of what appealed
to him about her. Nothing like a woman who didn't back
down. Right now, however, her usual confidence seemed to be
missing.

"Why not?" he asked.

"Look at them."

Instead of shoving the stack his way as he thought she'd do,
she handed him one at a time. Sounding a bit like a nervous
tour guide, she told him how she'd found Ghost Cave and the
trouble she'd initially had getting decent pictures of the petroglyphs. If she'd spotted his erection, she gave no indication.
Unfortunately, it showed no sign of fading.

"I'm not going to say anything about how long I've been
keeping the cave to myself." She handed him a picture of mini-
mally drawn figures in a battle scene. "It's public land, government property really. Just thinking of some bureaucracy
charging in and taking over . . . I loved knowing I had this all to
myself."

She hadn't said anything to him. Why not? Somewhere in

the midst of all their rutting, surely there'd been time for conversation.

Years ago, Santo and Addie had shown him a couple of boulders on their property that had random stick figures and squiggles that had been done by Native Americans. There'd never been a discussion about sharing their find with local historians, let alone the feds, but that would have changed if they'd been the ones to find Ghost Cave, wouldn't it?

Maybe Cat had run out of words, because she handed him the next four photographs without first explaining what she believed they represented. His heartbeat had been a bit rapid when he'd walked in here, a condition he chalked up to thoughts of their physical relationship. With each picture, he felt less and less in control of his body. Going by the muted lighting at the edges of each photograph, he had a pretty good idea how dim the cave's interior was.

Had Cat worn a jacket as defense against the chill? Had she ever felt as if she weren't alone, that perhaps the souls or spirits of those who had created the drawings still lingered?

"You weren't afraid?" he asked.

"It crossed my mind that the cave might not be as stable as it looked, but I figured I could get out in time."

"Could you?"

When she stared at him, the look in her eyes rocked him. Today wasn't just about her showing him her find. The thing was, he'd already suspected that.

"All right, maybe I couldn't," she muttered, "but I didn't and still don't believe the risk was that great." She lightly ran her fingers over the edges of the sheet she was about to hand him. "Have you ever done something because you felt you had no choice?"

Hell, yes.

"That's the way it was for me. It didn't take long to realize I'd been handed an incredible gift."

"Gift?"

From the looks of it, she'd just braided her hair, but that didn't stop her from trying to run her hand along her scalp. "I hope you aren't making fun of me."

"I'm not."

"I want to believe you, Matt. Need to. Do you comprehend how incredible and rare this is?" She went back to risking a paper cut. "Most people go their entire lives not experiencing anything like this."

With each word, he became more aware of her, something he didn't believe was possible. "No, they don't."

"Maybe—probably—there's nothing more at work here than chance. Shit happens. Sometimes it's good shit. I was in the right place at the right time, end of story."

Except she didn't believe that and with his heart reaching double time, neither did he. *Stay on track. Be her confidant, nothing else.* "What's next?" he asked.

It wasn't his imagination; she didn't want to hand him the facedown photograph she was holding. He didn't want to see it, somehow knew he'd be changed by it. And yet what choice did he have?

"Just study this, all right?" She slid it toward him with unsteady fingers. "Take your time."

Trapped and excited, he turned it over. The ink hadn't had long to dry, which meant he risked smearing it. Still, he couldn't withdraw his fingers from the exquisitely created pack of wolves. They'd been depicted as individuals, and yet, as far as he could determine, they were equals. He didn't believe there was an alpha. Holding his breath, he ran his forefinger over each muzzle. Still not breathing, he touched the first eye.

"I understand," Cat whispered. "Impossible to ignore the detail, isn't it."

"The eyes are alive."

Instead of touching his wrist as he sensed she wanted to, she pulled back. "I thought the same thing. Matt, they're looking at . . . Are you ready to see what it is?"

He hadn't been prepared for anything that had been happening recently and would give anything to have his physically strenuous but emotionally simple life back. Damn it, he'd worked so hard to get to this place.

"Show me."

She started to hand the next shot to him, only to stop. "I'm hoping Helaku can explain. If anyone can, it's him."

He'd seen the old Paiute maybe a half dozen times since Santo and Addie took him under their roof. At first he'd barely been aware of Helaku's presence. But Helaku had kept studying him with his ancient eyes as if looking for something. *Leave me alone,* Matt had wanted to demand, but what if Helaku said he didn't know what Matt was talking about? Better to keep his distance.

The last time the two men had been under the same roof had been during a farming career day put on by the local 4-H and held at the high school. Along with other ranchers, Matt had sat on a panel first explaining their operations and then answering questions. Helaku had been one of three Paiutes who talked about how their ancestors had used the land. At least that's how things had started. Before long, however, Helaku's description of how ancient Native Americans tracked both prey and enemies had everyone spellbound. When he started talking about his ancestors' belief in nature's spirits, something had opened inside Matt.

Looking up, he locked eyes with Cat. "You're friends with Helaku?"

"I'm not sure I'd call it a friendship. I couldn't respect him any more than I do."

Are you stalling? her eyes asked. *Of course not,* he wanted to retort, but he'd picked up on her tension, either that or he was getting vibes from whatever was on the back side of that piece of paper.

Determined not to give away his reaction, he turned the photograph over. At first he didn't understand why she'd made such a big deal of this wolf drawing. Then he compared the pack in the lower right with the one that dominated the sheet.

Bigger. Stronger. With impossibly black eyes and a stance that screamed alpha. No doubt about it, the other wolves were in awe of it or intimidated or both.

Same as him.

The house sounds faded, and there wasn't enough air in the room. He felt hot and cold, numb and super-sensitive. Scared.

Hell no! Not scared, not him.

"Is the perspective off?" he asked when he could speak. "The artist made him larger because, hell, I don't know why."

"Here." Cat thrust another paper at him. "I stepped back a bit when I took this one so you can clearly see the difference. The way the others are looking at him, I believe everything was drawn at the same time."

"Deliberate? Not artistic license?"

Her silence gnawed at him, said she knew more than she was ready to reveal. Willing himself to do the last thing he wanted to, he studied the alpha's every detail. He'd seen bulls carry themselves like this with testosterone running through them and making them fearless.

Oh, damn, the oversized wolf had balls and a long, thick, erect cock.

The longer he stared at the intact male, the more his own erection grew. If he had hackles, they'd be standing on edge.

"Why?" he muttered. "What was the point of this?"

"Matt?"

Alerted to her hesitant tone, he turned his attention from the photograph to her. He could smell her sex.

"What?"

Looking as if she'd never seen him before, she hurried to her feet and positioned herself on the opposite side of the table. Cows distanced themselves from bulls when they weren't ready to be bred, but her scent said she needed to be mounted.

"I don't think having you come here was such a good idea." She nodded at what strained for freedom between his legs.

"Too late. I'm here."

"Yeah." She licked her lips. "You are. Matt, you've seen everything I think I'm going to show Helaku, but that isn't the last picture I took."

The blood surging through his veins made listening and comprehending all but impossible. "It isn't?"

"No. I thought..." Leaning forward, she picked up the photographs he hadn't yet seen and held them to her chest. "Yesterday I believed showing them to you was a good idea. Now I'm not sure."

He could overtake her in a single leap. "Why not?"

"Because you're scaring me."

Her words got to him. Touched a core of responsibility he'd nearly lost. "I don't want to, Cat. I'm sorry if I am. Go on." He indicated what she was holding. "Show me."

Nodding, she slowly turned one of the pictures over so he could see it. So he had no choice but to acknowledge what was there. The longer he studied it, the more alarmed he became. Alarmed, damn it, not scared.

"I know where that was taken," he said, "the very spot."

How is that possible? her eyes said.

At a loss for words, he took the photograph from her and dropped it onto the table. His mind processed what he was seeing and yet it didn't. With the surrounding vegetation for perspective, he had no doubt of the flesh-and-blood wolf's size. Even with shadow blurring its features, the piercing black eyes made their impact. Cat had captured everything from the tips of the wolf's forward-pointing ears to his bushy tail. There was no doubt of the wolf's sex.

"How far away were you?" he finally asked.

"Maybe twenty feet."

Twenty feet was nothing. The predator could have covered that in a single leap. Still looking at what he hadn't fully processed, he tried to force himself to relax. Bottom line, Cat was safe.

Maybe there'd never been a hint of danger.

Maybe the wolf had deliberately revealed himself to her. What did he mean, *maybe?*

"Matt?"

"What?"

"You're tearing the photograph."

Damn it, she was right. The thing was, he didn't remember picking the shot up again. Dropping it, he went back to studying the incomprehensible. A bull heading for a corral full of cows had nothing on this living, breathing alpha wolf. Cat's shot had frozen the beast, but there was no doubting his potential and deadly purpose.

"The prints you found," she said, "belong to him."

Hopefully there was only one wolf this size. The thought of any more made his blood run cold. Then he looked at Cat again and chill became heat. His muscles flexed and tightened. She'd taken unbelievable pictures of a massive predator and had shared them with him. Now he had to deal with it.

Had to deal with what was happening to him.

15

Even before Matt moved, Cat sensed what he was going to do. Feeling as if she might explode, she backtracked. Arms at his sides, he stepped around the coffee table and headed for her.

"Don't."

Going by his expression, he either hadn't heard or her warning hadn't penetrated. He'd started changing in indefinable ways from the moment she showed him the oversized-wolf cave painting, His eyes had darkened until they mirrored the wolf's, and his gaze had grown predator-sharp. Even without fangs, he seemed less human.

Warning herself not to look at his erection, she reached behind her for the nearby recliner. Her fingers brushed an arm, but instead of trying to put the stupid, useless barrier between them, she stood her ground.

"What do you think you're doing?" she asked.

"What we both want."

Damn the man for being right! No way could she deny that along with distrust, fear, and confusion, heat warred for her attention. He was still human; she didn't dare lose sight of that. But the human was being swallowed by something else.

"Just because you're turned on doesn't mean I am."

"Yes, you are."

"How can you say that?"

"I can smell you."

Smell. No doubt, then, that his senses were sharpening because her sex *was* becoming fluid and was warring for her attention. "I just took a shower."

"Doesn't matter."

Going by his rough tone, she guessed talking was becoming difficult. Even as she tried to process what that said about what was taking place in him, she gave thanks for her confusion. After all, how could she possibly want to fathom everything?

Even as he closed in on her, she fell in love with Matt's smooth stride. He didn't simply walk—he glided. With every step, his thigh muscles strained the jeans. His legs couldn't possibly be becoming larger and yet—

Powerful male hands reached for her. Alive with emotions she had no words for, she watched as her wrists disappeared under his fingers. He gripped her hard and harsh, the message clear.

Today was all about having his way.

Drawing her arms around his waist so she was off balance and hard against him, he thrust his crotch at her. "Take it."

Demand he leave me alone. Lie and say you don't want him. "Not like this. Matt, it won't work. Our clothes."

Holding her at arm's length, he looked down at her. Trepidation and anticipation warred within her. Even drunk she'd never felt like this.

"What do you want?" she asked.

"Strip."

Maybe she should point out how hard that would be without the use of her hands. Instead she waited. Watched. Hummed.

"You heard me, Cat. Enough with the clothes."

She tried to lift her arms only to surrender to his greater strength. Drumbeats echoed inside her. When finally he released her, she remained in place before him. The compelling beats seemed to be coming from him.

Fluid and confident, he stepped to her side and grabbed her braid. "Do it."

He applied just enough pressure that she had no choice but to look upward. The ceiling offered neither comfort nor explanation. Lost in sensation, she started in on her blouse buttons. She'd debated cutting her hair short only to chicken out because she was afraid that would take more work. Braids and ponytails were easy and practical.

Today she acknowledged another reason for keeping the length.

Done with the unbuttoning, she pulled the shirt out of her waistband and shook it off her shoulders, which was no easy task. Instead of helping, he continued to keep her off balance until the garment fell to the carpet.

"Bra."

The drumming inside prevented her from being sure she'd heard him correctly, but what did it matter? She had no use for clothes this morning. If not for his hand between her shoulder blades, she might have fallen backward. Trusting him when she knew she shouldn't, she accepted his support while she fumbled with the damnable fastening. Finally the bra lay on top of her blue cotton top. Her breasts felt as if sandpaper had brushed over them.

"Enough," she said to the ceiling. "This is killing my neck."

Without a word of apology, Matt pushed against the back of her head. Even as relief streamed through her neck, she nearly begged him not to release her braid after all.

Not trusting her reaction if she looked into his eyes again, she tackled her jeans. Her hands hadn't been this unsteady since she'd taken the pictures. Dispensing with her jeans was relatively easy. On the other hand, the idea of standing nude in front of Matt terrified her. The only thing she knew about the panties she still had on was that they ended just shy of her navel.

"What about you?" she asked. "Am I the only one who—"

"I do what I do, when I want."

Unless you aren't sure what you want, she silently finished for him. The photographs half a room away dominated the space. They had something—maybe everything—to do with Matt's mood.

Thinking to mention her concern, she faced Matt full-on. The moment she did, her heavy breasts and the juices in her pussy stopped her thoughts. Matt had become a mountain, a fierce beast, nearly inhuman. Granted, he still wore everything he'd had on when he'd walked into her place, but she could see through the layers to the truth about this man she'd once thought she knew.

"I . . ." Not sure what she'd been going to say, she drew her braid over her shoulder and started fingering it. Her other hand zeroed in on her cunt. The ache in her neck didn't matter— only the one laying claim to her cunt did. Sex, soon. Sex, different and yet familiar.

As if he'd tapped into her thoughts, Matt's gaze narrowed. She'd once watched a cougar slink toward an unaware rabbit. Torn between wanting to warn the rabbit and letting the cougar do what nature had designed it for, she'd stared. And stared. Achingly slow movement had ended with a burst of power and speed. Her hand clamped over her mouth, she'd watched the cougar tear the rabbit apart.

Matt's stance reminded her of the cougar's.

With a thumb hooked through her panties' waistband, she reached out to touch the recliner. On the heels of an indrawn breath, Matt grabbed her and threw her into the chair. She landed awkwardly low on her spine with her breasts shaking and her feet sliding on the carpet. Grabbing her panties, he ripped them off.

"Stay there!"

Teeth clenched, she struggled not to let his size and fierceness overwhelm her. Had she ever felt this helpless, this alone? *Alone.* How could that be when Matt was here with her?

"It's the wolf picture," she said. Her breasts flattened out, making her erect nipples even more prominent. She didn't try to close her legs, because Matt wanted her like this—exposed and vulnerable. "It has some kind of impact on you. An influence. I felt the same way when I saw the wolf."

"You don't understand."

Maybe. Maybe not. Either way, what did it matter?

He planted his hands on the armrests and positioned himself between her legs. Much as she ached to touch him, she didn't because what if she did something to set him off?

"I didn't want to come here," he said, his tone husky and raw. "I knew it wasn't safe."

"For who, you?"

He nodded, then frowned as his attention slid from her face to the rest of her. "Maybe you too."

"Then leave." It wasn't what she wanted to tell him. "Get out of here before you do something you'll regret."

The corners of his mouth lifted, but she'd never call that a smile. "Wrong, Cat. I'm not going to regret this."

Working slowly, he braced his arm on the chair back on either side of her head. That done, he too-slowly leaned into her. Blanketed her body with his. Despite her resolve, she tried to escape by pressing her body into the recliner. He was fully dressed in contrast to her nudity and too strong for her to stop him from doing whatever he wanted.

He wanted sex. He'd said he could smell her, but she wasn't the only one giving off base messages. She'd never seen him

more aroused. What did that make her, his prey or fuck part-
ner?

"You aren't going to leave. That's the last thing you'd do
now," she said.

"A predator never backs down," he told her.

"That's how you feel, like a predator?"

He answered by baring his teeth. Knowing what he had in
mind, she nevertheless turned her head to the side and exposed
the side of her neck. Too late, she tried to change direction only
to freeze as his teeth raked her flesh. Her fingers digging into
fabric, she drew a mental picture of how he looked standing
over her. All-powerful.

A jolt of pain nearly made her cry out. Now her mind's eye
pictured his teeth fastened over her tendon. If he'd drawn
blood, would the taste propel him to bite even harder?

She'd concentrate on breathing; yes, that's what she'd do.
She wouldn't acknowledge the fiery knot in her belly or the
warmth leaking out of her to stain the recliner. Most of all,
she'd deny what Matt was turning into.

He'd stopped biting and was lapping at her neck before new
possibilities started forming. Granted, he'd become everything
the word *macho* represented; that didn't mean he'd stopped
being human. Her imagination had gotten away from her,
nothing more than that. Relief dampened her lashes and made
her eyes burn.

Then he pressed his hands against the outer sides of her
breasts and her tears dried. "Your freedom has always been important to you," he muttered. "Your independence."

Hot, she dug her nails into the recliner. "So has yours."

"You wanted my body but not the rest of me."

Was that true? "That cuts both ways, Matt. The few times I
tried to get you to talk about personal things, you shoved me
away."

"Did I?" He didn't sound convinced or as if he cared. "There's no shoving me away today, is there?"

The firmer the pressure against her breasts, the more the sensation resonated in her core. Squirming, she reached for his wrists only to have him knock her hands away. Instead of going back to what he'd been doing, he grabbed her around the waist and hauled her higher onto the recliner. His features blurred as he again leaned over her and lapped at one nipple and then the other.

"Oh, God!"

Matt repeatedly bathed her nipples. Mewling like some lost kitten, she raked her nails over his forearms. Her world swam, and her pussy tightened.

"Matt, oh God, Matt."

Closing his teeth over her right nipple, he lifted his head a little and drew her breast upward, sending something hot grinding into her belly. Desperate to regain some measure of control over her senses, she arched her back. He continued to pull.

"Shit, no. Please."

When he released her, another heated wave assaulted her. Instead of trying to get away, she offered her other breast to him. His tongue roughly flicked her nipple. Mindless, she grabbed hold of the hair at the top of her head. *You're killing me,* she came too close to admitting.

Then he was gone. Disappeared. Leaving her to drown. Too confused to move, she listened for the sounds she both needed and feared. Seconds later, his heavy breathing told her he'd stepped behind the recliner. Other sounds left her with no doubt that he was taking off his clothes. Tearing at them really. *It* was going to happen.

Hands she both worshipped and feared grasped her shoulders. Matt hauled her about until she was crosswise on the recliner with her head dangling over the side of one armrest and her legs over the other. Then he forced her arms over her head. When he let go of her, her fingertips brushed the floor. Blood rushed to her head. She could only hold it up for a few seconds, and each time she did, her attention went to his naked form. Even upside down, he looked incredible.

Overwhelming.

He gathered up her breasts. "Mine."

Her flesh was stretched over her belly and hip bones, sending uncontrollable sensations to that part of her body and from there to her totally exposed sex. Despite her conflicted emotions, she'd give anything to feel his hands on her there.

"This is how you should always be. Accessible to me."

Talking while in this position was nearly impossible, yet she had to try. "Just hanging there waiting for you? You don't give a damn about my needs."

Muttering something unintelligible, he switched his focus from her breasts to her ribs. Working strong and slow, he ran his fingers over the ridges and valleys. Weak and frightened, she tried to lift her arms so she could guide his journey.

"My head. It's killing me."

He didn't say anything. Should she repeat herself or remain silent? Leaving off his exploration of her midsection, he again took control of her waist and positioned her so one armrest supported the back of her head. The other provided a resting place for her buttocks. The only way she could keep her back from sagging was by bracing her elbows on the seat. Her body became limp, and she studied Matt through half-open lids.

His stance as he stood over her reminded her of a predator studying a recent kill. He widened his stance. Thrusting up from his dark nest of pubic hair, his cock served as the ultimate challenge and promise. Forget the consequences. She longed to cup her hands around him and draw him to her sex.

Ah, God, her sex!

Squeezing her eyes shut and then opening them, she stared like the idiot she'd become at Matt's incredible body as he moved between her legs with his hands down where she couldn't see them. Could only feel them.

Matt's fingers now lay over her hip bones with the heels of his hands and thumbs pressing down on her stretched-tight belly. She couldn't move. Freedom was a gift given to someone else.

"I smell you," he muttered. "The strength of your need."

Of course he could. No way could she hold back the fluids leaking from her. Wet heat leaked over her rear opening and from there to where? Probably into the recliner fabric.

Done in. Matt's possession.

"You're ready to mate."

Don't say anything. Refuse to get down to his level.

"Can I hold back?" he continued. "Stop myself from jamming my cock into you?"

"Why does that matter?" She stared at the ceiling so she wouldn't have to look into his eyes.

By way of answer, he handed her a low growl. She jumped when his thumbs touched her labia, then added a moan when he touched her again. Need slithered over her. The next time he stroked her outer sex, helplessness engulfed her. No way could she get out of this damnable position.

Matt's hands pressed against the joint between hip and leg, slid up her to cover her hip bones, raced down her thighs only to glide upward again. The sides of his thumbs laid tracks along her inner legs. He stopped, damn him, an inch shy of her pussy.

If not for his rough, rapid breathing, she'd believe his self-control knew no bounds.

On the move once more, finger pads probing at her belly, ribs, navel. Sanity slipped from her control and left her to thrash her head about. The keening sounds were coming from her, but how could that be when she'd never made such noises before? Never felt so lost.

"Matt, please, I can't—"

He silenced her by lowering his head and exhaling a hot breath over her drenched labia. Spent air licked at her opening. Gone, she struggled to separate her legs even more. She wouldn't say another word, refused to beg.

Beg for what?

The question without answer made her slow to acknowledge the strain in her shoulders and arms. Then, desperate for relief, she lowered herself a few inches. Unfortunately, that increased the pressure on the back of her neck.

No begging!

"I need this." Matt's hands crept over her body, the journey slow and deep, never touching her pussy. "You under me."

Under his control, he meant. Helpless to stop him from doing whatever he wanted. At the moment he was closing in on her knees, going at it a quarter inch at a time while her sex dripped. Now she could smell herself, the scent urgent and harsh.

Sensation pulled her deep inside her lightning-touched body, and for several seconds—or was it minutes?—she knew nothing. Then it came to her that although Matt's long, broad hands still blanketed her thighs, she could no longer see him. Alarmed, she forced her head off the armrest. There he was, damn him! Kneeling between her legs. His breath a constant torture to her pussy.

Do you want me dead?

Driven by an emotion she couldn't give a name to, she struggled to lift herself off the recliner. Grunting, Matt pressed against her inner thighs, and although she resisted, in the end she had no choice but to give in. One of her legs now butted up against the chair back while the other hung over the end of the seat. He had her. In every way a powerful male could control a female.

"Do you know what you're doing?" she demanded.

"Priming you. Taking you to where need takes over."

A woman not crazy-wild to have her sex invaded might be able to make sense of what he'd said. She, however, didn't care. The stranger that was Matt intended to drink of her body fluids. She needed to accept and prepare. Climb on top of the insanity wrapping itself around her and hold on. Hold on.

Instead of using his tongue or lips, however, he came at her with his thumbs. Coated with her juices, they slipped like butter over her pussy. Maybe she should have fought. Protested at least. But when he drew her sex lips apart, she fell into a place framed by jumping nerves.

Except for her pussy, her body no longer existed. Gone was awareness of her uncomfortable and helpless position. Her arms trembled, yet the burning muscles became part of a larger whole, a woman drifting in willing, helpless anticipation.

Matt's thumbs, better suited for gripping reins or branding irons, reached her opening. They waited, barely touching as if willing to give her time to comprehend. Instead of gratitude, however, she fought down an urgent scream. Damn it, she needed to be penetrated!

Don't tell him. Let it happen. Wait until he's ready and then ... and then ...

A finger—it didn't matter which one—slipped into her. For a moment, the feeling of fullness calmed her. Then a second finger joined the first, pushing her channel apart. Moaning in need, she nevertheless struggled to free herself.

"Why, Cat? You know you want this."

Yes, she did. Yes, she needed. But it was so much, her pussy no longer belonging to her. Her entire body gone.

Matt, who knew her so well, the physical part at least, let his fingers rest. Even so, she couldn't stop her inner muscles from clamping down around him. Damn but she loved the sensation! Loved Matt skewering her.

As her sex channel clenched repeatedly, an intense burning sped through her and threatened to come out the top of her head. Maybe this was some weird kind of climax, the best her short-circuiting body was capable of.

Matt flexed and straightened his fingers. Although dizzy, she tried to convince herself she was strong enough to stay on top of everything he threw at her.

Then his thumb touched her clit.

Sobbing, she again fought to lift herself off the recliner. Gasped, screamed maybe. Cursed him while her muscles held his fingers inside her. Still pressing, he rolled her clit about. Some alien sensation powered into her. Sounds escaped. Her body whipped about, and the back of her head against the arm-rest burned. Her arms caught fire.

"Matt." *Help me.*

Early in their relationship, she'd told him her clit was super-sensitive. Damn her for being so honest! And damn him for trapping her rapid-firing nub between thumb and forefinger. Lost in the wild current that was her climax, she fought both him and herself with all her pitiful strength.

"Stop it, stop it!" The words scraped her throat.

Silent, Matt hauled her off the recliner and onto the carpet, stopping her release. The fibers scraped the back of her shoul-ders, buttocks, and legs. Sunlight had invaded her living room, and the brightness stood in sharp contrast to the darkness sur-rounding this man.

Straddling her, Matt folded his arms across his chest and stared down at her. His erection dominated. Once again she likened him to a predator after a successful hunt. Fear slithered through her, yet she'd never felt more alive. More needful.

When he opened his mouth, she prayed for the courage to

handle whatever he said. Instead of speaking, however, his lips became a harsh line, and his eyes narrowed.

Questions bunched inside her, but anything she said would reveal too much. Expose her in ways even nudity couldn't.

She couldn't keep her gaze from sliding from his face to his chest. Going lower, she clenched her fists in preparation. There. A fully aroused man's cock. Matt's cock. Wanting one thing.

Her.

Dropping to his knees, he drew her legs apart. Just like that, her muscles abandoned her. Instead of entering into the space he'd created, he hauled her toward him, deeply bending her knees as he did. As he ran his hands under her buttocks and lifted them off the carpet, she ordered herself to look into his eyes. A single glance, however, and will deserted her.

He positioned her so her ass rested on his thighs with her head low and blood sliding into it. Unable to concentrate on what he had in mind—like she didn't know—she flung a heavy arm over her eyes. Darkness cradled her.

Just like that, she stepped into a bottomless pool overflowing with hot, swirling water. Somewhere out there, the world waited. Reality hadn't disappeared; it just didn't matter anymore.

A touch of cock against clit. Light and yet possessive sliding over her labia. Promise waiting at the entrance to her sex. Jangled and loose at the same time, she drew in as much air as her lungs could handle. In her mind's eye, she saw her juices flow out and over his cock's tip.

"Mine." The word expanded to fill the room. "You're mine."

Too gone to respond, she tried to lift her left arm off the carpet. Failing despite the Herculean effort, she surrendered to a world of nothing and everything.

Familiar and unknown pressure again centered her attention on her opening. When he entered her, a chuckle escaped her, but she stopped it in midsound so she could concentrate on sensation. Had he been this thick before, this heated? The invasion continued, pulling her channel apart and seeming to fill her throat, heart, mind.

By turn, her pussy became weak and then strong, simple vessel accepting whatever happened to it followed by furious need. During those needful times, her sex clamped onto his, and she struggled to suck him deep into her. Sweat slickened her.

A chain of sharp, short masculine grunts made her wonder if he was trying to keep his vulnerability from her, but her body, which knew his so well, had found the truth. Each harsh thrust came from a man lost.

Feeding off him, she dove into release. Her world swirled, started to tip only to straighten and then career in another direction. Giddy, she dug her heels into the carpet. This time when he powered into her, she was ready. They slammed together. Reality splintered and she imagined wild animals united by lust. Her nostrils filled with a musky scent.

"Damn you, Cat! Fucking damn you!"

16

Still kneeling, Matt extended his arms behind him and braced his body on them. Except for the feminine form curled on her side near his feet, the world lacked definition. Looking as spent as he felt, the woman planted an elbow on the carpet and half sat up. The way her gaze kept slipping off him made him wonder if she was drugged.

Who was she?

Bit by bit, his muscles quieted. Instead of the weary self-satisfaction that marked his first minutes after a climax, he was becoming more and more alert. His sense of smell was keen, and he could hear the horses moving about in the nearby corral. A single blink put an end to the room's hazy quality.

"Are you going to say anything?" she asked.

Cat's voice. Yes, he knew that. "Like what?"

Her nostrils flared. "Like apologizing for not first making sure I was on board with what just happened."

What the hell was she talking about? She'd wanted sex as much as he had. Hadn't she?

His muscles flexed and charged, strengthening with every beat of his powerful heart. A small herd of wild mustangs called his acreage home, and although he cursed them for eating what the cattle needed, he'd never once entertained the idea of trying to get rid of them. How could he when watching the compact creatures run reminded him of the meaning of the word *freedom*? He'd watched stallions fight over mares in heat and had twice studied mating mustangs.

Yes. Mating. A stallion proclaiming dominance over a mare trapped by nature's heat flowing through her.

Unexpected dizziness brought him back to his body. He had no idea how he'd gotten to his feet or why he'd chosen a wide-legged stance. An insistent whisper from his cock sent his hand to cradle it.

"No way." Cat stood and began backing away from him. "Absolutely no way you can get an erection so soon after..."

She was right, and yet the longer he held his cock, the heavier it became. His balls ached. When he was fully erect with precum dotting the tip, he tore his attention off himself. Cat had backpedaled so she now stood at the opposite side of the room. True to her name, she assumed a half crouch with her gaze locked on him and her arms lifted and hands fisted.

"Get dressed, Matt. Pull your boots back on and get out of here."

Drying moisture painted the insides of her thighs, and her nipples were hard. Throwing her head back, she scraped her palms over her breasts. "Don't read anything into this. I'm still riding the climax you backed me into."

Much as he wanted to again insist she'd wanted sex as much as he had, he couldn't find the words. Truth was, he didn't trust himself to put a coherent sentence together. His muscles felt too big for his skin, his jaw powerful enough to crush bone.

Half expecting to see paws instead of hands, he tore his attention from Cat and looked down. Both confused and reassured by the sight of fingers and palms, he stroked his erection. Fire licked at his groin and then banked down a little. He could stay on top of what he was feeling. Maybe.

"Did you hear me?" she demanded. "I want you out of here."

Why? he asked with his eyes, because his throat had locked down.

Her long blink said she'd heard the silent question. "You're freaking me—Hell, no you aren't! I mean it, Matt. Either you walk out of here in the next thirty seconds or I'll make you."

How?

"If necessary, I'll call the sheriff, tell your friend Bob Wilton that you've gone off the deep end."

He wasn't near any end; he simply was. Simply existed.

Surrendering to the powerful sensations arcing through him, he started toward her. With every step, he became more in awe of his thigh and calf muscles. They were capable of running endlessly, long loping miles broken by short, great bursts of speed. He *saw* himself launch his naked and rangy body at an unsuspecting prey, maybe a deer. Expertly sidestepping a terrified kick, he closed his fangs around—

Fangs?

Labored breathing pulled Matt back into Cat's living room. She had one hand to her throat while the other hovered over her pubic area. Her meaningless words swirled around him. He needed to listen, to understand, to acknowledge her emotion.

But how could he when something was descending on him? Enveloped by what was both fierce and savage, he surrendered to the compulsion to look out her front window.

A wolf stood near Cat's roses, looking in at him with bared fangs and knowing eyes.

From where she crouched with her back pressed against a wall and escape a million miles away, Cat tried to see what had captured Matt's attention. His stance reminded her of the barn cat as it focused on a hapless mouse. The nameless and feral cat usually stayed out of her way and would run if it spotted her coming, but all bets were off when it was in hunting mode. Then nothing but killing mattered.

"What is it?" Did she really expect an answer. "What do you see?"

"Wolf."

"No!" Afraid for her horses, she left the wall's safety.

Careful to keep as much distance as possible from Matt, she inched toward the window. Her familiar front yard with its flowers and gravel circular driveway awaited her. The only life-form she could see consisted of a spider intent on creating a web in the window's upper-right corner.

"I don't see anything," she told the man who invaded her living room and, earlier, her body.

If her statement surprised him, he gave no indication. "He's waiting for me."

Chilled, she again looked out. Then, not knowing what in the hell was happening, she faced Matt full-on. He'd changed from the man who'd scratched her itches. The form might be familiar, but he was different inside, less human.

"What does he want from you?"

"My soul."

Keeping her legs from collapsing took her full attention, and by the time she trusted herself to keep on standing, he'd started toward her. Despite her determination to face whatever he threw at her, she placed one leg and then the other behind her. He kept coming. On the brink of panicking, she realized he wasn't interested in her after all. Instead, he was heading for the window. His cock remained swollen, yet he didn't seem aware of its condition.

"Tell me what you see?" she asked when she was looking at his back.

"He's real and yet he isn't. His eyes . . ."

Matt, what's happening? "What about them?"

"So black. Like midnight."

How many shocks could her system take? she wondered as she realized he was talking about the massive predator she'd taken pictures of. Why couldn't she see it now? "Ghost Wolf," she whispered.

"He wants me."

"No! He doesn't. Matt, I don't see anything. You're imagining— Matt, look at me!"

Instead of doing as she commanded, he remained at the window with his hands pressed against the glass. She couldn't wrap her mind around the full impact of his nudity. Neither could she make sense of what he'd just said.

Could she?

Matt needed her. He'd had a breakdown of some kind, a sudden and total disconnect from logic. He wasn't crazy. No one lost their mind that quickly.

Praying she could bring him back, she swallowed down her fear and reached for him. Her first attempt failed for lack of courage on her part, but damn it, she was only going to touch his shoulder. How hard could that be? Feeling removed from what she was doing, she watched as her fingers made contact with his shoulder blade. Power pulsed through him and into her.

Alarmed, she fought the impulse to pull back her hand. He hadn't responded to her nails on his flesh, which meant she needed to do more to get through to him.

Not breathing, she spread her fingers over the top of his

shoulder. Another wave of hot strength and energy shocked her. Effortless and silent, he spun toward her. His eyes were like ice, frozen. Lost and frightened, she flattened her hands over her breasts.

"Mine." His voice lacked animation. "You belong to me. Just as I belong to him."

"No. Matt, you're wrong. You don't know what you're talking about."

"I've never been more right." Only his mouth moved.

She couldn't talk him through whatever had happened to him after all, not today and not this way.

"This is my home," she reminded both of them. "Only I have a right to be here, and right now I want you out of it." She jerked her head at his discarded clothes.

"He's waiting for me," Matt said tonelessly. "He's weary of being alone."

He had to refer to Ghost Wolf. Snippets of things she should say occurred to her, but she rejected them because she sensed he wouldn't listen anyway. Maybe he was incapable of processing anything.

Except what Ghost Wolf had told him.

"He doesn't know you." No way would she acknowledge the insanity of what she'd just said. "Certainly he hasn't been talking to you."

"Not with words, but that doesn't matter."

Before she could ask for an explanation, if she'd been going to, Matt pressed the heel of his hand to his forehead. His expression changed to something between exhaustion and impatience. Much as she longed to massage away his weariness, she didn't dare touch him.

The two of them were standing naked in the middle of a simple living room with the sun pushing the temperature to the limits of comfort. For the first time since early childhood, she was comfortable nude.

No, not comfortable. Truth was, whether she wore anything or not didn't matter right now.

"Matt, you have responsibilities back at your place; I know you do. What's on your agenda today?"

His nostrils flared and he pulled back his lips to reveal strong, white teeth. Caught off balance, she looked down. His cock continued to dominate his presence.

"Fine." Hating her small and wary tone, she tried for strength. "Maybe you don't give a damn what you do today, but I don't have the same luxury." Still not taking her attention off him, she took the first step toward her clothes. "I have horses to feed and—"

Matt leaped. One instant he looked dead on his feet. The next he became an imposing blur. Instinct driving her, she dodged to the side. If it had been anyone else, she might have been able to escape his grasp. Turning with a predator's grace, he snaked his arms around her and hauled her against his chest.

With her arms anchored against her sides, she could barely struggle. Still she fought the larger, stronger man as she'd never fought anything in her life. The instinct for survival didn't drive her. Instead she vowed to do everything she could to get through to him.

"You don't want to be doing this. Matt, you know you don't!"

"Be quiet!"

Lifting her off her feet, he started to carry her over to the couch. She rammed her knee between his legs. He grunted but didn't release her.

"Don't do this! Don't do this!"

No matter how wildly she tossed herself about, Matt easily

hauled her to the couch. Making it appear effortless, he hoisted her higher and threw her backward onto the cushions.

Her brains rattling, she blinked repeatedly to get him to come back into focus. For a moment she saw something that wasn't quite human, but that had to be shock, not reality.

Instead of holding her in place as she was afraid he'd do, Matt again folded his arms across his chest. She drew a crazy comparison between his stance and that of a playground bully after bloodying a smaller student's nose.

"Fine." She ground out the word. "You're bigger and stronger. What have you proven?"

Much as she hoped for a reaction from him, his disconnected expression didn't surprise her. Obviously he believed he was in control, she told herself. He could do what he wanted when he wanted.

"There's a word for what you have in mind. A pretty ugly one. Do you want to say it or should I?"

Nothing, not even a blink.

"Go on! Get it the hell over with. You want a place to shove your pecker—go ahead and do it. But it'll be the end of us, Matt. Think about that. Everything we had going destroyed because you're horny, or whatever's wrong with you."

He slowly lowered his arms until they hung at his sides. Studying him, she both loved and hated him. Was afraid for him and wished she'd never met him.

"Watch me," she said. If he asked where her calm and courage came from, she wouldn't be able to say. "Pay attention because I need you to understand what it means."

Even though his gaze held hers, she couldn't be sure how much he was processing when she ran a forefinger between her labial lips. Determined not to let it shake, she held up her hand. "Do you get it? There's just the tiniest bit of moisture there. I'm not ready for sex. I don't want it this way."

"Sex?"

The word sounded foreign, almost as if Matt had never said it before; either that or he didn't understand the meaning.

"What's going on inside you?" *Don't touch him. It's too dangerous.* "Can you tell me that?"

When he didn't so much as open his mouth, she wondered if he'd lost the ability to speak. Accustomed to parents whose interaction with their child was minimal, she couldn't wrap her mind around the connection between her and Matt.

A frightening and maybe deadly connection.

About to remind him of her warning about calling 911, she stopped. He'd only laugh, if he was capable of laughing, and give her another vivid example of his domination.

How long had he been staring down at her, seeing and yet not seeing? Thinking thoughts she couldn't grasp.

"I need to get up," she informed him as calmly as possible. "I don't like feeling like this." Could he guess how close she'd come to admitting her helplessness?

"No."

"No, what?" Hearing his voice turned her inside out.

"You'll try to escape."

Escape was what a prisoner or captive did. Another wave of fear slammed into her, and she couldn't speak. Her world compressed, and everything became about survival. Later, if she was still alive, she'd get Matt the mental help he needed.

Determined to focus on more than just surviving what was left of the morning, she forced herself to ponder what help was available. Sparsely populated as this area was, he'd undoubtedly be taken to Portland. He'd have to be locked up, of course, for his own protection as well as the public's. Maybe he'd be given drugs. And therapy. Lots of therapy, during which a shrink would pull his deepest, darkest secrets out of him.

Movement ended the image of a shackled Matt lying on a couch. He was reaching for her, bending over her as he did.

Once again his too-dark eyes sheltered his thoughts. His nostrils flared, and his teeth stood out.

"No!" She slapped his cheek with all her strength.

A howl rumbled out of Matt. Instead of attacking her as she fully expected, he stumbled back a step. His hand went to his cheek.

I didn't mean... I only wanted... Matt, forgive me.

Spinning on his heels, he loped over to his clothes and boots, picked them up, and headed for the door.

It slammed behind him.

17

"No, no, I don't need to talk to him," Cat told Addie when she phoned Coyote Ranch the next morning. "He, ah, was in a hurry when he left yesterday. I just, ah, was wondering if everything was all right."

"Right?" Addie dragged out the word. "He's working overtime if that's what you mean. Headed out to the east pasture around dawn. Cat, do you mind if I ask you something?"

I'm not up to answering anything. "All right."

"Okay, did the two of you have an argument?"

"What makes you...I'm not sure what to call it." She looked down at the cotton shirt and jeans she'd hurried into right after her shower because clothes provided a necessary shield.

"Sorry," Addie said. "What happens between you and Matt is none of my business, except I couldn't love him more if I'd given birth to him. He's hurting—is that the right word?—and I hate seeing that. Is there anything I can do?"

About to tell Addie no, she reconsidered. Matt had come to live with Santo and Addie when he was a boy. In all likelihood, no one knew more about him than the woman who'd opened her home to him.

"Can I come over?" she asked. "You're sure Matt won't be back for a while?"

"Pretty sure. You want to come right now?"

"If it's all right with you."

Her rugged, physical life had lined Addie's features and grayed her hair. She had a ranch wife's permanently tanned hands with short, practical nails and a multitude of small scars. Like Cat's, Addie's forearms sported muscles. Cat had no doubt that the rest of the older woman's body carried out the same message of strength. She wore no makeup, her shoulder-length hair looked as if she cut it herself, and her clothing was a clone of what Cat wore.

The house at Coyote Ranch was positioned so its shadow covered the front porch where the two women sat drinking iced tea. Cat had parked her truck near the porch so she could bail if Matt returned unexpectedly. What she hadn't figured out was how she'd explain her exit to Addie if that proved necessary.

"I don't know if I'd still be here if it wasn't for Matt," Addie said once the weather and hay price discussions were over. "Oh, I guess I could hire a foreman, but it wouldn't be the same. This land has its tentacles around Matt's heart, same as it does mine. As it did Santo."

Cat figured Santo and Addie had been married at least thirty-five years. In that time, their separate selves might have essentially merged. If so, Addie had lost a key part of herself. Although she and Matt hadn't had nearly that much time together, she, too, felt incomplete without him.

"Was it always like that for Matt?" she asked in an attempt to get the conversation going where she needed it to. "He felt connected to the ranch from the beginning?"

Addie laughed, and for a moment her eyes lost the grief buried in them. What was it like to love someone that much? "Hardly. He was too young to be a sullen teen, thank goodness, but he had so many of the symptoms that sometimes I wanted to shake him. Even though he knew he had nowhere else to go, he didn't want to be here."

"How did he come to live with you? I heard rumors—"

"I'm sure you did."

"Is his father in prison?" Cat stared at her hands. "I never knew how to bring that up."

"Prison," Addie muttered. "Crazy how things get turned around. I take it you and Matt haven't talked about his past."

Or about mine. Lifting her head, she met Addie's gaze. "That sounds as if Matt and I don't have much of a relationship. Maybe we don't."

"I doubt that. You wouldn't be here if you weren't concerned for him."

Concern barely touched at what she was feeling. Along with confusion over his inexplicable behavior was a lingering fear of him. And sexual energy. More energy than fear. "So Matt's father isn't in prison?"

Addie shook her head and leaned back in her chair. She stared at the horizon. "Maybe Matt doesn't want you knowing his story, but I have the feeling you need to. One thing I'm sure of, it's essential if you're going to understand him."

"I want to." *I need to.*

"Let me start by explaining why he came to live with us. His mother was my father's second cousin."

"Was? Is she dead?"

"No one knows. She hasn't been heard from in years."

The more Addie said, the more chilled Cat felt. Matt's parents, who'd never married, had been in their teens when he was born. His mother had just turned fifteen while his father, a high school dropout and seasonal ranch hand, had been a month shy of nineteen. Matt's mother, Heather, continued to live with her parents while his father, Kaga, often came to see his son. Heather's mother took care of her infant grandson while Heather reluctantly went to school.

"Heather's parents are deeply religious, absolute fundamentalists," Addie said. "My understanding is that Heather wanted to have an abortion, and if they wouldn't sign for her to go to the clinic, she wanted to put Matt up for adoption. However, Grandma and Grandpa wouldn't allow it. She'd sinned and was going to pay for it."

"That's all they cared about?"

"Apparently. How unfair that was to Heather and Matt. And to Kaga, who wasn't in any position to support his son, a son he dearly loved."

"I'm glad to hear that. Kaga? What an unusual name."

Addie turned her attention to Cat. "He was Native American. Paiute."

Shocked, Cat covered her mouth. "Matt never said anything about that."

"I'm not surprised, because he was determined to put his past behind him. When he turned thirteen, he told me he considered himself reborn. Thirteen was when his life began."

"What was so awful about his childhood?" She had to force the question. "Oh, God, was he abused?"

Looking pensive, Addie slowly shook her head. "As far as we know, not physically. I wish I could say the same about emotionally."

Considering his grandparents' religious beliefs, Cat thought she understood. However, as Addie continued, Cat realized she'd had no inkling what Matt had gone through.

When Matt was around three, Heather fell in love with a man fifteen years older than her, a man who wanted nothing to do with a small child. Heather had run away with the man, and although she resurfaced from time to time when the lover of the moment—the older one hadn't lasted long—turned out not to be Prince Charming or she ran out of money, she never played the mother role. No one had seen or heard from her since Matt's ninth birthday, which she'd celebrated by calling and talking to him for maybe five minutes.

In contrast, Kaga never missed a birthday or holiday. He lived a few miles from Matt's grandparents and paid every penny of child support he could afford. As far as anyone knew, Kaga never had a serious romantic relationship, let alone got married or had other children.

"Kaga didn't talk much, especially not to Matt's grandparents, who resisted his every effort to be a father," Addie explained.

"Why were they so hard on him? Didn't they understand that a child needs parents?"

"To their way of thinking, Kaga's sin in creating Matt was even greater than their daughter's because he was older. Kaga—I've seen a picture of him and he was a rugged, handsome man—had no family."

"None at all?"

"I'm just repeating what I've been told. Believe me, getting anything from Matt's grandparents was like pulling teeth. They could do no wrong. Sinners were all around them, but they were saints raising a sinful child according to God's law."

"Sinful? He was a little boy."

"An illegitimate child whose mother had abandoned her family and a father who didn't go to their church, so of course was going to hell."

Cat had come to Addie hoping to learn more about Matt. Now she'd give anything to know more than the little she'd been told about Kaga.

"Kaga tried to be a father to Matt because Matt was the only family Kaga had," she said, on the verge of tears for a man she'd never met.

"Exactly." Addie went back to her study of the distance. "When Santo and I went to pick up Matt, we talked to neighbors, teachers, even the police. We learned more about both Kaga and Matt's upbringing from them than we ever did from his grandparents."

"How did the police get involved?"

Addie sighed and closed her eyes. "Two reasons. One, Matt kept running away, and because there was nothing else they could do with him, the police kept bringing him back to his grandparents' place. Two"—Addie's eyes opened—"Kaga had problems."

Instead of asking her to explain, Cat waited the older woman out. Learning so much in such a short amount of time was exhausting, either that or her sleepless night was getting to her. If she could, she'd wrap comforting arms around both of them.

With Matt, a hug would soon turn into something else.

"He went crazy. Insane."

"Oh, no!"

Addie sighed again. "I don't know how long things were bad for him before he took off but—"

"Took off?"

Addie stood, walked over to the railing, and faced Cat. Leaning against the wooden support, she rested her elbows behind her. "For a while. Then he came back but . . . I know it sounds as if both of Matt's parents deserted him, but the circumstances and outcomes were entirely different. Heather was too immature and self-centered to understand what it meant to be a mother. Kaga gave his son, maybe the only person he ever loved or who ever loved him, as much of himself as he was capable of."

Unable to ignore the need for movement, Cat joined Addie at the railing but didn't turn her back on the setting because she needed to know if Matt returned—Matt whose innate sexuality still had a powerful grip on her.

"I wish he'd told me about his father," she muttered. "I wonder why he didn't."

"He only rarely mentioned Kaga to Santo and me," Addie said. "When he first came to live with us, we were up to our necks trying to learn how to parent a lost and closed-in kid. We told ourselves he'd talk when he was ready, but maybe if we'd pressed, he wouldn't have had all those nightmares."

Sick for the boy Matt had once been, Cat wrapped her arms around her middle.

"For the longest time, Matt didn't want me to touch him," Addie continued. "He was okay with Santo; they had a bond from the beginning. But I think he didn't know how to relate to women, whether he could trust them."

"Given what his mother did, I can't blame him."

"I know. Anyway, the first time I held Matt was during one of his nightmares. Afterward, I was there for all of them. The things he said . . . either he'd seen his father fall apart or he imagined what it must have been like."

"What did he say?" *I'm sorry, Matt. I hate doing this, but what choice do I have?*

Addie turned toward her; tears glittered in her eyes. "He kept calling out to Kaga. He'd beg him to relax and calm down, to stop saying the things he did. He, ah, talked about a knife."

"Oh my God. Do you think Kaga tried to kill Matt?"

"If he did, he didn't hurt him."

"You're right. He doesn't have a knife scar." Too late, Cat realized what she'd just revealed.

For the first time since she'd begun talking, Addie smiled. "Honey, you aren't telling me anything I don't know. Something I need to tell you. It might help you understand Matt better. Kaga committed suicide. With a knife."

Light-headed, Cat gripped the railing. She couldn't speak for thinking. Finally she said, "Do you think Matt saw? That that's where his nightmares came from?"

Now it was Addie's turn to hug herself. "I asked him. After he told me he loved me, I let him know he could tell me anything and I'd honor it. He said he wanted to but the words wouldn't come out. He believed it was better for him to put the past behind him."

Still light-headed, Cat faced the land that defined Coyote Ranch. She felt as if she'd come here knowing nothing about her lover. In a few minutes, Addie had opened a door to Matt's past, maybe a Pandora's box.

"What kind of mental illness did Kaga have?"

"Matt's grandparents said it was the devil's work, that he was being punished for, and I quote, 'fornicating with a child.' "

"Damn them. Did they tell Matt the same thing?"

"What do you think?"

If the two were here right now, she wasn't sure she could stop herself from slugging them.

"Apparently," Addie continued, "Kaga never had professional help. From what the police told me, he withdrew more and more. He'd always been a good worker, but he stopped showing up at the several ranches where he worked part-time. He no longer paid rent on the cabin where he lived, and when they came to evict him, there were signs he hadn't been there for a while."

"What about his belongings?"

"His personal stuff was gone. Matt said Kaga loved to read, but there weren't any books left behind."

"Where did he go?"

Addie's mouth lifted, but it wasn't a smile. "The police didn't know, but Matt told me he'd set up a camp. He took Matt out there a few times. From Matt's description, the camp was pretty disorganized, with rotting food and piles of dirty clothes. I've concluded that Kaga reverted to traditional Native American ways in some respects. He lived off the land, tracked and hunted. Prayed to the spirits and went on spirit quests."

This was all too much! The thought of a boy trying to comprehend what was happening to his only parent made her want to cry.

"Information overload?" Addie laid her hand on Cat's shoulder.

"Yes. So, ah, how did Matt wind up living with you?" That, hopefully, would be easier to deal with than Matt's chaotic childhood.

Leaving the railing, Addie sat down again. She looked older than she had a few minutes ago, but then the conversation had taken its toll on Cat as well.

"Those damnable grandparents, those so-called relatives, decided Kaga wasn't the only one with the devil in him. After his body was found, they no longer wanted Matt under their roof. They called all of their relatives who still spoke to them and told them they'd give Matt to them if anyone wanted him. Whoever it was had two days to come and get him. Otherwise they were going to take him to the freeway and leave him there."

Because she didn't trust her legs to support her, Cat sank back into the chair next to Addie.

"That's where my father came in. He called me—I'd heard about the crazy relatives, of course—and asked if Santo and I wanted a son."

A son. Not just an abandoned child to feed.

"Of course we said yes." Addie pressed her hands to her stomach.

Blinking at the tears that wouldn't stop, Cat covered Addie's hand with her own. "Thank you."

"For?"

"For being such a good person. For being what Matt needed."

Addie squeezed back. Seconds passed as the women stared at each other. "What are you thinking?" Cat finally asked.

"I'm trying to decide if you're who Matt needs now. Something's bothering him. It's more than concerns about what happened to Beale and having the damned wolves bothering the cattle. Okay, okay." She shook her head. "I didn't mean to curse. They are what they are—predators."

And more.

"I just wish they'd go away," Addie continued. "Maybe that'd take the pressure off him, although I'm not sure—"

"I've been doing some research," Cat interrupted, because she didn't want to hear what Addie might say next. "Several ways of coexisting with wolves have been implemented in places like Montana's Blackfoot River watershed area. Ranchers there are placing electric fences around calving lots. Stringing bright flags onto pasture fencing seems to be working, and volunteer horsemen keep an eye on the wolves and let ranchers know if they get near their herds."

"I wonder if that might work here?"

"It's worth a try, if we can get ranchers to listen." *And if Ghost Wolf isn't part of the mix.*

"I'd like you to talk to Matt about this." Addie pulled free. "Others will listen to him. At least they would before . . . Whatever's wrong with him, I'd be willing to bet it isn't sexual frustration, right?"

Cat dropped her gaze. "I don't think so."

Addie laughed. "Honey, I may be an old woman, but I'm not dead. But my man is. I know what it feels like not to be getting any."

The sound of an approaching vehicle stopped whatever Cat might have said. So far, it was only a distant hum, but no way could she get herself to relax. "On that note," she muttered, getting to her feet, "I need to leave. I've been putting off my riding students lately."

"Why?"

The easy thing would be to keep her back to Addie while she headed for her truck, but Addie had revealed too much about Matt for her to take that way out.

"You aren't the only one who's worried about him."

"My guess is, you're seeing changes I'm not and I'm seeing a lot."

You have no idea. "Yes."

Addie cocked her head. "Guess I was wrong about him being gone. Are you going to stay or leave?"

"Leave."

"I'm sorry to hear that," Addie said as she stood and walked over to Cat. She held out her arms. "I need a hug."

"So do I."

18

Not *again. Not so soon.*

No matter how many times Matt ordered himself to relax his grip on the steering wheel, he kept forgetting, or rather the truth was his thoughts insisted on returning to what had awaited him when he'd reached the fencing near the north-side seasonal creek. Just yesterday, a group of some twenty cattle had been in the area, but he'd seen no sign of the well-fed cows and calves. Range cattle were always on the move, but they just didn't pack up and leave grassland unless something herded or chased them away.

The wolves.

The moment he'd gotten out of his truck, he'd known he was being watched. The Cat-thoughts and Cat-memories that had settled under his skin disappeared. As his father had done when he'd lived off the land, he'd gone into survival mode. Reaching into the cab for his rifle, he'd reassured himself that the bullets he'd loaded long ago were still there.

"What do you want from me?" he'd asked.

The words were barely out of his mouth when several wolves appeared. At first they were far enough away that he hadn't been sure how many there were, but thanks to their easy lope, he'd soon counted four. While he'd reached behind him to assure himself that the driver's door was open, they came within a hundred feet.

Instead of crowding his space or taking off when he hollered at him, the pack had stopped and studied him while a brisk wind ruffled their thick fur. He'd seen enough cougars and coyotes to know how predators looked when they were hunting. The pack wasn't.

"What do you want from me?" he'd repeated. He'd been mildly surprised when they didn't reply.

Then the wolves had swung their heads to the right and bared their teeth. *Shit,* he'd thought. *Shit.*

Ghost Wolf. Suddenly there, standing above him and the pack, his fur untouched by the breeze.

"They don't want you here." He'd nodded at the now-growling pack. "They don't accept you."

They have no choice.

That's when Matt, who couldn't remember when he'd last run from anything, had jumped into his truck and peeled away, tearing the dirt track as he did.

By the time the ranch house came into view, he'd calmed enough that he'd half convinced himself he'd imagined that Ghost Wolf had spoken. He'd tell Addie he'd changed his mind about fence mending and had returned for a horse so hopefully he could find the missing cattle. She wouldn't question his decision, which meant he wouldn't have to tell her the truth—a truth he wasn't sure he could voice.

Another truck was coming toward him on the narrow private road leading to the ranch. Lost in thoughts that kept crashing into each other, at first he paid scant attention to the vehicle. Then everything fell together.

Cat.

What had she been doing here, and was she leaving to avoid him?

Of course she was.

Fine with him. Other than an apology he'd have to rip out of his gut, he didn't have anything to say to her and couldn't comprehend that she'd want to speak to him. Why, then, was he pulling over to the side and stepping on the brakes?

She came alongside, started to slide past him, then stopped. "I didn't think I'd see you," she said out her open window.

"Otherwise you wouldn't have come, right?"

"Right."

The sun slammed against her features, so he could barely make them out—either that or he was incapable of concentrating.

"You were talking to Addie about me."

"Yes. What are you doing back so soon?"

Don't say a damn word. "I saw them. *Him.*"

Cat's head had been back a bit as if in defiance. With his admission, her body snapped to attention and then sagged. "What happened?"

Having expected her to ask who or what he was talking about, he hesitated. The top she was wearing today had a scoop neckline, modest by all accounts, or it would have been if his truck wasn't higher than hers and he couldn't catch glimpses of the breasts he no longer had any right to.

"Nothing," he lied. "I'm thinking the pack scared off my cows."

"You didn't see a carcass?"

"Or buzzards."

Maybe that satisfied her because she nodded. He'd give anything to read her expression, or would he? "You said *him.* Ghost Wolf you mean."

Strange. They could barely talk to each other anymore and yet they'd effortlessly agreed on what to call the massive predator.

"Yeah."

"Damn. Matt, did you feel as if you were in danger?"

"No." He wasn't sure about that.

Cat stroked the steering wheel. "Look," she said, "I have to go."

Go. "When will I see you again?"

"I don't know. After . . . what happened, I need my space."

And I don't trust myself around you.

Unable to think of anything to say, he faced forward. Only then did he realize he'd placed his truck in park—because he'd hoped she'd want to talk to him after all? Turned out he was wrong.

Just as he'd been wrong to think Ghost Wolf had tried to communicate with him.

Can't we start over, Cat? Go back to what we had. The rutting, our bodies winding together until I can't tell where I leave off and you start. Losing myself in your pussy, trusting my cock to you.

Cat would never understand the man. Of course, she'd never understand the whole thing with the wolves either. Maybe the two were connected.

What did she mean, maybe?

At least Matt's eyes hadn't looked as dark and wild today as they had earlier, but that might have changed the moment he touched her.

Same with her, she acknowledged as gently rolling Coyote Ranch grassland stretched out around her. Despite her resolution not to think carnal thoughts, Matt's voice had set off small fireworks inside her. If his voice was capable of knocking her off her emotional pedestal, she could only guess how she'd react to his knuckles running over her cheek and down the side of her neck.

What did she mean, guess? She knew. There was no denying that she kept tightening her buttocks muscles and pressing her thighs together even with her foot hovering over the gas pedal as she rolled along.

Matt had seen both a wolf pack and Ghost Wolf earlier today. That's what she needed to think about.

Damn it, she should have encouraged him to talk about it. After all, who else did he have to share the experience with?

Maybe she should turn around. Her foot drifted from gas to brake. Even as she told herself she needed to think about this some more before she did anything, she stopped the vehicle. Leaning her forearms on the steering wheel, she rested her forehead on the backs of her hands.

Matt had gone through hell while growing up. He'd probably been too young to understand what was happening to his father as Kaga fell apart, but even worse, he hadn't had anyone to turn to. Just as Kaga hadn't received any mental help, neither had his son.

The son who might have seen his father take his life.

Damn it, what was wrong with her? This wasn't about her; only Matt's emotional well-being mattered.

That and the wolves.

Groaning, she lifted her head. It didn't matter that Matt was nowhere around. She still needed to talk to him, and if her voice drifted out the open window and found its way to his ears, so be it.

"Matt, this is like being in a storm, a furious whiteout. We're both caught in it, you more than me. Things we can't comprehend have happened. You seeing Ghost Wolf today might not be the end of it. Hell, I know it isn't." Shaken, she sucked in hot air that did nothing to calm her.

"Maybe you're asking yourself if what happened to your father is happening to you. You're scared; you have to be. Could be you're thinking that this . . . this thing with the wolves is part of the insanity that—No, you aren't insane!"

Wasn't he? an insistent voice asked, but she shook it off. Matt coming at her like some bull elk during rut wasn't the same as Kaga going on weird spirit searches and killing himself.

She *had* to calm down. Otherwise, she'd never be able to decide what she needed to do. One breath at a time, emptying her mind so hopefully logic and a plan of action could take form. She'd study the peaceful surroundings and think of the cycle of life here that began with calving season. Matt had helped countless four-legged babies into the world and breathed life into some of them. He was a good man, loving and sexy.

Sexy.

Sensation rippled between her shoulder blades and raced down her spine. Damn it, didn't she have any defense against Matt's impact on her? Wishing she had some cold water to throw in her face, she bemoaned the lack of AC in her truck. At least there'd be more of a breeze once she started moving again.

Cat reached for the gearshift but didn't complete the movement. There'd been nothing in the grassland, not even a bird from what she'd been able to tell. Yet there *he* was, standing close enough that she could see into his dark eyes, his large head held high, his back straight, and his stance ready for action.

Get the hell away from me, she wanted to command Ghost Wolf, but her throat refused to form the words. God, but he was beautiful! Frightening and mesmerizing at the same time. Logic said there was no way he could have gotten from where Matt had seen him to here in that amount of time, but maybe logic had nothing to do with it.

She could handle studying Ghost Wolf from a distance of maybe a hundred feet by refusing to ponder how he'd gotten so close without her seeing him approach. Then he started walking toward her, and she screamed.

He looked as if he were stalking her with his head lowered and nose twitching in reaction to the smell of her fear. There was a slow-motion quality to his steps. Maybe this was his way of telling her he had all the time in the world to do what he wanted to her.

Lifting his head, he howled.

Another scream tore at Cat's throat. Gripping the shifter with numb fingers, she yanked down. Mindless to the possibility of damage to the truck's suspension system, she punched the gas. Holding on to the steering wheel with one hand, she tried to fish her cell phone out of her front pocket. Her unfeeling fingers closed around it only to lose control. The phone clattered to the passenger's side floor.

No calling Matt. Nothing but getting away.

To Matt's relief, Addie didn't say much about the time she'd spent with Cat, because he wasn't sure he'd be able to respond. Citing concern for the missing herd, he'd saddled a horse and taken off but not before grabbing extra bullets and his binoculars. He'd debated having one of his hands join him, but this was something he had to do himself. The danger was his alone.

Three hours later, he was herding the cows and calves to a pasture much closer to the ranch house. He'd found the herd about a mile from where he'd seen the wolves, their agitation telling him that they, too, had spotted the predators. Four wolves could easily take down a calf, so why hadn't they?

Cat!

Alarmed, he pulled on the reins and studied his surroundings. What had that been, a soundless warning from her? Maybe a cry for help?

Yeah, right. She'd been on his mind all day, that's all.

Disturbed by his inability to put their relationship into perspective, he turned his attention back to keeping the small herd going. He needed an intervention or exorcism, maybe incantations designed to cast out evil spirits or a cleansing ceremony handled by a shaman.

Shaman.

Rolling his shoulders, Matt first tried to stop his thoughts from diving into the past and then gave in to what he knew had to be done. Either he acknowledged his father or he'd spend the rest of the day fighting memories. He'd deal with the memories and then park them back into a corner of his mind until they insisted on coming out again, as they always did.

During the year before his father had taken his life, he'd repeatedly clung to Matt. Sometimes he'd beg Matt to rip the voices out of his head. Other times he'd insist that as soon as he completed the steps necessary for becoming a shaman, he'd drive the voices out himself. All he needed was for Matt to accompany him on his spirit searches. They'd fast and pray together until the spirits revealed themselves.

It was crazy talk; that's what Matt had thought back then. Yes, only his father loved him, and he was grateful for that love. He needed it. But strange and scary things had started happening to Kaga. He stopped acting like a father.

"Is that what you want?" Matt blurted. His horse's ears swung back toward him. "For me to forgive you for the way your insanity impacted me? If I do, if I acknowledge that you had no control over what happened, will you leave me alone?"

Of course his father didn't answer; he never did. Instead the dead man nibbled at pieces of Matt's mind.

A sudden thought had Matt sitting high in the saddle. Shit, what if that explained his inability to keep his hands off Cat? Was his damnable mentally ill old man trying to take his son down the same path?

Cat!

The back-to-back barrel-racing training sessions had gone well. Listening to the two seventeen-year-olds giggle, Cat wondered if she'd ever been that silly. Hopefully not. Probably not because her parents would have never allowed it. Bottom line, she'd enjoyed the girls' enthusiasm and felt good about what they'd accomplished today.

Now the two were gone, she'd fed her horses, and it was time for her to get something to eat. Instead of going inside, however, Cat continued to watch the roan mare pick through hay. Betsy was pregnant but because she wasn't due to give birth until spring, she hadn't lost her girlish figure. Of course, the term *girlish* was relative. No one would ever call Betsy lean and mean.

Burying herself in work today had been good for her, Cat acknowledged. For hours she'd focused on what paid the bills. Okay, so Ghost Wolf continued his residence in a part of her mind, but at least she'd stopped feeling overwhelmed by recent experiences. She also had a plan, thanks to a call to Helaku, who'd said of course he'd look at her photographs whenever she brought them to him.

And if Helaku didn't sound surprised by either the call or her request . . . chalk that up to her overactive imagination.

The roan blew out a breath, which sent hay scattering. Cat tried to swallow. How long had it been since she'd had something to drink? She tried to put her mind to what she could fix for dinner only to have her thoughts slide to Matt.

She should have called and let him know he wasn't the only one who'd seen Ghost Wolf today. Once she had, she'd apologize for cutting and running when their paths crossed on the road to his ranch. Somehow she'd explain that the things Addie had told her had knocked her off balance emotionally and she hadn't been in any shape to talk to him.

Except talking wasn't what she was interested in.

Raking her fingers down her braid, Cat went in search of enough air to, hopefully, counter need. Yes, fucking. Not talking. Two bodies threatening to combust and clothes being yanked off and hands grasping body parts.

No matter how dangerous the act, she couldn't stop herself from running her hand between her legs. Pressing her middle finger against her opening, she pretended it was Matt's cock.

Forget dinner. She'd stumble into her bedroom and masturbate, or maybe she'd rip off her clothes and sprawl on the recliner where Matt had used and abused her.

Damn, she needed abuse!

Flattening a hand over her flaming cheek, she opened her legs even more and added another finger to the rough massage. Could she make herself come like this? Climax out in front of Mother Nature and ancient Native American gods?

Surprised by the thought, she forced her hand to still. Her fingers remained against her crotch, however, ready for action. She'd been raised by parents who hadn't given religion the slightest priority and seldom went to church herself. As central Oregon had spun its web around her, she'd embraced Mother Nature. If she was going to believe in anything, it would be land, sky, and water, because without those things, this incredible place wouldn't exist.

If only she knew more about how and what Native Americans worshipped.

At that, a mental lightbulb went on. She could start self-educating herself by getting on the Internet. Armed with purpose—and distraction from sexual heat—she planted one boot ahead of the other. Before she could take another, however, a new sensation struck.

No, not new. Just more than she could handle.

Compartmentalize, yes, that's what she'd do. Ghost Wolf had found her again. He stood on a nearby rise, completing a triangle with her and her house being the other two points. The horses paid no attention. The wolf pack wasn't with him. He was glaring at her—no doubt about it, glaring. Hatred streamed from him and threatened to burn her.

Logic, getting done what needed to be done. One step followed by another. Arms at her sides and hands lifted a little in case... in case what? She needed to fight Ghost Wolf? Lots of luck with that. Concentrate on getting the walking done. Head like an arrow for the front door. Give thanks because all it would take was a quick turn of the knob. Less than a minute and she'd be inside. Safe.

Unless Ghost Wolf could walk through walls.

No matter that she reached for self-control with every bit of strength she had in her, the possibility that he was a ghost unhinged her. Clamping her hand over her mouth to keep from screaming—which might have shattered her—she broke into a run.

So did Ghost Wolf.

Out of the corner of her eye, she noted how perfectly every muscle worked with the others. Unlike dogs, whose back ends often tried to outrun their front legs, Ghost Wolf moved like flowing mercury, like a waterfall. Coming toward her. Overtaking her. If she wasn't so afraid she couldn't reach the house in time, she would have applauded his grace.

Breathing like a freight train, Cat took the three steps leading to the porch in a desperate leap. Ghost Wolf's breath seared the back of her neck and arms. Screeching, she grabbed the knob with both hands and twisted, bending back a nail as she did. She squeezed through the opening, ripping her arm on something, and whirled, slamming the door and leaning against it as she fumbled with the lock.

Outside, Ghost Wolf breathed.

She hadn't bothered with a dead bolt; who locked their doors out here? If the beast threw himself against the door, would it give way?

A massive wolf in her living room, claiming the space and backing her into a corner much as Matt had the last time he'd been here.

Was something of Matt in the creature?

To her surprise, she laughed. Then because she had nothing to do except listen to claws scraping on the porch floor, she pondered whether she was on to something or out of her mind. Nothing came together, no logical explanation, not even a supernatural one—not that she knew anything about the supernatural, which until the past few days she hadn't believed in.

Time for a course correction. She was no longer a cynic. She could no longer scoff at ghost hunters and psychics. When it came time to write her memoir, this chapter would be a doozy.

One not a soul would believe.

Except for Matt.

The claw sounds faded and then ended, leaving her in silence. After checking to see if she'd indeed engaged the flimsy locking device, she sprinted across the room and pushed *the* recliner in front of the door—like that was going to do any good.

She had to go to the window to see if Ghost Wolf was still around, but what if her presence prompted him to leap at the glass? Shaken by the thought of blood staining his fur, she gripped her upper arms and hugged herself. Maybe the beast didn't bleed.

"What are you?" she breathed. She wondered if he could hear her. "I don't understand. That's the hell of it—I don't understand."

Don't you?

Closing a hand over her throat to stifle a shriek, Cat waited out the impossible. The question had to have come from her subconscious. No way could the beast out there have spoken to her.

Forcing one foot in front of the other, she slowly killed the distance between herself and the picture glass window she'd always loved but now feared. She'd bought this place as much for the unspoiled setting as for the practical acreage. Maybe in reaction to her parents' insistence that she couldn't, wouldn't, and shouldn't live here, she'd insisted the fifty-year-old house was perfect. What did they mean, isolated? She was surrounded by horses, antelope, deer, rodents, snakes, insects, and more bird species than she could ever identify.

She'd fallen heir to several thankfully neutered barn cats and an elderly hound. After Roscoe died last year, she'd needed time to mourn the loving dog. Now, as soon as it was old enough to be weaned, she'd take ownership of one of Daria's puppies—two if Daria had her way.

But would a dog be safe here?

No matter how slowly she walked, Cat eventually reached the window. Not giving herself time to chicken out, she all but pressed her nose against the glass and cupped her hands against her temples to block out the glare.

Nothing. The trees she'd planted swayed to the wind's tune, and butterflies and hummingbirds laid claim to her roses.

For the first time since moving here, she feared her solitude.

After back-stepping, she dug out her cell phone. Out of habit, she started to call Matt, but she couldn't. Didn't dare.

But if not him, then who? No one, not even Helaku, would believe what had just happened.

Staring out the window again, she acknowledged that it wasn't just the solitude she couldn't deal with. She suddenly hated this place she'd believed she'd always love.

As for Matt, how in the hell did she feel about him?

Beyond the physical, that is, she amended, because she'd die needing his body plastered to hers.

19

Matt should have driven to Cat's place. Okay, so the road was a less-direct route than cross-country, but a horse was slower. Keeping the six-year-old pinto to a trot, he mentally replayed what he'd done since getting the cattle in place earlier today. After closing the gate behind the small herd, he'd gone to the barn where he'd rubbed down the quarter horse he'd used for the roundup. The whole time his hands had been at work, his thoughts, hell, more than that, had fixed on Cat. At the same time, he acknowledged that caring for the horse had been a personal act, flesh touching flesh.

Maybe grooming had tapped him into Cat, although more likely muscle memory was responsible for his dangerous fixation. His body responded to hers in every way possible, just as hers had to his. Beyond all reason, he'd known he couldn't let the day end without seeing her again.

Without reassuring himself that she was all right.

Damn it, Ghost Wolf had it in for him, not her. The creature had no reason to hate or harm her while... Groaning, he pressed the heel of his free hand to his forehead.

He couldn't think worth a damn, couldn't comprehend why Ghost Wolf wanted him dead, if that was it. Instead of working his way through the question, he'd saddled the pinto because he needed to feel something living under him and had taken off for Cat's spread. The time factor involved in getting to her hadn't concerned him until he'd covered some three miles, and of course by then it was too late to turn around.

Even with the saddle between him and the pinto, the animal's heat seeped into him. Lifting himself off the leather, he tried to release some of the pressure on his half erection. During those moments when the rough terrain distracted him from thoughts of Cat, his cock settled back into its natural state only to spring back to life each time she stormed into his mind. Despite his attempts to convince himself there was no reason to be concerned for her welfare, he couldn't shake off horrific images of fangs ripping into feminine flesh.

I'm a mess, Cat. Any chance you'd fuck my brains out so I no longer have to think?

Not long after taking off, he'd carried on a mental conversation with Ghost Wolf. He'd pulled out one argument after another for why the predator had no earthly reason to want anything to do with him, but therein was the rub—*earthly* didn't factor in.

Okay, he'd ride to Cat's place and hang around, unseen of course, until he'd convinced himself that neither Ghost Wolf nor the pack was around. That done, he'd return home, before dark.

Why did that matter? He wasn't afraid of the dark.

Or rather he hadn't been for years.

The land around Cat's spread was nearly as flat as the proverbial pancake on three sides with a small hill to the west, which was where Matt and his mount now stood. He liked being able to look down without her knowing, but he also felt disloyal. She'd made it clear she didn't want to see him today or for the foreseeable future. The hot and heavy and simple relationship they'd enjoyed was behind them, history. It was time to sever what little remained of their ties so he could focus on staying alive.

On learning what the hell was happening.

When the pinto lowered his head and pulled at grass despite the bit in his mouth, Matt started to pull up on the reins, but what did it matter? Other things were much more important.

His body felt as if it were becoming electrified, the sensation an unwanted reminder of the time he'd inadvertently touched an electric fence while standing on wet ground. The stinging shocks also reminded him of what it had felt like to want Cat so badly he hadn't cared about the consequences—or her.

Yeah, that had been him, a dumb, stupid stallion determined to shove himself into the nearest pussy. Fortunately, the *mare* had been equally in heat.

Still fighting the electrical charges, he stood in the stirrups while studying every inch of land below and around him. He'd done the same earlier today while trying to convince himself that the wolf pack wasn't near his herd. As soon as he'd assured himself Cat was safely in her house, he'd—Wait, was she in there? What if she was somewhere else, outside alone?

Her truck was parked between the house and barn. Surely she hadn't taken off on foot.

Telling himself she might be in the barn, he pressed his heels against the pinto's sides, but before the animal could start down the hill, he stopped him and dismounted. Maybe the pinto would stay around; maybe he would take off for home and hay. Matt would deal with that later.

He'd taken a half dozen or so steps when he realized he wasn't simply walking. Instead, every movement felt like gliding. The more territory he covered, the more right what he was doing became. Not only did he no longer feel as if he'd touched a live wire, but also a sense of peace was taking over. This might be Cat's land, but he, too, belonged here. The wind-sanded dirt and rocks welcomed him, waited for his boots to press down on them. These smells were part and parcel of him and the breeze essential to his genetic makeup. If necessary, he'd explain that to Cat, but hopefully she'd be so glad to see him and strip for him there'd be no need for an explanation.

Yes, she was here. In the house. He knew because her scent was separate from that of sage and earth. Pausing, he drank in the familiar and new and wrapped himself around her essence. A moment later, he stiffened. Unlike him, she wasn't comfortable in her skin. After a few seconds spent listening to her heartbeat and finding her breathing's rhythm, he acknowledged something else: Cat wanted to be anywhere except where she was.

Why? She'd always said she loved her land. Nothing had happened to change how she felt. Nothing except for Ghost Wolf.

And the way he'd acted around her the last few times.

He was trying to come up with an explanation for his aggressive behavior—no easy task when he simply wanted to be—when a new sensation tore into him. His already-alert senses sharpened.

There. Ghost Wolf. Coming from the back of Cat's house and striding toward the corral that held her horses.

Fascinated, Matt watched as the great creature silently approached the nervous horses. He'd never heard of a wolf pack taking down a healthy, fully grown horse, not that it mattered. Only right now and Ghost Wolf did. Whinnying in alarm, the horses crowded the corral's far end. One broke free of the group. Bucking and galloping by turn, it repeatedly circled the confining enclosure while Ghost Wolf settled himself on his haunches and watched.

The strength in Matt's legs increased with every step as he

headed toward the corral. He felt no need to run, and what thought fragments entered his mind soon slipped away. Somewhere deep inside lurked the possibility that his life might be in danger, but it didn't matter.

As another horse joined the panicked one, Matt started to run his hand over his middle only to stop and frown. What was the old hunting knife with its sheath doing tucked into his waistband, and why had he thought he might need this particular one?

"No! Goddamn it, don't you dare!"

Cat's voice turned Matt toward the house. The front door slammed behind her. Holding a slender fire poker over her head, she hurried down the stairs and toward the still-sitting Ghost Wolf looking like a mother grizzly defending her cubs.

"Don't!" Matt warned as he hurried toward her. "Stay away from him."

Openmouthed, Cat gaped at him. "What are you doing here?"

Instead of admitting he didn't know, he said, "You can't beat him. He'll kill you."

That's not what I'm here for.

Not believing what he'd just heard, Matt struggled to divide his attention between woman and beast. Moments ago he'd believed he belonged here as he'd never belonged anywhere. Now he wished he was anyone except who he was.

"Did you hear that?" Cat's question barely reached him.

"Yes."

"Oh, God!" Cat tried to run her fingers into her hair only to be stopped by her tightly done braid. "I don't believe this is happening."

Ghost Wolf had stood up while Matt's attention was on Cat. The predator's two-hundred-some pounds on a nearly six-foot-high frame dried his throat. Battling awe, disbelief, and something he refused to name, Matt simply accepted that Ghost

Wolf existed. That done, he once more turned his attention to Cat, who continued to hold the fire poker like a weapon—a useless one.

Was the knife he should have gotten rid of years ago any better?

Every line of her body said she was willing to do whatever it took to save her horses. She had to be afraid, yet she faced the predator square on, which earned her his utmost respect.

More than respect, he amended, because Cat barely resembled the woman he'd believed her to be. She'd cast aside the civilized, sensitive, and sensual nature that had served her up to now, and she'd become an animal.

This beautiful creature ready to pit her puny weapon against a killer clawed at his sanity and reached deep inside to the beast he'd never before acknowledged. Feeling animal himself, he studied the female of the species they'd both become.

When she started walking again without taking her attention off Ghost Wolf, her reckless courage enveloped him. He breathed in her raw scent until it touched his cock and settled into him.

I didn't expect that from you.

"Who is he talking to?" Cat demanded. "You or me?"

"Maybe both of us."

Her eyes narrowing, she shook her head. "Oh, hell, it doesn't matter. Listen to me, Ghost Wolf, or whatever you call yourself. If you hurt one of my horses, I'll kill you."

How?

Mouth hanging open, Cat shook her head. In the space of a couple of seconds, she'd gone from mother grizzly to confused woman. "I don't know," she muttered. "Somehow."

You can't. I'm timeless. Never-ending.

If asked, Matt couldn't have explained why he was walking toward the woman who'd spent more time naked than clothed around him. Even with his ability to think splintering, he didn't want her standing alone.

Stop!

"Why?" he demanded of Ghost Wolf. "What does what I do matter?"

You're mine. You belong to me.

"No!" Cat screamed.

Yes.

"Why?" she demanded. "And what does hurting my horses have to do with—"

I wanted to see how you'd react to a threat.

Pressure built along Matt's temples. Maybe Ghost Wolf's unspoken words were responsible.

Perhaps Cat realized something was happening to him, because she stared at him with eyes that said she'd lay down her life for him.

"Leave us alone," he told Ghost Wolf. The pressure in his skull continued to build, and he massaged the sides of his head. "You're a wolf. You belong with the pack. They accept you."

They do as I command, but I'm not one of them.

"Who are you, then?" Cat demanded.

As Ghost Wolf turned his attention from him to her, Matt chastised himself for not asking what might be the most important question. At least his headache had leveled off. As long it remained like this, he could concentrate. And maybe, somehow, he'd comprehend how this conversation could be taking place.

Who am I? You found the answer in the cave.

"I don't understand." Cat sounded young and frightened. "The drawings, you mean?"

Dismissing Cat with a curled lip, the creature settled his gaze on Matt. Time passed, each moment heavy and densely layered. The longer he fought to meet Ghost Wolf's dark stare, the more he felt himself being drawn back in time to when his mentally out-of-control father had insisted he could see the past, present, and future in his son's eyes.

"Stop it," Cat blurted. "What are you doing?"

Pulled out of memories he thought he'd buried, Matt blinked the scene back into focus. The wolf creature now stood less than twenty feet away. Even with everything he had to comprehend, Matt pondered why Ghost Wolf's nostrils weren't moving.

Maybe the beast wasn't alive.

I need you. You more than the pack I've waited for all this time. Knowing you were nearby kept me going. Without you—

"Matt, can you hear me?"

Angry, Matt spun toward Cat. His intention had been to demand she shut up so Ghost Wolf could finish. However, everything changed when his attention settled on her. Her eyes widened as her gaze slid to his cock.

"Now?" she asked.

Nodding, he slid his hand over his erection. In his mind's eye, her clothing no longer existed. Instead she stood naked and ready for sex, her body saying that nothing else mattered.

Don't let her do this! You belong to me, not her!

"No, he doesn't," she insisted. "You'll destroy him while I'll . . . Matt, please."

Cat continued to hold on to the poker but no longer carried it as if it was a weapon. She remained naked to him, with every muscle and bone more beautiful than anything he'd ever seen. Even as the fresh pounding in his brain threatened to bring him to his knees, he knew he'd crawl to her if he had to.

No, Matt, no!

A snarl pushed past Cat's mouth. Hurtling the poker spearlike at Ghost Wolf, she rushed to Matt's side and clamped her hands around his wrist. "Come with me! In the house, we'll be safe there."

Wind-borne laughter circled around Matt as Cat dragged him up the stairs. He should at least look back at Ghost Wolf, should say something to let the creature know how deeply the words had touched him and that he was glad her weapon had missed. He would have if Cat wasn't so close, so warm and alive.

Breathing heavily, Cat yanked on the door and shoved Matt inside ahead of her. She didn't know how, for a few seconds, she'd been stronger than Matt. She also shook off the frightening thought that a creature capable of speaking without words wouldn't let a door stop him.

After locking the door, she again pulled the recliner into place while Matt stared expressionlessly at her.

"Your knife," she said, still out of breath. "Cut him if he tries to come in."

"He won't."

"How can you say that?"

"I know."

Maybe he did. Today anything seemed possible. As much as she wanted silence in here so hopefully she could determine what Ghost Wolf was doing, she couldn't get her heartbeat to quiet. Leaving Matt to stand like a living statue in the middle of her small living room, she walked to the window and looked out.

Ghost Wolf stood where she'd last seen him. He must have known she was studying him, because he glanced down at the poker she'd insanely tried to hit him with. Shaking his head, he pulled it toward him with a front paw. Then he lifted a rear leg and peed on it. She nearly laughed.

The wind must have picked up, as evidenced by the dust swirling about in her dirt parking area. Strange that she couldn't hear a single gust strike the side of her house. Remembering that Ghost Wolf had been heading for her horses when she'd first spotted him, she waited, not breathing, to see if he'd start toward them again.

Instead he left. Simply left. One moment Ghost Wolf stood

in the middle of dust and flying dirt. The next he no longer existed.

Undone, she stumbled around so she could look at Matt, placing her hand on the windowsill for balance as she did.

"You didn't see that, did you?" she asked the man who as far as she knew still hadn't moved a muscle. "He disappeared, evaporated. Something. Matt, what is happening?"

"He wants me."

"Oh, God, I know what he said but—"

"Don't."

Wild horses had long called this part of the country home. Although there was concern that their numbers might increase until there wasn't enough food for the herd, she'd relished her occasional glimpses of them. Most fascinating was a well-built black stallion with several battle scars and an impressive harem that hung out on nearby government land.

Now, looking at Matt, she half believed she was looking at the stallion again.

"Don't what?" she managed.

"Talk about him, not now."

Why not? she needed to ask, but right now she didn't trust Matt. Maybe it was the comparison with the stallion that had her thinking this way, but she couldn't find anything of the modern man in the cowboy with his wind-tangled hair, dusty boots, strong chest, and try-to-ignore-me erection.

"He was talking to me, not you." Matt looked around at the living room as if he'd never seen it. "He wants nothing to do with you."

As much as she needed to point out that it wasn't that simple, she didn't. "What are you doing here?"

Drawing in a breath that expanded his chest when that was the last thing her nervous system needed, he rammed his hands into his back pockets. After giving the knife at his waist a distracted glimpse, she filled her own lungs.

"Here? I don't know," he said.

"You don't . . . I'm glad you came."

"Are you?"

How could she possibly answer with her nerve endings splintering? So this was what it felt like to be caught in class 5 river rapids, tossed about with no way to reach the shore or stop herself from striking looming boulders. She'd give anything to start the day over.

"I don't know what would have happened if I'd been alone." To hell with not letting a certain name pass her lips. "Ghost Wolf was going to attack my horses."

"No."

"What makes you say—"

This man she didn't understand stopped her by lifting his head. "He wanted you outside."

"He, ah, could have come in here."

"No, he couldn't. He's like the pack, a wild creature. He avoids human enclosures."

The explanation made a terrible and undeniable kind of sense. Feeling both empathy for Ghost Wolf and relieved, if Matt was right, she turned her attention back to the high-desert land that was her home. Ghost Wolf hadn't returned.

"What about you and walls?" Both wanting and dreading the movement, she faced Matt. "I had to pull you inside just now."

"Why did you? The last time we were together, you said you never wanted to see me again."

Never. Surely she hadn't used that word. "I can't think around you." It was only part of the truth.

Matt pulled his hands out of his pockets. One went to the knife nestled against his middle, and he withdrew it from a faded leather sheath. "Cat, you asked what brought me here."

"Yes."

"I kept thinking about you today. Heard you."

"Oh."

After stroking the knife's dull side, he placed the weapon on the lamp table where the recliner had been before she'd turned it into a doorstop. "You were crying for help."

How long ago had Matt walked into her life, and what, if anything, had she done with that life, before his arrival? A brand of energy that made her think of winter storms and Brahma bulls surrounded him. At the beginning, everything had been about sex, hungry bodies feeding off each other. Even as she'd been drawn to his strength and competence and things unspoken about his past, she'd told herself she knew him.

What a damnable naïve and horny fool she'd been.

"I thought about you too," she told him, afraid to close the distance between them. "Maybe that's what reached you."

"Maybe."

When he started toward her, she fought to remain in place, but instead of touching her as she did and didn't want, he positioned himself near the window. She stepped aside to give him full access, responding to his heat as she did.

"Where did he go?" Matt muttered.

"I don't know. It, ah, was . . . Suddenly he wasn't there."

He pressed a hand against the glass as if trying to reach beyond it so he could touch the too-large wolf. "He's lonely."

Reacting to Matt's somber tone, she grasped his free hand. Only then did she force herself to acknowledge what may have been the biggest mistake she'd made today, maybe forever.

"Because of what he said about wanting you?" she asked.

Still looking out, Matt shook his head. "He's been waiting for the wolves to return. All those decades since the last one was killed, not knowing if any would come here again, it's been hell for him."

As tears stung her eyes, she laid her head on his shoulder. "You feel sorry for him?"

"Don't."

He didn't have to say another word for her to understand his warning, but it was too late. Today had been too much.

Matt was all she had.

"I mean it," he said, and pushed her away. "You don't know what you're putting me through."

"Don't I?" A roaring filled her head, and her skin felt as if it were breaking free from the rest of her.

Despite his cocked head and the whisper of a smile, a million miles separated them. If they so much as touched again, they risked dropping into a pit where need waited to swallow them. Going by what strained against his jeans, she sensed he was in danger of exploding. Much as they wanted that explosion, it meant returning to the limited relationship they'd had before.

Which hadn't been enough.

"We've never made love," she told him. "Have you ever wondered why that is?"

Broad shoulders lifted. "What's this about, Cat?"

Trying to find normalcy for the first time. Trying to find us despite Ghost Wolf. "Think about it. Making love is something people who care about each other do. What does that say about you and me?"

He stood with the window and her world behind him. She wouldn't be surprised if, as Ghost Wolf had done, he slipped through the glass and floated away.

"I can't think," he muttered, pinching his forehead.

Because Ghost Wolf had a hold on him. Although she'd give anything to massage away the pressure in his head, she took his free hand and laid it over her breast. Took the risk.

"You don't have to think," she whispered. "That's what I'm here for." *Why I'll do whatever I have to to save you.* "What does lovemaking mean to you?"

She held her breath as he opened his mouth. Instead of answering, however, he closed his eyes. Where had he gone to? What secret place was he taking shelter in?

"I'll tell you what it means to me," she said. *The needs I buried under the fucking that defined us.* "Commitment and vulnerability. Taking my lover's body slowly. Spending the night reaching mutual climax. Trust. Mostly it means trust."

When Matt lowered his arm, she noted the red splotches where his fingers had pressed against his skull. He rocked back and forth, making her think of a horse roped for the first time. If she said or did the wrong thing, would he bolt? Maybe it was all he could do not to attack her.

"I want to trust you, Matt, but I don't know if I can."

"I understand."

His eyes were still closed, and he'd done nothing to acknowledge her presence. "I'm not sure if you do, but maybe it doesn't matter right now," she told him. "What are you seeing?"

"Him."

Ghost Wolf. Of course.

"He isn't in here. There's just the two of us and maybe the only chance we'll have to see if there's anything between us. Come with me, please."

20

Cat had led Matt into the bedroom and had him sit on the side of the bed. After placing his knife on the nightstand, she'd removed his boots and socks and unsnapped his jeans. Then she'd helped him stand so she could pull the worn denim over his hips and down his legs. Three times he'd reached for her. Three times, asking herself if she was doing the right thing and if she could see it through, she'd placed his arms back by his sides.

Because the bedroom was at the back of the house, she couldn't see where Ghost Wolf had last stood. Instead of being relieved, however, she fought the impulse to run back into the living room. The look on Matt's face, or rather the lack of one, kept her next to him.

Matt had always embraced life. It fascinated him and he'd never been a bystander, so why was he so different today? Putting off asking something she might not get an answer to, she sank onto the carpet and helped him step out of his clothes. Her face was scant inches from his cock, but she couldn't work up the courage to touch him there, let alone take him into her watering mouth. Shaking, she ran her hands down his thighs.

"He's waiting for me," Matt said.

I know and that terrifies me. "If, as you said, he's been around all these years, he can wait a little...Why you?" She clamped her teeth around the unwanted question.

"I don't know. Cat, I don't know if I'm ready for this." He brushed his erection.

If that was true, it was a first. Always before— "Take off your shirt."

He slowly unbuttoned and shrugged out of the garment. She rocked back on her haunches, which provided her with a too-vivid view of his cock. Still not touching him, she placed her fingers over her thighs and looked up at him.

Fine stubble shaded his jaws and chin. In contrast to his deeply tanned forearms, the sun's impact on his chest was less. He wasn't looking at her, and as earlier, he'd gone motionless.

Matt was waiting for her. The next move and the ones to come after were up to her. Even more unnerving, she needed a reason for what she was doing.

Neither of which she had.

Hoping to hide her confusion behind action, she awkwardly got to her feet. Matt gave her a glance. Then his gaze turned inward. Studying him, she acknowledged that they weren't alone after all. Some part of Ghost Wolf shared the space with them.

"You don't belong here," Cat told the creature.

Wrong. I have every right.

"I don't want to hear this." She didn't know what to do with her hands. "You already said— Go away!"

No.

"Don't argue with him," Matt said. "It won't change anything."

"You want him around? An audience?"

Taking hold of her shoulders, Matt turned her so her back was to him. Her shirt served as a pitiful defense against his fingers, and it was all she could do not to lean against him. Any other time she would have.

"I'm worn out mentally and physically," he muttered. "Done in. I haven't felt like this in a long time, and I hate it. Don't want it."

Even though his admission brought her to the brink of tears, Cat held her breath, certain Ghost Wolf would say something. When he didn't, she nodded. "Do you remember when it was simple between us and sex defined everything?"

"It's never going to be like that again."

"No, it isn't."

"I've never seen your hair down," he said after a short silence. "Why do you always corral it?"

"What? Because it's practical this way."

"Enough with the practical, Cat. I want it down."

Did you hear him? she asked the spirit creature watching them. *He's thinking of us, not you.*

For now.

Much as she tried, she couldn't suppress a shudder. "Easy, easy," Matt reassured her. "You're all right."

Wondering if he hadn't heard Ghost Wolf's warning, she handed him a less-than-honest chuckle. "That's debatable."

As he went to work on the band she'd secured the end of the braid with, she tried to rest her hands on her hips, but they slipped off and down her thighs. Fascinated by what he was doing, she leaned forward a little to ease his access. Braiding her hair had been as much a part of her morning routine as brushing her teeth.

Watch, then, she told Ghost Wolf. *Watch and envy.*

This time there was no response.

Instead of simply pulling the three strands apart as she did, Matt slowly worked his fingers into her hair. Here he was, stark naked and vulnerable and sought by something neither of them could comprehend. Instead of stripping her or insisting Ghost

Wolf tell him what had brought them together, he concentrated on what was long overdue for a cut.

Are you still here? she questioned. *Of course you are. How does it make you feel knowing he isn't thinking about you right now?*

You're wrong.

No, damn it! She wasn't going to let Ghost Wolf destroy what might be the most important thing she and Matt would ever do together. The beast's voice in her head was just that, a voice.

The rest of him was elsewhere.

"There," she whispered as her still-wavy hair settled on her shoulders and ran down her back. "Thank you."

Matt finger-combed her hair. His nails slid over her shoulder blades and spine.

"Wait." She dragged her T-shirt over her head, which caused her hair to fill with static electricity and cling to the fabric before settling around her face, half blinding her.

"Let's see," Matt said.

She faced him, pulling hair away from her mouth as she did. Still expressionless, he brushed the rest off her forehead, cheeks, and neck. Then he stepped back. Left her alone.

"It's beautiful that way. You're beautiful."

If she could believe his gentle tone, she wasn't the only one who wanted these moments together to last, but maybe he was dividing his attention between her and the creature determined to claim him.

Wasn't going to happen! Not as long as she was alive.

"Earlier," she said, "you told me not to mention Ghost Wolf. I didn't succeed then, but I hope to now because you and I need to be together, just the two of us. Different from the other times."

"Different how?"

Her swollen nipples were so sensitive she could barely stand to have her bra against them, so she reached behind her and unfastened it. She handed the garment to him.

"Why haven't we spent a night together?" she asked. "Addie's at your place but you could have come here."

"You never asked."

Rendered mute, Cat cupped her breasts. Any more emotional hits today and she might not survive. Kneading her nipples distracted her, and as long as she didn't meet Matt's eyes, she could get through the next few moments.

"Neither did I," he said. "What would you have said if I had?"

"I don't know." The admission clogged her throat. "I'm used to waking up alone. What we had was great and I guess . . . Matt, I'm sorry." Pulling courage around her, she lifted her head only to falter. In this lighting, Matt's eyes and Ghost Wolf's seemed the same color.

"Don't apologize," he said. "We knew what we were doing."

Did they? More likely hormones had so defined their relationship that there wasn't anything left for other elements. By the time they'd finished having exhausting sex, she'd only wanted to sleep. Alone and safe from his body's impact on hers.

Oh, shit, she'd been afraid of him.

As afraid as she now was of Ghost Wolf?

"My head hurts," she admitted. "My brain's on overload."

"Yeah, I know."

Of course he did; his expression and dark, glittering eyes told her he'd reached his own limit. Taking another bite of courage, she unsnapped her jeans. She thought he might finish the job for her, but he didn't. Leaning over, she untied her tennis shoes and pushed out of them, followed by the rest of her clothes. An outsider might conclude that sex between them was mechanical, but she needed it this way. Clothing first, then hopefully showing Matt how much he meant to her.

And learning the same from him.

"Lie down, please." She indicated her bed. "On your stomach."

Frowning, he slowly and hesitantly obeyed. Once he was in position with his head propped on his bent arms and facing her, she climbed onto the bed next to him. Whatever he'd done today had left him with a layer of sweat same as her, but then they were physical people. Leaning down, she lapped at the small of his back.

He stiffened. "Oh, God."

"Relax, please."

He didn't, but then had she really expected him to be able to? When she again ran her tongue over him, her pussy clenched and her nipples tightened anew. Closing her eyes did nothing to quiet her physical reaction. Neither did placing her thumbs against his shoulder blades and massaging him there, but she kept on task by reminding herself that right now was about him.

Keeping Matt with her.

The stare from an unseen source continued to burn her. At any moment, Ghost Wolf might reappear, but she'd deal with that then. Matt was under her, prone but not easy in his skin, his head lifting occasionally and his breathing without rhythm.

Thinking of him, only him, she repeatedly kissed the back of his neck while running her hands over his ribs and spine. He'd adjusted his cock before settling onto the mattress, so hopefully he'd found a comfortable position. If not, she'd soon learn.

"Your body says everything about you." She spoke with her mouth close to the base of his neck so her breath could run over him there. "For too long all I thought about was how sexy it was, but that's only the half of it."

Moistening her lips, she lightly ran them over the top of his left shoulder. He shuddered anew. Smiling, she slid the pads of her hands along his sides. The last few times they'd been together, he'd in essence stormed her, demanding sex and pushing all her buttons. Scaring and exciting her. Now, hopefully, she'd show him another way.

Keep him with her.

"You'll never make it as a cover model," she told him. "Too many scars and that uneven tan would have to go. You're older than the pretty boys, and your muscles come from work, not weights." Shifting position slightly, she pressed her thumb pad into the base of his spine. Grunting, he arched off the bed. "All in all, not the type they're looking for."

"Shit, Cat. And the point of this is?"

Desire, determination, maybe desperation was the best she could come up with.

She waited for him to relax again before trailing her hair along the length of his spine. Ignoring the kink in her neck, she guided the hair he'd set free over his buttocks.

"The point is, I know some things about you, Matt." Again shifting, she ran a short-nailed finger between his ass cheeks. "Not everything I need to, but it's a start."

Grunting, he tried to turn onto his side. She stopped him by placing her body on top of his with her breasts pressing against his back.

"You're not going anywhere, because for once in your life you aren't the one in control."

"What control? This—damn it—this isn't the first time."

There it was, another example of how little she knew about the man inside the perfect-to-her body.

"Tell me." She punctuated her command by slapping one buttock and then the other. "About the other out-of-control times."

The air itself seemed to take a breath. Freezing, she waited out the sensation and in the silence that followed, she knew she'd said the wrong thing.

"I'm sorry." She kissed the places she'd just slapped. "I have no right asking." On the brink of letting him know what Addie had told her, she gnawed on her lip. "We're all entitled to secrets, but if there are too many of them, the relationship suffers. There has to be a certain amount of honesty."

"Does there?"

A brick wall, no way of making Matt open up.

"All right. That's up to you, Matt," she managed. "I love having sex with you, but if we're ever going to move past that, there has to be trust."

This time when he stirred, she let him turn onto his side. His cock reached for her, and it took everything she had not to lose herself in the invitation.

"We aren't alone," he said.

"I know."

"It doesn't bother you?"

"Bother? This is the last thing I want to happen, certainly the last thing I ever thought would, but it is. What do you want me to do, deny it?"

Something in his expression made her wonder if that's exactly what he needed to hear. Sighing, she stretched out next to him and propped herself on her elbow with her knees slightly bent. Her breasts sagged. He captured both in his workman's hand.

"I love how sensitive they are," he said. "That first night when we were being introduced, I couldn't keep my eyes off them."

Feeling protected and unnerved, she said, "I noticed."

"That didn't bother you? I thought you might tell me to take a hike."

Matt had spoken at little more than a whisper. She didn't know whether that was because he hoped to keep their conversation private or because saying what he had wasn't easy for him. Outside, the summer afternoon pounded down on the dry earth and made the animals lethargic. In here, energy was a living force.

If she wasn't careful, she'd fall into its heat.

"I developed physically early," she told him. "Having my mother haul me into a specialty store to outfit me with bras was traumatic."

He released one breast and enveloped the other, so his calloused hand scraped and sensitized. Wet heat bloomed in her already-moist pussy.

"I thought girls can hardly wait to grow."

"Some maybe, I don't know."

"You didn't share that stuff with your friends?"

"What friends?" She started to wince in reaction to what she'd just said only to shake her head and lower herself onto her back. Pins and needles attacked the arm that had been under her as she rested her hands on her belly. "I moved around so much that a lot of the time I was homeschooled by tutors. Hard to develop friendships that way."

Matt sat up and crossed his legs. His knees and shins pressed against her hips. Her attention went to the cock barely out of reach. Extending his hand, he lightly trailed his fingers over her pubic hair. Her head roared.

"This isn't the first time you've mentioned moving around while you were growing up. I'm sorry I didn't ask you to explain earlier."

"So am I." Her fingers ground into her belly. "Now. Back then, well, you know."

"What happened? Something about your parents' jobs?"

In too many ways, Matt was in uncharted territory, land she'd never traveled over. If she was ever going to learn more than what Addie had told her, she first had to give something of herself.

Incapable of thinking and looking at him at the same time, she stared at the ceiling and fought to ignore the fingers tracing the lightest of trails through her pubic hair.

Her parents had their own business, she told him. Several

years before the birth of their only child, they'd parlayed their organizational and social skills into a service that put on conventions and conferences. Among their clients were corporations, professional organizations, and recreation groups. They still handled everything from venue selection to menus to travel plans. In addition, they were responsible for setting up the meeting rooms, getting bartenders for the open bars, and supplying everything the speakers needed.

"They've run conventions in major cities both here and abroad," she said as his hand headed for her crotch, and her ability to speak faltered. "Because they have to be there in advance of and after the event, they hauled me everywhere. My favorite were the events held at resorts. I learned to ski and surf. Picked up a little French and Italian."

"You've been so many places while I . . . What brought you here?"

Matt needed her sober and clearheaded, something he wasn't going to get as long as he kept touching her this way. Hating what she had to do, she took hold of his wrist. Instead of placing his hand on his own body as she'd thought she would, she rested it on her belly. He settled his other hand next to it.

"Talk," he said. "While you can."

And while you're here to listen. Alarmed by the thought, she searched the room for signs of Ghost Wolf's presence.

"My parents love what they do. They call themselves gypsies, albeit wealthy ones because they're so good at their jobs. For a while they had an apartment in downtown Chicago, but we were there so seldom they gave it up. We stayed in furnished places wherever the conventions were being held. The last I talked to them, they were renting one of those extended-stay executive places in Los Angeles. I hate that city."

"I've never been, never wanted to."

Cat didn't remember closing her eyes, but not seeing Matt made talking easier. Also, this way she could focus on his rough warmth against her belly. Beyond trying to keep emotion out of her voice, she told him about the day that in retrospect had brought her here. As had happened countless times while she was growing up, she was alone two days after she'd turned seventeen. Her parents had just bought her her first car. More to the point, they'd called the dealership where they'd leased their vehicle and told the salesman to deliver whatever was in the best condition with the lowest mileage on the lot but not to go over $7,000. It turned out to be a six-cylinder yellow pickup truck so light in the rear end she could hardly keep it going in a straight line.

Despite the abominable color, she'd done what any teenager would do. She'd taken it out for a drive. She'd headed east, hoping to get out of the city and into the desert where she'd find quiet and breathing room.

"I got lost. I kept getting stuck in traffic and thought I'd lose my mind. When I got low on gas, I drove around in circles looking for a station. Then I ran out of gas while waiting in line. Fortunately, a couple of men pushed me; then one had to show me how to pump the gas while other people laughed. By the time I was done, I was even more desperate to get away from it all."

Desperate? Yes, she'd said the word. Opening her eyes, she found him staring down at her and nodding.

"Did you find the city limits?"

"Which one?" She tried a light tone she didn't feel. "The cities all run together in the L.A. area. And, no, I never found the end to the congestion. Finally a police officer pointed me in the right direction and I got back to where we were staying." Taking hold of Matt's wrist again, she brought his hand to her cheek. Even with the loss of his fingers near her sex, she didn't regret what she'd done. "My folks were at the convention center, so I walked to it. I was too frazzled to consider getting back in the truck. There were people all over the place, staff, caterers, press, early arrivals. Dad nodded in my direction. Mom didn't acknowledge me."

"Oh, Cat, I'm sorry."

"Not the first time," she managed as he lightly rubbed her cheek. She didn't care if he found her tears. "I turned around and walked back to the apartment, bumping into what seemed like more people than I had on the road. I spent the evening in this immaculate and impersonal apartment watching a National Geographic show about Alaska."

"Wishing you were there."

"*Needing* to be there—not the cold but the space."

"That's when you learned you weren't made for city life?" He kissed her on the nose.

She touched where his lips had been. "You've never done that."

"I should have. You were only seventeen, which means you couldn't just pack up and leave."

"No." Even with Matt beside her, memories threatened to swamp her. "But that experience and others taught me that the life my parents chose wasn't for me. And that I came in second to their career. I can't believe they thought they could groom me to take over the business. They're extroverts while I'm . . . I've become a country hick."

Nodding, Matt guided her into a sitting position so they now faced each other with their knees kissing. He rested his hands on her thighs while hers knotted at the base of her belly. The juices he was responsible for dribbled down her to stain the inexpensive bedspread.

21

_____

"After my father died," Matt said, "and I was sent to live with Santo and Addie, I thought about leaving. Heading for the bright lights."

"But you didn't."

"I couldn't."

"Why not?"

"For a long time I didn't know. Although I didn't have a driver's license, I knew how to drive, but where would I go? Would any other place feel like home? How did you feel the first time you came here?"

"Love," she whispered.

"With the land?"

"Absolutely."

Matt's hands slid along her thighs and from there to her hips, while her thoughts fell apart. Ghost Wolf could be standing invisible in a corner of the room. Hell, he might be about to attack and tear her apart. But until or if that happened, she'd lose herself in Matt and the things they were saying to each other.

"Just like that, the first time you saw all this nothing, you were hooked?"

"Immediately. Completely." Her skin jumped both where his hands lay and at her waist where she thought he'd head next. "I've told you that, haven't I?"

"If you did, I wasn't listening."

Matt could be so honest. Yes, there'd been many times when he held silence and action up as barriers against their getting to know each other, but she didn't believe he'd ever lied to her.

"Because," he continued as he spread his fingers over her sides and started upward, heading for her breasts, "I couldn't think around you."

"Couldn't? Past tense?"

"I'm trying to change. Hell of a time, isn't it, with everything blowing up around us."

"There is a sense of urgency." The words were barely out of her mouth when she wondered if she'd heard Ghost Wolf laugh. "Matt, do you think he's capable of ending everything for us? Killing us?"

Planting his hands under her armpits and pressing so her breasts were pushed out of shape, he drew her across her folded legs toward him. "That's not his intention."

Keep talking. Don't let his body break you down. "What makes you so sure?"

Matt shook his head. "I just know. Ghost Wolf needs me. He won't destroy me."

With his thumbs against her nipples and her nipples straining and needful, she ran her hands around to his buttocks. Despite the awkward position she'd placed herself in, she couldn't imagine letting it end unless—

"He doesn't feel the same about me," she said into Matt's chest.

Releasing one breast, Matt lifted her chin. She had no choice but to look at him. "I won't let him hurt you."

He couldn't make good on that promise; they both knew that. But hearing the words filled her heart with heat. She'd never asked herself if she could fall in love with Matt; they didn't have that kind of relationship.

Or rather they hadn't until a few days ago.

"You'll take that knife and fend him off with it?" she asked.

"Knife?" He glanced at it. "Yeah, that one. He's still here, you know, some part of him anyway. The air is heavy with him."

Matt was right, damn him. No matter how desperate she was to throw his words back at him, she couldn't. "How can he do that, separate his essence from his body, if that's what he's doing?"

"Because he's different."

"Beyond our comprehension," she whispered, when that touched only the edges of what they'd been experiencing.

"For now." Matt looked so sober she grew alarmed. "It smells good in here. What's that, roses?"

Trying to keep up with the sudden change in subject, she nodded and explained that she dried some of her roses so she could place them in bowls in her bedroom. Two were on top of her dresser.

"Where'd you learn something like that? Did your mother—"

"Hardly." Somehow her hands had wound up on the insides of his thighs, scant inches from his cock. "It's one of my few domestic skills." She wondered if Matt's mother cared about her home, but then he wouldn't know. Besides, his cock was killing her concentration.

Ending her interest in Ghost Wolf.

His expression bland, Matt looked down at her hands. For the second time today, he ran his fingers into the hair at her crotch and she knew they'd come to the same place.

Alive, scared, and excited, she cupped her hands around

what as far as she was concerned was the most important part of Matt's anatomy and leaned over their legs until her spine protested. She managed to draw his cock head into her mouth but couldn't keep it there.

"Sorry. My technique needs work."

"Your technique is perfect. Everything about you is."

His words surrounded her, then splintered under a hollow growl. Chilled, she tried to determine where it was coming from only to stop because Matt had again taken hold of her chin and was forcing her to look at him.

"I mean it—I won't let him hurt you," he said.

Fresh tears burned her eyes. When she nodded, she did so with every inch and ounce of her being. He pushed her away from him, turning her as he did, and she found herself standing on the carpet with her back to Matt and him holding on to her wrists so her arms were behind her. She recalled that earlier time when he'd manhandled her.

Matt released her, leaving her with nothing to do except let her arms fall to her sides. Aware of her naked body, she faced him to discover he'd slid to the side of the bed and was sitting with his legs over the edge and his cock waiting for her.

A second growl, softer than the first, stopped her.

"He doesn't want this to happen." Matt indicated his erection. "Because he wants me to himself. But he can't stop us."

"How do you know?" Her mouth didn't want to work. At the same time, her body softened.

"He already would have if he could." Running his hands over his thighs, he sat straighter. "His body's elsewhere."

Did that mean they didn't have to concern themselves with what was behind the growls? Despite the question, she really didn't care. She believed Matt. Only that mattered.

His words and what he was offering her.

Wiping her sweating hands on her thighs, she put an end to

the distance between them. When their knees touched, she stopped and pressed his legs together. That done, she waited until he lifted his gaze from her crotch to her face.

"Me riding you?" she asked. "That's what this is about?"

"If it's what you want."

Want! Hell, the word didn't come close. Bracing her hands against his thighs for support, she straddled him. She came down slow, glad he was guiding himself into place.

Into her.

Long, slow, and strong.

The bed had come with the house, and although she'd bought a new mattress, she hadn't gotten around to getting another frame to replace the one that had been built higher off the floor to accommodate an elderly man's decreased physical ability to get up and down.

She gave thanks for her procrastination.

Resting her hands on Matt's shoulders, she carefully and slowly lifted herself off him. His features went out of focus, either because they were so close or because she couldn't concentrate on anything except what was taking place inside her pussy.

He'd become her. Two separate human beings connected in the most primal way. Vulnerable and honest to the max, with their separate flames coming together to create a firestorm. Liquid heat ran over her body to turn her both heavy and weightless. Tightening her sex muscles, she again settled her legs and buttocks against him.

"Shit!" His fingers dug into her hips as he pushed her upward again.

Fucking Matt became mechanical and soul-felt, with her body desperate to reach climax and her heart reaching out, hoping to touch his. Her breasts jiggled with every move. The burning sensation in her legs carved a hot path to her cunt until she swore every part of her from the waist down was having sex.

"Slow it. Just a little."

At first doing sex according to Matt's pace seemed impossible; how could a wild mare cease galloping? But he used his hold on her to control her pace, driving upward and into her as he did until they became one in all the ways that counted.

Her fingers cramped, yet she couldn't get them to relax. Matt's shoulders were hardened by his life. Surely he could take everything she gave him. Cracking open an eye and looking down, she stared at her wildly flopping breasts. Nearly laughed. Her entire body was in motion as she jackhammered Matt. One second her sex muscles held him prisoner. The next they reached their limit and let go.

He came at her, pent-up energy firing through him so he all but knocked her off him.

"Ride him!" she cried.

"Yeah? Who's doing the most bucking?"

Great question, one she couldn't answer. After giving herself a moment in which to regroup, she took Matt's cock so deep she swore she tasted him. Eyes closed again and head back, she clutched him with her renewed strength and again straightened.

He started to slide out. "What . . ." she started to say. The rest of her thought evaporated under her body's heat.

Matt came after her, lifting himself off the bed and arching, again burying himself inside her. Owning every inch.

A sound without a single human note to it rolled out of her. She couldn't remember how to hold her head up. Something brushed her back, distracting her from fucking and being fucked.

Ghost Wolf?

The brushing sensation repeated, and she relaxed. Laughed. Her hair, which Matt had freed, was trailing over her back and igniting her nerves.

The wind here could be brutal in summer, the hot, dry heat sucking all but the rudiments of life out of those who called it home. At the same time, air movement reminded humans and animals alike that they were part of a whole called nature.

Nature had slipped over her, making her less woman and more wild animal. Even with sweat streaming off her, she was content. Blown about by flames of her and Matt's making.

Something slammed into her and threatened to knock her to the floor. A long, low scream tore up her throat and escaped. Her body curled in around her sex, broke free, came together again.

"Holy shit!" Leaning back, Matt powered himself into her. "Oh, damn, damn, yes!"

"Yes!" she screamed so her world would know. "Yes, Matt, yes!"

Despite the pulsing sensation in the air, Matt remained on his side, studying Cat.

"What are you looking at?" she asked. Although her breath touched him, he held back from embracing her.

"You."

"I know that." She blew several hairs off her lips. "In case I haven't said, that was incredible."

He couldn't agree more. She started to smile and nod only to lift her head off the pillow.

"Do you hear it?" she asked.

"The breathing?"

"Yes." She gnawed on her lower lip. "You're still here, aren't you, Ghost Wolf? What is it, you want to see what happens next?"

Suddenly angry, he sat up and slipped off the bed. Hands fisted and body—except for his exhausted cock—tense, he glared. "Leave us alone, damn it!"

I can't.

Matt whirled in the direction he thought the thought-voice

was coming from. "Don't say that! Just get the hell out of here."

You have no reason to be afraid of me.

The bedding rustled as Cat joined him. "What about me?" she asked. "Should I be afraid?"

He's mine, not yours.

Fear lashed at Matt, compelling him to clutch a naked Cat to his side. Even with his nerves alert, he couldn't completely dismiss her warmth. As much as he wanted to demand to be told why Ghost Wolf had said what he had, he knew he wouldn't get an answer. He also knew she wasn't in immediate danger.

But if there were no walls for her to hide behind?

"I'll talk to you," he told Ghost Wolf. "Stand face-to-face with you and listen to what you have to say, but not now. And not if you don't leave us alone."

Once again, he had the feeling that the air itself was breathing. A lonely air.

"That's the way it has to be," he continued. "She comes first. You don't own me."

Not now anyway.

"Go to where you came from. Return to the pack. Do whatever you want but do it away from me."

For now.

22

"It was a threat," Cat said. "He's not done with us."

"He's never going to be." Matt waited until he'd gotten his pickup over a particularly rough spot before glancing at Cat. "We need to know why he's selected us."

"Us? Matt, it's you he's after."

As soon as the air had settled down, if that was the right explanation, Cat had grabbed her cell phone and told him she was going to ask Helaku to see them as soon as possible. Maybe the old Paiute couldn't tell them anything, but she felt compelled to show him the photographs, all of them.

"Me," Matt muttered, and forced himself to relax his hold on the steering wheel. Cat was right. They had no choice but to accept Helaku's invitation to come right over, so why did he wish he was doing anything else?

"You sound surprised," she said.

"Did you expect anything different?"

If his retort bothered her, she showed no sign. "I know I shouldn't. Ghost Wolf has made no secret of his obsession with you." She slapped the passenger door. "I hope metal is the same as wood and his body can't get past this either. Insane. Absolutely insane. And yet reality."

Damnable reality when he'd give anything to be back on her bed listening to her talk and telling her things he'd never believed he'd tell anyone. Sealing their words with more sex.

"My mother didn't want me," he said, because he needed to start somewhere. "Until Santo and Addie took me in, I didn't know what belonging felt like."

Her still catlike green eyes bore into him. "What about your father? Addie told me some things about him, his mental illness, his—"

"She told you he killed himself, right?"

"Yes."

They reached the county road, which meant he'd be able to look at her even less than earlier. Maybe it was better that way, easier at least.

"Does that bother you?" she asked. "Maybe you're upset because she confided in me."

"No." He had to mentally repeat the word before he fully believed it. "She thought you needed to know."

"It wasn't just that, Matt. I came to her because I didn't understand what was happening to you."

"When I started acting crazy."

"Don't say that! You aren't. Just because your father—"

"You weren't there."

Cat stared at him until he half believed she could see through him. "But you were."

Tell me, he heard in her tone. He'd never spoken a word about the last day of his father's life, but that had been a boy's attempt to deny the unbearable. Now the time for the truth had come.

"I wasn't when he killed himself." Right now the road was empty except for the occasional farm equipment lumbering along. Still he didn't look at her. "But earlier in the day and shortly after."

"Did you find him?"

"Yes."

That December day that changed the course of his life hadn't begun any different from the hundreds before, he told her. Kaga had been *living* in a lean-to he'd built about a mile from where Matt was staying. Through spring, summer, and fall, the lean-to had filled Kaga's need for a place to keep his few belongings, but now the temperatures often didn't rise above freezing. Matt had stolen some plastic sheeting and several blankets, thinking they'd be better than his father sleeping on the ground. Kaga had passively watched while Matt made the improvements, but when Kaga sat on it, the plastic had made a crinkling sound.

"He said it hurt his ears and made it impossible for him to think—he was fixated on contacting the sun."

"Oh."

"That's an example of how his mind was working. Ancient Native Americans worshipped the sun, he told me. From what I understand, winter scared them. They feared the days would continue to get shorter unless they regained Sun's favor. My dad believed he could keep winter from coming if he did certain things. I kept begging him to move into a nearby abandoned barn at least, but he said he needed to remain where he was so Sun God could find him. I told him he was crazy."

"How did he respond?"

Matt shook his head. "I don't think he heard. He didn't act like it. Cat, his emotions were all over the place, high one minute, low the next. He thought *they* were out to get him."

"They?"

"The world. Police. It kept changing."

"I'm so sorry."

"So am I. Mental illness . . ." The term swirled around him to remind him of how many times recently he'd wondered if it applied to him. "It's hard on the sufferers and everyone around them."

"Was he diagnosed?"

"He didn't trust doctors. I tried." *Not hard enough obviously.*

"You were a child. There was only so much you could do."

To the left were the twenty or so acres where Randy Thompson grew his hay; to the left were basalt rimrocks with evergreen skeletons at the base. And next to him, Cat with her awesome body. "Maybe." His throat closed down and then opened. "I used a bike I'd found and fixed up to ride out to where he was staying. That last day, I'd hooked a wagon to it so I could bring the bedding stuff to him. Thinking about everything I'd done to try to help only to hear him spout more nonsense, I did what I'd sworn I never would. I called him crazy."

"Yes."

Don't say anything more, Cat. Just listen because I don't know how long I can keep going. "After that, I climbed back on my bike and pedaled out of there. The last thing I said to him was that I never wanted to see him again."

"You didn't mean it."

"No, I didn't, but it took me hours to calm down long enough to admit what I'd done. I was the only one he'd let get close. He needed me."

She touched his arm. "No more than you needed a father, but he wasn't able to give you that."

"I couldn't stop thinking about him." The emotional mountain was ahead of him. The hardest words yet to be said. "Instead of going home after school, I went back out to his camp. The whole time I was on my bike I knew it was going to be bad. If there'd been anyone I could turn to . . . A couple of years ago, I'd given him a knife for his birthday."

"The one you've been carrying?" she softly asked.

"Yeah." *Keep going. Get it all out. Don't lose yourself in her voice.* "The people I had to live with didn't believe in allowances. I stole the knife because just once I wanted to have something to give him."

This time Cat's fingers lingered on his arm. "Of course you did."

Gripping the steering wheel until his fingers cramped, he studied the land that owned his soul. "That's what he used to kill himself with."

For too long there was only the sound of the engine and tires. Then Cat undid her seat belt and slid over so their hips touched. She rested her hand on his thigh. "And you saw—"

"Yeah." *His lifeblood staining the bed I'd set up for him.*

"Oh, God. Please tell me you didn't blame yourself."

"No." Releasing the steering wheel, he briefly covered her hand with his. "Maybe it was a coping mechanism, but I told myself nothing would have stopped him from finding a way out of his hell. Maybe that damned knife was a gift in more ways than one."

She rubbed his thigh, causing sexual energy to shoot through him. "Did, ah, did he leave a note?"

Keep going. Give her everything. "He'd drawn something in the dirt. I destroyed it before I brought the police out."

"What a nightmare." She sounded on the verge of tears. "Knowing you had no one to turn to, no one to hold a boy who—What was the drawing of?"

Without warning, Ghost Wolf's spirit appeared, floating on the air outside the cab. It was waiting to hear what he had to say. He'd go to his grave believing that.

"Two stick figures," he told both Cat and the creature that had invaded his life. "A man with his arms around a child."

23

Helaku lived west of Lakeview in a cabin on land owned by someone the old Paiute called his nephew. Cat's understanding was the *nephew* was a relative on Helaku's dead wife's side who'd invited him to stay as long as he wanted. Before the arthritis in Helaku's hips curtailed his horseback riding, he'd been the driving force behind natural horsemanship. Although he was still involved, these days he spent much of his time researching his people's history for a book he was writing for the University of Oregon Press.

Life was to be lived for today, he'd told Cat when she asked about his project, but today couldn't be fully appreciated without an understanding of what had gotten people to that point.

Instead of sharing Helaku's wisdom with Matt, she said nothing as they headed behind the nephew's house to a small, weathered structure. How could she put words together in the wake of what Matt had told her on the way here?

Unlike her and Matt's places, Helaku's didn't have a front

porch. Someone had added a roof extension that kept rain away from the front door. Standing under the overhang with the large envelope holding the photographs against her breasts, she knocked.

You're here, Ghost Wolf. Somehow you accompanied us. Stay outside. That's all I ask. For Matt's sake.

The door opened and Helaku, who was no taller than her and dressed in a faded flannel shirt rolled up at the sleeves and baggy jeans, acknowledged his visitors. He didn't immediately invite them in but studied her and Matt in turn. Then his gaze went to the land. Old, dark eyes widened. "Now I understand," he said.

Instead of asking the Paiute if he, too, sensed Ghost Wolf's presence, Cat held up the envelope.

"I know," Helaku said before she could speak. He nodded, which caused his long, sparse gray hair to rise and fall. "The time has come."

Cat had been in the cabin before, but that didn't stop the artifacts filling the living room from stealing her breath. The High Desert Museum had chosen Helaku as caretaker for everything from fragile reed moccasins and ancient deer-hide dresses to spears, bows and arrows, stone knives, and fishing implements. An employee at the museum had told her that Helaku's collection—the Paiute collection really—far exceeded what the museum had. Did Ghost Wolf know about it? Hell, maybe his spirit was in the room right now.

"My God," Matt whispered. He'd shaken Helaku's hand, but instead of taking the chair the older man indicated, he walked over to a glass case filled with pictures taken of traditional Paiute life by early white photographers. "I had no idea..."

Matt was taller and stronger than Helaku, but at the moment her lover made her think of a young and uncertain boy. He didn't seem to know what to do with his hands.

"I know you didn't," Helaku said. Joining Matt, he pointed at something Cat couldn't see. "That's my grandmother, and the baby in the papoose carrier is my father." His knuckles grazed Matt's arm, reminding her that she'd touched Matt on their way here. She'd give anything to have his body to herself. "When you're ready, I'll show you everything."

Nodding, Matt trudged over to the chair and sank into it. She couldn't tap into his emotions.

"We could talk of things that don't matter," Helaku said as he joined Cat on the couch, "but that would only put off what needs to be done." He jerked his head at the envelope she'd placed on the couch between them.

In the past, Helaku had been so talkative she'd had trouble getting her questions out. She didn't know what to make of the change. Maybe he was reluctant to touch the envelope. Not wanting to, she drew comparisons between how Helaku was acting and how Matt must have felt while riding out to his father that last time.

Unable to keep her hands from shaking, she undid the latch. She wasn't sure how well Matt could see the photographs from where he sat. As she'd done with Matt, she began by telling Helaku where and how she'd found the cave and the trouble she'd initially had taking decent pictures. She took out the first picture and handed it to Helaku.

"Ah," he muttered. "Finally." In contrast to Helaku's weather-blasted features, his bright eyes shown.

"Finally?" Matt said.

Helaku ran a ragged nail over the stick figures. "My grandparents told me," he whispered. "I knew this place existed; they wouldn't lie."

"You've never seen it?" Matt asked.

Blinking repeatedly, Helaku shook his head. "My grandparents and others of their generation didn't share it with their children, because they feared whites would find out. When he was dying, my grandfather said it was better for the cave to be lost forever than for what was sacred to be desecrated."

"So no one has seen Ghost Cave since your grandparents—"

"My people call it Grizzly's Home."

"Oh."

"According to the stories handed from one generation to the next, an ancient warrior following a grizzly was the first to see the small opening and large space behind it."

"Wait a minute," Matt said. "You mean this warrior crawled into a bear den?"

Helaku shrugged. "He was on a spirit quest."

For the first time since coming in here, Cat met Matt's eyes. Helaku's explanation made sense, kind of.

Picking up the envelope, Helaku placed it on his bony knees and drew out the next photograph. It was as if he knew not to try to absorb everything at once. "If I were my grandfather," he said, "I would build a sacred fire out of manzanita and oak and hold this in the smoke."

"Why?"

"To bless what was created by Paiute but captured by a white. To ask the spirits for forgiveness."

For a moment, Cat thought Helaku was accusing her of the desecration he'd mentioned earlier, but going by how he lightly stroked the envelope, she told herself his gratitude overran everything else.

One by one, the photographs emerged. Helaku held each one up so light from the nearest window reached it. He mumbled under his breath while occasionally nodding but said nothing. Torn between watching the Paiute peel back the past and watching Matt, she wondered if she'd survive today intact.

Her place smelled of dried roses while Helaku's held the not-so-subtle scent of sage. Maybe she was getting high on it, because she could only stare when the old man thrust the petroglyph of the wolf pack looking at Ghost Wolf at her. "Matichu," he said.

She reluctantly took it from him. "What?"

"Matichu. Guider of all spirit quests."

Matt was on his feet and standing over her without her knowing how that had happened. He took the picture from her. "Explain," he said.

"Wolves are pack animals," Helaku began. "My ancestors admired that quality more than the predators' hunting prowess. According to my grandfather, the old ones—he never considered himself old—were simple humans who learned from studying the creatures around them. They didn't want to act like prey animals. If they were going to survive the harsh world they found themselves in, they'd better learn how to conduct themselves like predators."

Hearing Helaku use modern speech to describe something ancient kept her from getting sucked too deep into the past. Still, she was afraid she might lose touch with the present at any moment. Maybe Ghost Wolf—or Matichu—was responsible for this drifting sensation.

"The old Paiutes followed bears, cougars, wolves, and other predators. They tried attacking the way a cougar does, but most times the deer or elk—even rabbits—got away. Their success rate increased dramatically when they hunted in a group. Mirroring wolf behavior regarding protecting and rearing their pups increased the Paiute survival rate. That's when, over time, of course, my ancestors—yours, too, Matt—determined that wolves were at the top of the food chain. And thus the most sacred."

Cat thought Matt might object to what Helaku had just said. Instead, now looking at a home surrounded by what of the Paiutes had survived the centuries, Matt nodded. Had she ever wanted to touch him more than she now did?

"So," Matt said, "Paiutes prayed to Matichu before going on spirit searches?"

"Yes." Helaku smile highlighted the wrinkles at the corners his mouth. "I tried it myself. Because my parents were determined to assimilate, to focus on being Americans and not Indians, they didn't pass on most of what their parents tried to teach them. Consequently, it's taken me a lifetime to fill in the blanks." He took the photograph back from Matt. "I'm still learning. This"—he held the photograph against his chest—"is incredible. I'll die content once I've stepped inside Grizzly's Home."

Helaku's awe had Cat blinking back tears. There were only two pictures left for him to see but not until Helaku was finished talking. Going by the unease in Matt's eyes, she believed he felt the same.

"For all I know," Helaku continued as he studied the dramatic cave wall rendering of pack and massive wolf, "my grandparents' grandparents created this. It was their way of saying that everything, even other wolves, revered Matichu."

"Matichu," Matt said. "One spirit wolf, then? A single entity."

Helaku nodded. "Symbolic, of course."

Cold and hot, Cat looked up at Matt. Except for his eyes, his features were neutral. "No," Matt said, and took control of the envelope. "Not symbolic."

Don't do this! she wanted to scream.

Helaku placed the final cave photograph on top of the others on his lap. He studied Cat and then Matt before turning his attention to the nearly empty envelope. "Show me."

He knows. At least he suspects.

Matt was her lover, the lighter of all her lights, a complex and half-savage man. He didn't belong in this small cabin surrounded by the past. Instead he should be racing across the prairie with the desert air in his hair and the sun burnishing his skin.

Those thoughts and a familiar tightening in her groin distracted her from comprehending what Matt was doing. Working so slowly she thought she'd scream from the waiting, Matt pulled out the final photographs and fanned them over Helaku's lap. Leaning over, Helaku trembled.

"Matichu," the old man breathed at length. "Alive."

"I'm not sure we can call it that," she whispered. "The wolves that returned to Oregon are real, alive." Her fingers hovered over Ghost Wolf's/Matichu's muzzle. "He is something else."

"Tell me, Cat, what did you feel when you saw him?"

"Where do I start?" She tried a light tone she didn't feel. "Scared shitless, of course. In a way it was like being in a whiteout. If I panic, I'm dead. I knew I had to focus, concentrate. Take pictures."

"What about Matichu's emotions?"

Weren't they debating whether the great wolf spirit figure was alive? Did the old man really expect her to answer his insane question?

Yes, Matt's expression said.

"I have no doubt he resents me. Maybe he hates me."

"Because?"

Listen to your heartbeat. Concentrate on filling your lungs. Then say what you need to no matter how insane it sounds. "Matichu wants Matt. He wants me out of the way."

In another room a clock ticked. The refrigerator powered

up. Beyond these walls the wind increased. And inside Cat's head, something roared.

A dry weight settled over her hand, and she studied Helaku's weathered fingers covering hers. "I'm an old man," he said. "Because they love me, my children and grandchildren listen when I go on about our heritage, but I haven't told them about Matichu."

"Because you think they won't believe you?" Matt asked.

Helaku squeezed Cat's hand. "If they saw what she took, they would." He nodded at the final photographs. "But only then. Without this they would make fun of their ignorant and superstitious ancestors. A question for you, Matt. When did you first accept Matichu's existence?"

Matt started to ram his hands into his back pockets only to stop and caress the knife handle sticking out of the sheath at his waist. "I'm not sure. Do you know who Santo is—was?"

"Of course. One horseman knows another."

Watching Matt stride to the window and look out, she couldn't imagine ever feeling more in awe of and concerned for him. Sexual need barely mattered. Where was Ghost Wolf/ Matichu?

"Then you know how Santo died." Matt's voice was muffled. "I was with the group that found his body. When we were searching, I sensed something out there. Something new on the desert. More than an animal. Like a building storm."

"Ah, yes," Helaku said. "Well put."

"You never said . . . Did you tell anyone?" she asked.

"No." Spinning around, Matt fixed his gaze first on Helaku and then on her. "Matichu is here." He reached behind him and slapped the window glass. "Waiting for me."

"Yes," Helaku said.

"Why?" she managed. "Of all the people he—it—could fixate on, what makes Matt different?"

Silent, Helaku released her hand, got to his feet, and joined Matt. Together they faced the window, and the old man placed his arm around Matt's shoulder as best he could given the difference in their height.

"You can't hide," he muttered. "You must open yourself to the truth."

24

*A*re you ready for this?

"Are you ready for this?"

Startled because Cat had voiced the question he'd just asked himself, Matt loosened his hold on the reins and gave the gelding under him his head in preparation for the final climb to Grizzly's Home, as he now thought of it.

"I don't have a choice." Looking at her for the first time since they'd left the horse trailer on the desert floor below them, he noted how tired she looked. The day had been hell on her, on both of them, and it wasn't over.

"I'm sorry," he continued. "I should have waited until tomorrow, let you get some sleep first."

On the tail of a rueful look, she rubbed her right eye. "It's better this way."

"Oh?"

"Yeah. Less time for either of us to back out."

In a few minutes they'd reach the spot where she'd left her horse before when she came to Grizzly's Home. He didn't know how long the on-foot hike would take and refused to speculate on whether they'd be back at her place before dark. She was right. Today might represent the limits of his courage.

And hers.

In truth, a large chunk of him wanted her to bail while they were still on horseback. He might be willing to risk his life seeking answers. He had no right asking her to do the same.

"You don't have to do it this way," she said after several silent moments. "Come here in an attempt to get Matichu to reveal himself to you, I mean. Give him time. We both know he was outside Helaku's place. A little more patience on our parts and he might have shown himself."

About to tell Cat that something of Matichu's spirit-force was already in the wind, he decided not to because the words might tip him over the edge and strip courage from him. Reminding himself that, as a boy, he'd had the strength to ride to his father's camp knowing what he'd find, he squared his shoulders.

If he survived today, he hoped he could spend tonight in Cat's bed. That's what he'd use to keep him going. To face the truth Helaku had hinted at.

"Matichu and today's wolf pack are united in some way," he said. "Interdependent maybe."

"I don't think so."

"Then what?"

She drew her mare to a stop and dismounted before looking up at him. "I'm thinking about the petroglyph. The way the wolves regarded Matichu makes me believe they saw him as their alpha. Maybe their spirit leader."

Years ago his father had put his own spin on Native American beliefs. Matt had lost sight of what was based on tradition and what came out of Kaga's scrambled mind. "The drawing could be symbolic. Not . . . Hell, I'm not sure what I'm trying to say." Truth was, his own sanity felt as if it were slipping through his fingers. Maybe the only way of holding on to it, at least briefly, was by losing himself in Cat's body.

Not that he could now.

"Neither do I." She handed him the barest smile. It carved a path to his under-siege soul. "One thing I keep thinking—are you going to get down?"

Her question reminded him that he was still on horseback. Reaching the ground, he measured the distance between them. Too close and too far apart. "What are you thinking?"

She ran her hand down her braid to remind him of what it looked like loose and feminine. Sex. Quick and hard. Energy given and taken for what lay ahead.

"If Matichu wanted us dead," she said, "he would have already done it."

"How? He isn't flesh and blood, is he?"

Suddenly looking nearly as old as Helaku, she shook her head. "I don't know. He sure isn't smoke and mirrors. If you're right about what happened to Santo ... and what about Beale and those women hikers? Matichu's hand was in that."

"Maybe that's why we're here."

Instead of responding, Cat took a halter and rope out of her saddlebag. After exchanging her mare's bridle for the halter, she tied the horse to a bush. "Better do the same," she said.

Her suggestion got him going again. His intention, such as it was, was to walk to the cave and, if Matichu didn't stop him, crawl into the dark space and experience it firsthand. However, going by the air's heavy feel here, he wondered if he might not get that far.

"You're carrying the knife," Cat said. "I'm surprised you've held on to it all these years."

So was he, but every time he tried to get rid of it, he couldn't. Yes, the blade had ended his father's life, but it represented the only connection he still had with Kaga. Forgoing an attempt to explain, he took the lead on the deer trail. The sun was low in the sky with whispers of a cool night in the shadows. Behind him, Cat's boots made barely perceptible sounds. Once—if—this was over, he'd tell her how much he admired her courage.

Watching Matt's ass and the backs of his legs, to say nothing of his shoulders and lean waist, stood between Cat and what this afternoon was about. Living in central Oregon had introduced her to strong, resourceful, and brave men. She understood the courage it took to wrestle out a living here with the weather acting as one enemy and isolation another. Over the past few days with Matt, she'd come to understand strength's deeper layers.

In his own way, Matt was the alpha wolf.

What, then, did that make her?

Matt hadn't said anything, but the way he occasionally stopped and lifted his head as if testing the air told her that he, too, was aware of the weight, warmth, and warning on the breeze.

They'd soon reach the cave entrance, get down on their hands and knees, and crawl into darkness. They'd share their time with old petroglyphs, and the drawings would become more than images on photo paper for him.

And maybe Matichu would join them.

Wiping her sweating hands on her hips, Cat faced the possibility. Matichu couldn't or wouldn't enter something man-made, but what if nature had created the space?

Is that what you're waiting for? she silently asked the beast. *You want to trap us in there? No escaping, Matt's knife against your fangs?*

You don't understand.

"Ah, shit!" She pressed her hands against the small of Matt's back.

He whirled toward her. "What is it?"

"In my mind," she blurted. "Matichu telling me I don't understand. You didn't hear him?"

"No."

Matt withdrew the slender blade and held it in front of him. Then he wrapped an arm around her waist. His heat bled into hers. Anticipating more, her pussy tightened.

"Enough!" Matt's head swiveled one way and then the other. "No more playing this damn game, Matichu. What the hell do you want?"

Nerve endings scraped raw by Matt's closeness snapped. Even before she looked toward the cave, she knew what she was going to see. Beside her, Matt tensed.

Matichu, or Ghost Wolf, stood above them surrounded by dull black lava. His rich coat had picked up the lava's darker hue as had his eyes. In contrast, she'd never seen anything as white as his exposed fangs. It had to be his higher elevation but she half believed he was even larger than the other times she'd seen him.

She wasn't afraid. She'd come too far and waited too long for anything except the sense of a necessary task accomplished. Sucking in a long breath, Matt turned them so they faced Matichu head-on.

"Finally," Matt said.

Yes, finally.

In all her years of being around horses, she'd never seen anything as awe-inspiring as the world's largest wolf. Her earlier look at him didn't lessen the impact.

"You were waiting for us?" Matt asked.

I came with you. You sensed me at the old man's place. Don't tell me you didn't.

Matt's hold on her waist let up a little, maybe so he'd be ready to spring into action. "I have no intention of doing that.

Why did you wait so long to materialize? You could have at
Helaku's house."

This is better.

It was, Cat admitted. This confrontation or whatever it was
should take place on ancient Paiute land and among the three of
them.

"Why have you been stalking me?" Matt demanded. "And
trying to crawl inside me?"

Matichu lowered his head a little. *Don't call it stalking. I
didn't attack you the way I did the boy.*

"His name is Beale. You nearly killed him, damn it. You sure
as hell traumatized him."

In part so you'd know.

"Ah, shit," Matt muttered, so low she wondered if the *wolf*
could hear. "He was a substitute for me?"

The pack attacked him, not me.

"They didn't do it on their own." Her calm voice surprised
her. "You were behind the attack. You commanded the pack
to—"

I needed to test my power over them.

"Goddamn it." Releasing her, Matt positioned himself between Matichu and her. By stepping to the side, she was able to
keep an eye on the wolf while studying Matt's tense profile.
"By compelling them to nearly kill an innocent man? Don't
you get it? As a result, there are idiots out there determined to
blast the pack out of existence."

I won't let it happen.

"How? By waging war between wolves and humans? Wolves
lost in the past. They will again."

There didn't have to be war. Done right, man could find a
way to coexist with the predators, but that would happen only
if Matichu allowed the wolves to conduct themselves as nature
designed.

"All right, all right." She roughly ran her fingers down the side of her neck. "There's something... What you said about testing your control over the wolves—this is a new experience for you?"

"What are you talking about?" Matt said without looking back at her.

"I'm not sure. Trying to think things through. You've been here a long time, haven't you, Matichu? Centuries. Ancient Paiutes worshipped and revered you. Maybe they were afraid of you. If you controlled the wolves that once lived here as you're doing with the newcomers, I can understand why Paiutes created the drawings they did. They'd do whatever they could to keep you on their side."

Matichu had lowered himself onto his haunches while she was talking. If his cocked head was any indication, he was listening to her every word. Matt's strong back told her the same thing.

"You *are* one of a kind. Unique. Solitary," she said in little more than a whisper. "You keep yourself separate from humans because you have little in common with them while the wolves... they're the closest thing you have to family."

You're wrong.

25

_____

Confused, Cat rubbed her right temple. "What? Is there something the petroglyph didn't show?"

"Okay," Matt broke in before Matichu could respond, if he'd been going to, "so you tested your power over the relocated wolves by having them attack Beale and later by scaring those women hikers. What about the wild dogs? The pack killed two of them, but was it their idea or done under your command?"

The pack's. The dogs were competition for food, pitiful competition.

Matt hadn't mentioned dead dogs, but given everything that had happened lately, she wasn't surprised. The tension swirling around the three of them had her nerves on high alert. Strangely, much more stimulation and she'd climax just standing here.

A faint but sharp sound alerted her to movement from Matt. He'd started walking toward Matichu.

"Don't!" Springing after him, she tightly wrapped her arms around his waist. Still, if he wanted, he could easily shake her off. "Matt, don't risk—"

"What about Santo?" Matt demanded of the now-standing great wolf. "That *had* to be you. He died before the wolves arrived."

I hated him.

For a moment Cat believed Matt was going to attack Matichu. His body vibrated and a primal scent emanated from him. "Why?" he spat out.

Because of you.

"Me?"

You loved him.

"Oh, God," she heard herself say as a thought struck her. It was impossible, wasn't it? And yet… "Why does anything in Matt's life matter to you?" she asked, nibbling at the edges of what was opening up inside her. "Like I said, you're a solitary creature. A guide for the old Paiutes. Your role is—was—to help them connect with the spirit world. Isn't that enough?"

"The old Paiutes are gone," Matt said, with his back still to her and his tone now rough. "The wolves had been killed. That left Matichu with nothing. No one. Decades of loneliness."

For the first time, Matt sounded sympathetic toward Matichu, but that wouldn't last once his thoughts returned to Matichu's role in Santo's death. Praying she could keep him calm while opening what might be a massive Pandora's box, she touched her lips to the back of his neck. He started but still didn't acknowledge her.

"I'm sorry for you," she told Matichu, meaning it. "I didn't have much in the way of parents. Matt didn't have a mother and his father—"

I know.

Matt hadn't lived around here when his father was alive. Maybe Matichu had overheard her and Addie talking and then Matt telling her about finding his father's body, and maybe the Pandora's box's lid was about to open.

"I'm trying to understand," Matt said when it felt as if the silence had gone on forever. "What was the period after whites arrived like? You entered in a kind of limbo when the old ways ended? Maybe you went into hibernation until the wolves returned. No, that's not right. You were awake—is that the right word?—when you killed Santo."

I didn't kill him. I revealed myself to him. Tried to speak. His foolish horse panicked.

"I'm sure it did. And Santo, he was desperately trying to comprehend what he was seeing. By the time he started to regain control over the horse, it was too late."

Unlike a little while ago, anger didn't rule Matt's voice. He hadn't forgiven Matichu, but maybe he'd set hatred aside while trying to understand what she already comprehended?

What happened happened.

"In other words, Santo's death and the impact on those who loved him doesn't matter to you."

You have no idea what I've endured. You speak of hibernation. My soul shattered when a bullet struck the last wolf and the old Paiutes died and their children stopped coming to Grizzly's Home. When they forgot about me.

Tears blurred Cat's vision. Was it possible to be numb with disbelief while at the same time being locked into the creature's every word?

"Your soul died?" she managed, feeling she had no choice but to forge ahead. "But it, or something, is alive now. Otherwise, we wouldn't be having this conversation."

Matichu's great head lifted, and he stared at the sky. *So many seasons of nothing, of waiting, needing.*

"Waiting for what?" Matt asked.

Looking as if he'd long been wanting to have someone to speak to, Matichu nodded. *A way to become real again. To feel. To care. To connect with something.*

Matt tensed. "How did that happen?"

There was a soul, a broken spirit in need of a home. We came together.

Knowing what was coming didn't stop the shock from slamming into Cat. Matt gasped and the knife he'd been holding clattered to the ground.

You understand.

She did, barely, but this wasn't for her to say. Only her lover, her man, could speak the words.

"Whose soul, Matichu?" Matt demanded in the deepest tone she'd ever heard from him. "Or should I call you Kaga?"

You understand.

"I'm trying."

Reaching behind him, Matt dragged her to his side. Her boot brushed the knife that Kaga had killed himself with but that would be useless against Matichu, not that she wanted the savage and complex creature dead.

"When did the coming together happen?" she asked. "The connection with Kaga's soul." Was she really asking this? "How? He's been dead for years."

A fine tremor ran through Matt, prompting her to pray for a way to protect him from the incomprehensible reality. Matichu glared.

A lost soul simply is. It has no age. It floats here and there looking for a place to belong.

"And my father's soul came to this area because that's where I am."

Everything was so complex, a vast amount of information that boiled down to one thing. Matichu and Kaga had become one.

And because I wanted to reside in a spirit wolf's body.

"You?" Cat blurted. "Who is talking now, the wolf or the man?"

Both.

"Oh, shit," Matt breathed. He drew her to his side and kissed her.

Don't do that!

"Don't do what?" Matt demanded while she stared at Matichu's newly bared teeth.

Give yourself to her. You belong to me.

Now it was her turn to mutter, "Oh, shit." She should have seen this coming. Of course Matichu / Kaga wanted Matt to himself.

"You're wrong. I don't belong to you."

Struck by Matt's apparent calmness in contrast to everything she was feeling, she flattened a hand over his chest.

Stop! You have no right to him. Wolf eyes narrowed. The creature stepped toward them.

Reaching down, Matt snagged the knife and pointed it toward Matichu. "Dad, I forgave you for using my gift to you to get yourself out of the hell you were in. I've never known why I kept it, but now I do." He squared his shoulders. "If I use it on myself, you'll have nothing. Unlike your soul, mine would end."

Matt wasn't contemplating committing suicide; she'd never believe that. But what remained of his father might not know.

"I don't understand what happened," Matt continued. "I'm not sure either of you do. All we know is somehow Matichu and Kaga became one. What was it, Matichu? Suddenly you felt alive again?"

We awakened slowly, pieces at a time. You were here, growing up, becoming a man. We absorbed your energy. And when you met her and sex became everything, we took some of that heat.

"Matt," she whispered, "I'm sorry."

"For what? We didn't know what was happening." Again he turned his attention to the great wolf.

"You're right. Matichu, when you went after Santo, did you know the wolves were returning?"

I will not speak to you. Matt belongs to me, not you. Fangs again exposed, Matichu crouched. His powerful muscles tensed.

"Stop it!" Pushing her behind him, Matt stepped toward the beast. He now held the knife in both hands. "She's my future, not you. You can't claim me. Do you get it? You can't!"

If she's dead—

"Then you'll have killed me. Dad, I lost you years before you ended your misery, so I know what loss feels like. I can't do it again. I won't."

Matichu's muzzle wrinkled, making her think he was trying to pull in Matt's and her scents. Even with fear engulfing her, she remained aware of the arousal caused by Matt's presence.

I'm not crazy anymore, son. My mind's clear. I need you in my life.

A tear trickled down her right cheek. She didn't bother to brush it away. "Of course you do," she muttered. "But your son is a man with his own life. You have to let him live it."

Matichu—or was Kaga responsible?—extended a paw, only to draw it back. His ebony eyes glittered.

"She's right, Dad." Something, tears probably, clogged Matt's throat. "Everything has changed for both of us. You're in a predator's body, so I understand your impulses. I'm . . . I'm trying to forgive you and Matichu for what happened to Santo. If I do, will you forgive me for not being able to save you?" He ran his thumb and forefinger down the knife's broad sides.

You are my son. I would never fault you. My madness was beyond your comprehension. And mine too.

The beast was crying. Seeing his tears nearly dropped her to her knees. Whatever happened next was between Matt and his father—and Matichu.

"We have today," Matt said, "and tomorrow. The past is over. Do you understand?"

Knowing how important the past was for both Kaga and Matichu, she was surprised when the creature nodded.

"You want us to have a relationship," Matt continued. "So do I, but not if it's ruled by predator actions."

What do you mean?

"No more commanding the wolf pack to attack or stalk humans."

"He's right," she said, even though she'd just again vowed to remain silent. "Wolves' survival here depends on coexisting peacefully with humans and their animals. Otherwise, it'll become open season on the pack."

Maybe she was mistaken, but she thought she saw slow comprehension in the large, dark canine eyes. Some six feet now separated her from Matt, and yet she felt every inch and ounce of him. Wanted him with her whole body.

"She's right," Matt said. "What happens to the pack is in your hands—paws. Let them be wolves. They'll respect the boundaries humans set up."

Without the wolves I have nothing, unless it's you.

All right. So Matichu/Kaga didn't yet accept her. She could live with that, for now.

"Matt," she said, "the old Paiutes worshipped and depended on Matichu for guidance. What if that happens again?"

"How?"

He'd spun toward her before asking. Looking into eyes that reminded her of the great wolf's made it nearly impossible for her to go on. Still she knew what she had and wanted to do.

"By starting with Helaku." She looked at the creature as she spoke. "By bringing him to see and connect with Matichu."

Matt slid the knife back into its sheath and held out both

hands. Still watching Matichu/Kaga, she went to him. One leg went between his and their heat bled together.

"Will you do it?" Matt asked his father and the spirit creature he'd united with. "Show today's Paiutes yesterday's wisdom?"

I would love to, yes.

Epilogue

The long and emotionally draining day nibbled at Cat's muscles. Every time she tried to replay the conversation that had taken place at Grizzly's Home, all she got was fragments. Hopefully by morning she'd be able to recall the details. One thing she did know, she'd soon be getting in touch with Helaku.

She'd thrown together a couple of sandwiches and a salad while Matt tended to the horses. They'd eaten with their heads down, stuffing their empty bellies. Then Matt had lifted her in his arms and carried her into her bedroom. Prompted by his strong, weathered body and her own humming one, she all but parked her mind at the door.

"Wait a minute," she protested when Matt plunked her onto the side of the bed and, kneeling, started pulling off her boots. "You're acting pretty darn sure of yourself."

"I'm acting like a man who survived a storm and is celebrating."

She waited until her boots and socks were off and her jeans

unzipped before fisting her hands in his hair and forcing him to look up at her. He tried to pull free, but she was having none of that.

"The way I look at it," she said, "you've been more than happy to let Matichu and your dad mess with your libido lately."

"That's news to me."

"Yeah, right." No longer interested in exerting control over him, she released his hair and started in on her braid. "I've been jumping your bones long enough to know your standard operating procedure. You've always been quick on the trigger—no complaints there—but until a short while ago, you didn't pull that Me-Tarzan business."

Still kneeling, Matt placed his hands on her thighs. Holding on to her train of thought would be easier if his fingers weren't heading for her crotch.

"I'm not Tarzan. Never been near a jungle."

"You know what I'm talking about—the semi-bondage thing, exerting your rights." Done with her hair, she shook her head so the strands fluttered over her shoulders. Oh, to be rid of her top. "That was predator behavior. The wolf or spirit or whatever trying to take over."

Matt's fingers stilled, and his features sobered. "If I'd known what was responsible for—"

"Would that have changed things?" Groaning, she pressed the heel of her hand to her forehead. "My brain's used up. I don't think I can hold up my end of a conversation about the weather."

"I'm not asking you to." Planting his hands on her inner thighs, he spread her legs and nuzzled her jeans' covered crotch with his chin. "In fact, I'd like to declare a moratorium on thinking and talking."

It was dark out and getting cold. She should have closed her window. She would, later.

"You're forgetting one thing. This is my place."

Still holding her legs apart, he cocked his head. "Your point is?"

This was the Matt she'd initially lusted after. That man loved to make a game of sex, to take things light and hard.

Folding her arms across her breasts, she gave him her best glare. "I've put up with a lot of Tarzan behavior lately. You know what they say about variety being the spice of . . . well, however it goes. Tonight's about turning things on end, and if you don't like it, you can leave."

A shadow briefly stole Matt's amused expression. Instead of telling him she didn't mean it, she stood and unceremoniously shucked out of her jeans.

"If you want to see the rest of the merchandise"—she ran her hands under her top and cupped her breasts—"I suggest you match my level of undress."

"What if I don't?"

Good. There was the teasing tone she hadn't heard for too long. "Then I'll have no choice but to tackle that chore myself. However, if you want to reap the full benefits of tonight's menu, I suggest you get with the getting."

A few minutes later, nothing remained of their clothes.

"That was fast," Matt observed, and reached for her.

Wagging her finger at him, she dodged away. Her breasts with their erect nipples rolled with the movement, capturing Matt's attention. Just yesterday he would have thrown her onto the bed and climbed on top of her, but tonight was about reminding him that they were equals.

Or not.

"Hands by your sides, mister." She again folded her arms, but this time she anchored them below her breasts so the mounds stood out. "No touching the merchandise until you're given permission."

"You're nuts."

"I'll take that as a compliment. All right, here are the rules, and if you know what's good for you, you'll abide by them."

Assuming an almost military stance with his arms ramrod straight and his cock at a right angle to the rest of him, he glared.

"And if I don't?"

"Then you'll spend the night mucking out the barn instead of getting any."

His expression softening, he fixed his gaze on her pubic hair. The longer he looked at that part of her anatomy, the more aroused she became, not that she wasn't already. He might be going along with her game. That didn't mean he didn't have a few moves of his own.

"All right." She licked her lips. "Time for you to get on the bed."

He grunted. "Those are my choices? I get in position or it's out to the barn?"

"You got it, cowboy." Giving him a stern look, she jerked her head at the bed. "Assume the position."

He didn't ask what she had in mind, not that he needed to. After all, nothing was going to happen if she couldn't get her hands or other parts of her anatomy around his cock. Watching him plant a knee on the mattress in preparation for hauling the rest of his body after it, she admired his lack of self-consciousness in presenting his ass to her. She again licked her lips.

Matt crawled onto the bed on his hands and knees, then looked over his shoulder at her.

"A question, cowgirl. It's obvious I'm ready to service and be serviced." Reaching down and back, he gave his cock a shake. "I have a right to know if you're ready to reciprocate."

If he couldn't see her body vibrating, he needed to get his

eyes checked. About to hold up a trembling hand, she caught on.

"I suppose you have a point. All right, let's see if I can give you a sample."

Feeling foolish and excited, she slipped a hand between her legs. Two fingers went straight to her opening. Wet heat immediately coated them. She took a moment to collect as much sticky moisture as she could, then reached out and wiped her offering on Matt's lips.

He licked. "Yes, indeed, a prime sample. Comes from a healthy diet."

"And from lusting after a prime example of the male sex."

Matt continued to look sideways at her while she wracked her so-called mind for what she should do next. She was trying to decide between jumping on the bed or giving him another taste when he dropped to his belly and onto his back. He planted one hand behind his head. The other pointed his cock at her.

"Your call, cowgirl."

Yes, indeed it was. With her nipples tied in knots and her pussy leaking, she didn't need to do any more thinking. Stepping around to the foot of the bed, she climbed onto it, kneeing his legs apart as she did. Her shaking stopped. Lifting her head, she turned so the air from the open window cooled her cheeks. She spotted a pair of eyes buried in a predator's body looking in.

I can't think about you, she told Matichu/Kaga. *Tomorrow, yes. Tonight, no.*

Lowering her upper body, she drew Matt's cock into her mouth. Saliva flooded her cheeks.

"Ah, shit." Fisting her hair, Matt held her in place. "Now I know why I want your hair loose, so I can—Oh, God!"

Controlling Matt was so easy. So incredible. Her lips sealed themselves around his shaft, and she tasted sweet promise. Her head pulsed as she ran her tongue down his cock's underside. Was she floating over him?

Then his hold on her hair let up and she lifted her head, losing him as she did. She lapped at his cock until it glistened.

Another look out the window—a quick glance that gave her eyes no time to register what was there—and she straddled Matt.

Hungry for sex, she straightened, thinking to improve the alignment of cock to cunt. She reached down, thinking to guide him in, only to brush his hand, which was already around himself.

"Let me," he whispered. "Please."

Planting her hands on Matt's chest, she arched her back. His cock touched her opening. Slipped in. Hissing, she slowly lowered herself onto him. Became part of him.

Matt bucked upward, prompting her to grip him with all her inner strength. Wet slipped over wet, and his swollen length abraded her hot, soft channel. Her hiss became a scream.

Her body gathered, knotting in anticipation of meltdown. Mindless, she raked Matt's chest with her nails, then bent low to kiss him there.

She fell apart.

Hours later, she stirred to find her head on her man's chest and his arm around her. Listening to his light snore, she fell back asleep.

Outside, the great wolf looked up at the moon but didn't howl.

Turn the page
for a sizzling preview of
ROUGH PLAY,
by Christina Crooks!

Coming soon from Aphrodisia!

1
_____

The noise sounded a little like a mouse scratching behind a wall. The strangeness of it pulled Charlotte's gaze from her budget calculations. Daytime was when the apartment's mice should have the sense to sleep instead of scratching loudly enough to draw a predator's attention.

Charlotte looked back at her white plastic laptop. She frowned at the clicking-whirling noise it made. Maybe the computer had made the scratching noise? She hoped it wasn't about to break. She relied on the old laptop for her struggling matchmaking business.

The sound again. A metallic scratching.

The fish tank? She looked at it with a frown. No, the noise wasn't coming from her cloudy freshwater aquarium or its quiet motor. She needed to clean the water again, she noticed.

Her door rattled slightly.

The front door.

Someone was messing with the lock. Not the landlord. He had a key. Besides, he'd knock.

Charlotte's hearing zeroed in on the tiny scrapes, the metallic jiggling. Picking the lock? Breaking in to her second-floor home.

Her heart sped into a staccato beat and she leapt silently to her feet. She paced the tiny living room in a tight circle, trying to prevent adrenaline from fogging her thinking. What to do? "Okay," she whispered to herself. "Okay. Yell for a neighbor, call a friend, a boyfriend, anyone. No. There's nobody."

Nobody.

The realization stopped her steps. Half a year after her divorce finalized, and she was still solitary. She knew she should've forced herself to get out more, to meet people. To date. The solitude now impaired her options. She didn't know her neighbors, and aside from the ex himself, there was no one to call.

"Okay, okay, okay. No, it's not okay. Shit."

She started pacing again, and her mind started working again. "Gotta do something. Call the police, of course."

Following her own advice, she dove for the small flip phone next to her notebook. Its rounded edges squirted from her sweat-slicked grasp, falling to the hardwood floor. The crack of plastic, then the clatter of the battery projecting out across the room sounded calamitous.

The scratching sounds stopped.

Charlotte held her breath until small black dots swam before her vision.

She strained to hear. When she couldn't stand it anymore, she tiptoed to the door. She brushed it ever so lightly with the pads of her fingertips, leaned toward the peephole.

The door shuddered under a blow, jerking a scream from her. Charlotte stumbled back without having seen the pounder. The fist-slam against the door told her he was strong. She hoped her door held under that level of assault.

What if it didn't hold?

She curved into the same pacing circle, passing the broken

phone. She braced herself against the next loud noise, but it didn't come. She whispered to herself in the ominous silence, "Okay. Okay. Dead phone. Lunatic outside door. Go out the back sliding doors, jump. Crap. Go." Obedient to her own instructions, she'd half climbed over the balcony's wrought-iron railing when she heard the sound of knocking on the front door.

Polite knocking, not pounding.

She paused.

Was it a trick? As if she'd be stupid enough to just open the door.

Still she paused, with a reluctant glance down. It was a long way to a hard landing.

Another polite knock.

It wouldn't hurt to look.

This time she didn't tiptoe to the door, but stomped. "I own a gun! And my boyfriend'll be back any minute! And I have a vicious attack dog!"

She peered through the peephole.

"Dogs aren't allowed," her landlord said. He waited, lanky and familiar, his lean body propped against the iron railing on the concrete balcony. It was the exact same type of railing she'd just been climbing over in the back.

The guy couldn't be more than thirty, but his frown made him look old and mean. She hoped he wasn't feeling mean. She didn't have the full month's rent.

She also didn't have a boyfriend, gun, or an attack dog. Hoagie, her little brown and yellow mutt, wouldn't dream of biting anything but his toys and bones. He lived at Cory's anyway.

Her ex got the sweet little dog. She got the goldfish.

"Oh, man. Okay." Charlotte calmed her breathing, smoothed the front of her shirt. It clung to her sweaty skin and revealed more than she wanted to show her landlord, so she peeled it away and fanned the material to cool herself down. Her hands stopped for a moment. "Can I ask you something? Were you pounding on the door a couple of minutes ago?"

"No." He sounded impatient. His impatience convinced her he wasn't the same guy.

"Okay, just a sec." She walked toward her desk, stepping over the phone pieces, and quickly wrote out a check.

She opened the door with caution, looking past the landlord. "Did you by any chance see anyone? A man running away?"

"No," he repeated. He stared pointedly at the check.

"Because someone was trying to pick my lock," she continued, not to be deterred. "Whoever it was tried to break down my door." She held her check folded in one hand. "Could you please look at the lock?"

He sighed. He examined the lock. "Scratches. Could be from keys." He gave a cursory glance at the door. "The lock's intact. The door's undamaged. Seems fine now. Did you call the police?"

She bit back a number of replies. The police weren't high on her list of good guys lately. They hadn't managed to find her stolen car in the past months, and their swaggering presence while writing traffic tickets or sprawled in uniformed groups inside that donut shop down the road didn't do much to deter the brisk local drug trade. She often heard gunshots at night.

She frowned unhappily. Other than Cory, cops were the only lifeline she had. She really needed to get out more. It was past time.

At the moment, she shifted from one foot to another, wondering how to manage the landlord situation. "Yeah, I was about to call the police. But then, you showed up." She smiled brightly.

"Uh-huh." He held out his hand. His left hand. She noticed he wore no ring.

A man of few words. She could work with that. "The check is short. I'm sorry. The thing is, I have a small business I'm growing, and I can make it up to you in service. It's a matchmaking business. To help people locate dates and true love. I have many happy clients." A slight exaggeration. She'd *had* many happy clients. Now they were happily paired-off former clients.

His scowl deepened, but he withdrew his hand.

"So, what do you think of that kind of service?" she prompted. She offered him the check, a gesture of goodwill.

He glanced at it without taking it, then transferred his gaze to her. His scowl faded to a look of speculation. His thin hair hung in limp, unwashed straggles over his broad forehead. Nice eyes, though. And he had the body of a man who did some physical labor.

He suddenly closed his calloused fingers over the insufficient rent check as if afraid she might attempt to snatch it back.

He looked at her in a way she didn't like.

She spoke quickly. "Or, if you prefer, I'll just get the rest of the money to you in two weeks. That's when Burger Town pays me. Things have been tight, hours have been cut. And you know my car was stolen. Right out of the parking lot down there."

He didn't even look. Were thoughts of eviction crossing his mind? "Think about what I'm offering. Just consider it. I mean, you're not wearing a wedding ring. You're single, right?"

She noticed his slow smile and tried to ignore the glances at her body. "I'm a fabulous dating coach. Dating coach," she repeated when she saw the gleam in his eyes. "I help people meet people. I'm good at it. I charge a reasonable fee. Very reasonable."

"You're good at it, eh?" His nice smile turned into a leer. "In exchange for the rest of rent?" He eyed her apartment's door again, and she knew he wasn't thinking about her intruder. "Sounds like fun."

"Dating coach," she said again. "Nothing more. I don't do sex stuff. You seem like the kind of guy who could use a good woman." As his scowl returned, apprehension fluttered in her belly. "Okay, a not-so-good woman? An easygoing and fun one. Hmm."

"What, I look desperate?"

"Of course not! I just want to help—"

"I never need help when it comes to women." He pocketed her check. "I ain't interested. Besides, if you were any good at your business, what're you doing living here and working in fast food?" He gave her a pointed look, then turned his back. "Two weeks, then I get the rest of it. No excuses."

She felt her lips tighten into a grimace. He was definitely feeling mean. Too bad for him.

Too bad for her. Flipping burgers, even part-time, bummed her out. Though it was only until her business caught on. She had a gift for matchmaking. A real, honest-to-God gift.

She spent every spare penny on advertising her matchmaking business. But people didn't believe her when she claimed a 99 percent success rate of making matches that resulted in permanent relationships. They surely wouldn't believe her if she told them how she did it.

Nothing excited her as much as using her special skill. Nothing felt as satisfying as trusting her instincts and her prescient visions. Nothing thrilled her like consulting her X-rated imagination to hook up her clients. Well, almost nothing.

Her dangerous personal fantasies with always-faceless ravishers didn't count, she told herself. They didn't count at all. Those were strictly and permanently for fantasyland only.

She gave a brief shake of her head, dismissing the thoughts.

She watched the landlord's departure with a professional's assessing stare. He descended the worn steps of the fourplex with a furtive but muscular grace. Lower blue-collar. Very single. Probably frequented Riverport's numerous strip clubs. But he had a nice gruff voice, broad shoulders, tapered hips, and the smudged jeans and easy gait of a man who spent a bit of time outdoors. Not bad. Not her thing, but not bad. Who'd be into him?

Like images on a jackpot's spinning wheel, faces of women she'd known and counseled turned over in her mind. Jill, Vickie, Tina. All taken now, thanks to her. Tamara had moved to Southern California. But she could've totally seen Tamara being into him.

She asked the question of her special intuition, then watched the answer: Tamara getting it on with the landlord.

Charlotte stared into the stairway's handrail, its metal imperfections coalescing into the magic visions.

In her mind, Tamara rubbed against the landlord's strong body, clawing his jeans off with only a little less desperation than his own feral dive for her nipples as he shoved her shirt up over her breasts, jammed her bra up, too, and took first one breast then the other into his mouth. No finesse. But Tamara liked it. Rough and straightforward, a little dirty but nothing too kinky.

Charlotte leaned against the rough stucco of her building with a sigh and made the movie in her head stop.

Tamara was gone and the landlord didn't want to pay Charlotte for her matchmaking services. That was a problem. No one was currently paying her. She'd hooked up all the clients.

Well, all but the last woman. The difficult woman who represented Charlotte's only failure.

Charlotte pushed herself from the apartment building's rough stucco wall, ducked inside to grab her mailbox keys and outgoing mail. Maybe a check or a client referral would be waiting in the box.

Her maiden name listed on her mailbox still had the power

to bemuse her. She should never have married Cory. His face had never appeared in any of her visions.

Nobody's had, for her.

A breeze gusted, propelling a chill that lifted the hairs on her arms. Sweat cooled under her shirt. The wind probably heralded another of Riverport's frequent fall rainstorms, though the sun still beat down with noontime vigor.

Who'd dared to attempt to break into her apartment in broad daylight?

Would they have succeeded if she hadn't switched shifts at the last moment with a coworker? What if she hadn't been home? She supposed she'd have returned to find her few remaining belongings stolen. The divorce hadn't left her with much—she hadn't wanted much, just the dog, her exotic fish, and a little money to start her business.

Cory gave her the money and fish but convinced her to let him keep Hoagie at the house. Said the little dog they'd both raised from a puppy would be happier with his own backyard. He offered visiting privileges on weekends.

To her surprise, he'd honored her wish to stop by for a brief visit every weekend. Even more to her surprise, they got along better as friends than spouses. They'd never be close, though. Not after what he'd done to her.

Today she could've used Hoagie in her home. The little pup's barking might've scared off the lock picker.

She shivered again when she realized she might've returned home to find the intruder already inside, waiting for her.

She looked around with a careful, vigilant gaze.

Nobody.

Freaking herself out over nothing. The lock picker was long gone.

She opened the mailbox quickly. Bills, bills, ads, bills . . . aha, a big card.

Charlotte pushed in the outgoing mail—bills plus a wedding card to her latest satisfied client.

She returned to her apartment. She dumped everything with the keys and ripped open the big envelope eagerly. Another thank-you card. It came with wedding photos from some exotic island with lots of sand and palm trees. Charlotte grinned at the sight of the former client wearing nothing but a bikini bottom and a big smile. The card's handwritten message waxed eloquent with gratitude. The woman promised referrals. The clients usually did. Sometimes they even remembered to do it.

Charlotte gnawed her knuckle with the ongoing worry even as she enjoyed Tina's clear happiness in the photo. She remembered watching the couple's first movie. The woman's expression had stretched into sexual ecstasy as that very same smiling gentleman, now wearing colorful swim trunks as he posed casually next to her, screwed her enthusiastically.

Some women had all the X-rated movie luck.